# THE PRE-NUP

## BOOKS BY ARIANNE RICHMONDE

*The Wife's House*

*The Newlyweds*

*The Guilty Sister*

*The Breakdown*

# THE PRE-NUP

ARIANNE RICHMONDE

bookouture

Published by Bookouture in 2023

An imprint of Storyfire Ltd.
Carmelite House
50 Victoria Embankment
London EC4Y 0DZ

www.bookouture.com



ISBN: 978-1-83790-391-7
eBook ISBN: 978-1-83790-390-0

*For my husband.*

# PART 1

# ONE

"You don't remember a thing?" My husband looks down at me, his six-foot-four frame making me feel like he could snap me in two. Is he angry with me? Disappointed?

Lying on the couch, I shift my weight and cover my bare shoulders with a blanket. For some reason I feel cold, despite the Malibu summer heat. I blink up at him, shivering. My mouth is dry and I can hardly get the words out. "No, I don't remember a thing."

"Nothing at all?" His question unnerves me. His tone is not caring or placatory, but curious. As if he's hiding something. As if by my remembering, he'll be found out.

I shake my head. Lucas knows I have a migraine but has not given me anything to quell the pain. An unbidden tear escapes, sliding down my cheek. "Nothing. I remember nothing."

His gaze sharpens, his cool blue eyes narrowing as if he doesn't believe me, doubt etched on the corners of his lips. And when my expression of guile, of confusion, doesn't change, those lips crack into a small smile. A smile of relief, a smile that says he knows he's getting away with something.

Something cruel.

"Good," Lucas says. "I'm glad you can't remember what happened before our vacation."

The supposed "vacation." After he is gone, I flick through our Instagram feed once more. Our joint account @thefoxy-foxes showcases the perfect social media couple in love. The sort of couple that is not just happy but sickening enviable. Us on a beach in St. Martin. Sipping cocktails at a five-star hotel, which I know is a lie. Me in a bikini, frolicking in the turquoise waves. I recognize last year's floral-print bikini, yes. But I seem to be slimmer, and is my hair a tiny bit shorter? These photos were supposedly taken last week. Am I going crazy? No! This didn't happen. We were not on vacation in the Caribbean.

When someone reaches a professional level of gaslighting like my husband, thoughts of survival wend their way into your consciousness, like when you're hiking alone and get lost and can't remember which path to take to find your way back to civilization, to safety. When there's a strange man lurking in the trees and you sense you mustn't show fear and mustn't run, or it will make things worse because he could easily catch up with you and would be aroused by your fear and might hurt or even kill you. Yet you also know, without any doubt at all, that you need to get as far away from him as quickly as possible. That your survival pins itself on your split-second intuition: a savvy fight for your life.

All women have been in this precarious position at one time or other, haven't we? People assume we might encounter danger in dark alleys or down dead-end streets, or in remote locations like I just described. But in my case, it is happening right here, in my house.

In my *home*.

And my husband is the perpetrator.

# TWO

The first time Lucas brought me to his beachside house, three years ago, I was spellbound.

I'd gotten to know the classy guy in the suit, the slick attorney who turned heads wherever he went, but I hadn't met the laid-back surfer who was into photography and midnight strolls on the beach, and could tell me what all the constellations in the sky were and how to find the North Star.

"Ava," he said, as we strolled along the beach at dawn while pelicans flew in a V formation, skimming the ocean with their cries. "You're so beautiful."

I laughed. I didn't know whether to believe him or not.

"Don't move," he said. "Stay right there with the breeze in your hair." He skipped in front of me, walked backwards, pointing his camera at me, which was slung around his neck. He took it everywhere with him. I had spent the night at his house, but he had ushered me—like a true gentleman—to the spare bedroom, "So you get to have your own space," he had said. I was too drunk to drive home, and he persuaded me to stay, promising he wouldn't touch me. He kept his word, much to my dismay. The only reason I hadn't jumped his bones earlier in the evening was because I was scared he might not call me the next day. In the middle of the night, though, I snuck into his room, slipped under the covers beside him. I simply couldn't resist. That was that. We couldn't keep our hands off each other.

After the photo session, we spent the day on his back deck, watching the ocean turn various shades of blue, laughing and joking and telling each other our life stories. He didn't hint that it was time for me to leave like some guys would have, and I stayed again that night, and then the whole of the next day, borrowing his shirts and boxer briefs two days in a row. We ordered in pizza. It felt so good to smell him on me, to know he wanted me to stay. I loved this easy-going, fun side to Lucas. As sexually attracted as we were to each other, there was also a best-friend feeling I got with him. No judgment about my humble background, how I'd waitressed to put myself through college and that I'd never been abroad.

I sat on his lap pretty much all that first afternoon, his arms tight around my waist, as we looked out to the ocean, breathing in the scent of beach and fresh briny air while he told me all about the house. He was lucky enough to have inherited it from his grandfather, who had bought it eons ago before real estate prices shot to oblivion. By current Malibu standards, I thought the house was pretty funky. But in a good, charming way. A wooden, two-bedroom cabin-style with a back deck that looked like it hadn't been upgraded in decades. I loved its bohemian vibe.

Lucas had his chin resting on my bare shoulder, his blond hair lit up by the sun, our cheeks touching. "This place was built in the fifties," he told me. "It's one of the few original oceanfront homes that hasn't been turned into a McMansion and had its integrity and style destroyed, or worse, *actually* destroyed and replaced by a more 'opulent' structure of glass, concrete, and aluminum like some of my neighbors' homes."

"Like the place next door?"

He nodded. "The houses along this stretch of coastline are built on the sand, without a seawall. Still, it's weathered the earthquakes so far." Then he cupped my chin, turning my face toward him, and kissed me, at first softly, then deep and strong and decisive. "Not this earthquake, though," he said after the kiss.

I laughed. "That's one of the best come-on lines I've ever heard." We held hands then. I carried on chatting, feeling like I should fill in the gaps, that we had so much catching up to do. I felt like he was my missing puzzle piece and now my real life was just beginning.

"I love the way we're directly on the beach, open to the elements," I nattered, thinking how the house was perfectly situated. The night before, in bed, I screamed louder than I should have and the waves blocked out my cries of ecstasy. He was the sexiest man I had ever dated. He touched me in all the right places, and by the time my explosion came, I knew I never wanted to have sex with anyone ever again other than Lucas Fox. "It's perfect," I said. *He is perfect. This weekend is perfect.*

"That's why it's on stilts," he went on, his breath in my ear as if he was talking about something sensual, not simply a house. "It matches its environment and is authentically at home here in Malibu. Because, at its core, that's what Malibu's all about."

"I love the word Malibu," I said, stretching out each syllable with a slow drawl. "It sounds so exotic."

He tilted back his beer. "Whenever someone hears Malibu, they always conjure up images of rich people and movie stars. I guess nowadays, that's pretty much how it is. But they forget that Malibu started off as a surfer's paradise famed for its breakers, and before that there were ranches and farms along this rugged coastline. In fact, Malibu was founded in 500 BC by the Chumash, who were seafaring people who settled along its shores."

Suddenly I felt like the conversation had spun too far away from *us*, from our intimacy. I was nervous he'd want me to leave. I couldn't get over the fact he was into me. "I didn't know that," I said, not truly concentrating on the conversation, just talking for talking's sake, to stretch the day out further. "Where does the name Malibu come from?"

"It means 'where the surf sounds loudly.'"

*Where I sound loudly*, I thought, and smiled.

He never did ask me to leave. I stayed until dawn on Monday. Eventually I had to head back to my apartment to get changed for work.

My eyes now wander to the photo of me taken on the beach that romantic weekend, three years ago. It sits framed on the wall. Wisps of hair are blown across my face. The photo is black and white. I am looking into the lens, my lips parted in a gentle smile. Flecked with grains of sand above my eyes, my gaze is hopeful, expectant, as if waiting for Lucas to complete me in some way. There is also an almost imperceptible reticence in my eyes, a faltering, as if I knew in the marrow of my bones, he'd one day break my heart.

# THREE

I have a big painted box where I keep all my treasures, decorated with birds in gold, perched on leafy branches, a cerulean sky in the background. Every now and then, when I'm feeling nostalgic or blue, I pull out my special things. Hold them in my hands. The oldest thing I have is a toy car given to me by my dad before he abandoned us. I was only three years old. It isn't the usual present you might give to a little girl, but I loved it. A navy-blue station wagon. Later, after he'd gone, I imagined Mom and him getting back together, the car overflowing with us as a family. Brothers and sisters galore. Dogs and picnic baskets. That never happened. None of it.

Mom and I never saw him again. I have tried to locate him over the years. Mom assured me he was a drunk, probably dead in a ditch somewhere, but I never believed her. I *couldn't* believe her. Still, even with the internet and even after paying for a private investigator, I never found my father. I guess if somebody doesn't want to be found, there's not a lot you can do about it.

I pull out another treasure from my box.

A letter from Lucas. He handed it to me himself with a look

on his face I couldn't read at the time. That first weekend of passion had instantly led to pregnancy. I was terrified, because all I wanted was to keep the baby and was convinced Lucas would be horrified, that he'd want me to have an abortion.

*My beautiful Ava,*
*I know it's been fast and crazy and a surprise for us both, but I'm in love with you. You're funny and sweet and adorable in every way. I want to spend all my time with you. And, yeah, I can see us being together forever.*
*Let's do this.*
*Let's have this baby.*
*You're my North Star and I can't imagine my life without you.*
*Love you always,*
*Lucas xxx*

I still savor those words he wrote me, roll them around in my head, tears swimming in my eyes over the baby that never was. The miscarriage that broke me.

I dip into the other treasures in my box. There are various photos, dog-eared and love-worn. Me and my pony, Willow: the first time I fell in love with an animal, before I discovered the magic of dogs, too. We were so united, I used to ride him bareback. A photo of me and Mom from when I was little. Before my dad left. She's holding me in her arms, gazing at me lovingly. We are wearing matching sky-blue dresses. I have a lollipop in my mouth, my rosy cheeks fat and round.

I pull out another keepsake, feeling the softness of the crocheted wool between my fingers. A pale-yellow baby bootee. Yellow, because I didn't know what sex our baby would be. After we lost the baby, I squirreled this pair away in this box, just in case. Heartbroken, but hopeful.

*For next time.*

Teary-eyed, I put the box away, stashing it at the back of my closet. I hear the sound of Lucas's car in the driveway and dash to the mirror to check my face. There has been distance between us lately. The way he has been acting has made me sit up and pay attention, though he has an answer for every single thing and tells me my imagination is overactive. Maybe it is. I can't seem to trust my own judgment anymore. The whiff of someone else's perfume on the collar of his shirt ("a lady client who stank so much of scent it made me sick to my stomach. I had an excruciatingly long meeting—boy, am I glad *that's* over"). The smile stretched across his face the other evening as he was frantically typing away in reply to a text ("That project I was telling you about has just been green-lighted!"). Sometimes, when his phone rings, he checks who the caller is and doesn't answer, a shifty look in his eye ("I don't want anyone interrupting our quality time, honey"). The late nights at work ("You think I *like* working late? I'd so much rather be home with you"). The new collars for the dogs he told me he'd bought when I know how lazy he is about shopping ("They're like our *kids*, honey, I wanted to do something special"). The big cash withdrawal when he never usually pays in cash ("Busted! I was trying to surprise you with a gift so you didn't see the payment on our credit-card history!") All these things he has laughed away, and I wonder if I'm imagining things because of my own insecurities. A miscarriage can do that to you: make you lose your confidence. Even though it was nearly three years ago, it's as fresh in my mind as yesterday.

I greet him at the door with a hug. He stands back from me, drinks in what he sees and lets out a long appreciative whistle. I feel good. Sexy. Delighted by his reaction and basking in hope.

But he comes out with, "How come you're wearing heels? And makeup? You never wear heels." He says this in a grilling, suspicious way, like I've done something wrong.

"Because I feel like it," I respond. "Felt like a change."

With his eyes honing in on me in an icy-blue stare, he

quizzes, "Are you *cheating* on me by any chance, babe?" He cocks his head to one side, studying me as if to read something ominous behind my astonished gaze. The idea of having sex with anyone other than Lucas has never occurred to me. Nobody else attracts me. Not even rock stars or male models or movie stars. Lucas is the only one I want. The only one I see.

"Lucas! No! I can't believe you're asking me that."

He shakes his head, smiling as he does so. "I'm not convinced." His tone has changed somewhat. He's now making it seem like he's half joking. But he isn't. I ransack my mind, trying to think if I've done something—anything—to warrant this kind of left-field accusation. He wraps his arm around my waist and pulls me in for an intense, passionate kiss. His lips taste of the ocean and apples, or something sweet I can't quite place.

"Remember, Ava, you're mine," he says.

I breathe him in, lapping up the attention, forgetting my own suspicions, because in this moment, nothing else matters but us. In fact, his jealousy turns me on. He slides his hand up my thigh and finds the sweet spot between my legs. I moan in anticipation. He scoops me up and carries me to our bedroom, where we stay all afternoon. I feel almost like we've fallen in love all over again...

# FOUR

I am pregnant. The last thing I was expecting. My happiness overrides everything. This is what I have wanted for so long. And Lucas, too. All the suspicions and fears that have consumed me over the past few months seem to vanish. My wish has come true. A sweet anticipation swells my heart with love. With hope.

Lucas comes into the room with a tray. On a scale of one to ten on husbandish duties, I have to say that Lucas scores an eight, and on some days, a nine. Today he is hovering around a nine and a half. While I was sleeping, trying to shed a splitting headache, the dogs have been taken out on their walk, fed their breakfast, and here Lucas is, bringing me coffee and toast.

"How are you feeling?" he asks tenderly, setting the tray on the edge of the bed. His blue eyes are full of love. He lifts a tendril of hair away from my face, his fingers gentle on my skin. "I came in earlier but you were still conked out. Didn't want to wake Sleeping Beauty. Eat some toast." His gaze is loving as he brings the buttery toast to my lips, which is laced with my favorite honey. The fragrance fills my head with lavender and Provence. I open my mouth and let him feed me.

I chew and swallow. "Delicious."

"There's mint chocolate ice cream in the refrigerator, and while you were sleeping, I made mashed potatoes with chopped-up coriander."

"You didn't?"

"I did."

"That's so sweet of you." Lately I've been craving coriander, of all things. And comfort food like mashed potatoes and mac and cheese. Pregnancy has brought on strange desires.

He cracks that charming smile of his. "Actually, it was for selfish reasons. Keeping you happy makes my life a whole lot easier. And our baby has certain tastes."

*Our baby*. Those words sound so promising. He winks at me, a floppy blond lock hiding the other eye. The eye that holds secrets, intrigue. An eye that still renders me weak with its gaze.

He takes a long breath in through his nose, and his demeanor suddenly changes. The businessman returns, the one whose mission is unassailable. He glances at his Rolex. "I have to head on out. Can't be one second late or Dad will ice me out of the meeting."

I don't object. I know better than to get in the way of Lucas and his father. My attempts at championing Lucas's autonomy have failed over time. If Lucas were more of an entrepreneur type, he would have left his dad's law firm a long time ago. But he is weak. He cares too much about proving himself to Jack, about taking over his dad's business because that's what he was programmed to believe would happen ever since he was a young boy. This is the carrot that Jack has been dangling in front of Lucas for years now. Fox & Fox, except the "& Fox" part is still not set in stone. Fox & Co., as it is currently named, does not necessarily signal that it is a family business. In the last year, Jack has lost two accounts. Either he has lost his Midas touch, or it is a simple sign of the times, with clients searching to economize, but for whatever reason, Jack has transferred the burden of "climbing back to the top" to Lucas. He has made it abundantly clear that if Lucas cannot win this new account with the Japanese media company he's been courting for six months, Jack will sell Fox & Co. to the highest bidder and retire without giving Lucas "one damn cent."

"You were right all along," my husband tells me now. "I should have listened to you, honey. Should've walked when I had the chance, but after all the work hours I've put in, I want my money's worth. I'm going to show Dad what I'm made of. He'll see. I'll win this account. I am this"—he holds up his thumb and finger in a measured sliver of a centimeter—"close. I swear, by tonight I'll have the account nailed." Lucas stands up, handsome in a tailored, navy-blue suit and aquamarine silk tie that complement his eyes. Italian shoes polished to a high shine. He has even learned some Japanese phrases to impress the client.

"By the way," he says, glancing at the ceiling, "I meant to ask you. With your pregnancy hormones, being forgetful and stuff, we should get all the smoke detectors in the house checked to make sure they're all working."

"Sure. I'll see to it," I say, not liking his choice of the word *forgetful*. Then I give him my best smile and add, "Good luck for today. Eat 'em alive." I am parroting one of Jack's favorite sayings, *Eat 'em alive*. It usually goes along with *Swim with the sharks*.

Poor Lucas. He has always tried to be a shark, but has fallen short every time. The tough guy part of him is an act, a need to please his father. Still, I am not naïve. Before my pregnancy, there was a shiftiness in the way he was acting. Coming home late. Laughing at his text messages. Taking extra time over his appearance, even polishing his shoes. Little tells which show me he was lying, and the lying morphed into an insidious form of gaslighting, which I did not appreciate. The biggest tell of all? A diamond-hoop earring I found under our bed a couple of months ago when I returned from a job, after being away from home for a few days.

An earring that wasn't mine.

# FIVE

When Lucas leaves the room, I sit up in bed, appreciating our gorgeous view of the ocean and feeling so grateful about my pregnancy. Ariadne, one of our dogs, is nestled at my feet, half swathed by the comforter, luxuriating in an unusual, late-morning lie-in. I lost my job a couple of months back, so I've been able to sneak in a little extra shut-eye lately. My other dog, Sappho, has her head resting near my belly, where she is aware that a life is growing inside me. She knew, with her sixth sense, that I was pregnant before I had even missed my period. It's amazing how sensitive dogs are, how intuitive. I take it all in: the possibility of losing this—all of this—and a surge of dread and sadness well up inside me. I lost my mother to cancer last year. I have no siblings, and my father is as good as dead, too. Apart from my aunt, I have no family except my husband. It was a shock losing my job, something I didn't see coming at all. They "let me go." Nepotism runs rife in Hollywood, and I've been replaced by the daughter of the show's producer. With ten years' experience behind me as a script supervisor, a total newbie has replaced me, just like that. Two weeks' severance pay, and *Take care, Ava, drop by for a coffee any time, no hard feelings.*

It does worry me, because I have no savings left. The money I did have in my nest egg was gobbled up by the medical bill I owed the hospital after they told me there was nothing more they could do for my mom. I have always worked, always earned my own money, always been financially independent. The idea that I might not find a job in a town that is based around movie making, and in a field where I hold a pretty high degree of expertise, had not crossed my mind. But right now, my financial security is teetering on the edge of a canyon. I have nothing beyond this marriage, and our baby is on the way. Medical bills in the States are no joke. I wanted the best for my mom, as any daughter would. I didn't think twice about offering her the finest life she could possibly live during her last few months. I assumed my job would cover the costs. Not in a million years did I entertain the possibility of being made redundant and finding no other employment in the messy flotsam of being "let go." I'm still looking. I have three headhunters searching on my behalf. Who knew it would end up being so complicated?

I lay my hand on my belly so my baby won't absorb my anxiety. I am going to give this pregnancy everything I've got. After all, with no job right now, I certainly have the time to put in the work. I do it all: yoga, meditation, listening to podcasts about pregnancy, classes on nutrition and vitamins.

I take a calming breath and rest my gaze on my stomach. Tell myself that everything will work out fine.

*We are survivors*, I whisper. *We can get through this.*

But I can't seem to rein in my warring emotions. My eyes skate around the room as the thought of what's at stake if my marriage doesn't work out runs through my head. I try to push it away. I love my husband, despite everything, and making a nest for my family has always been a top priority for me. What if I was wrong about my suspicions of him cheating? He's just as thrilled about the baby as I am. We are a unit. This is the home we created together for our family, for our future. Everything in this house was chosen with love, by me, a woman in love. The blue and white joie de vivre curtains and cushions, the simple white of the walls that doesn't compete with the view, and where sunlight reflects shifting shadows and golden slabs of morning light around the room. The vanity, where my creams and French perfume sit side by side, the glass top sandwiching special family photos beneath that lift my heart every morning when I get dressed and set an upbeat mood for the day. The seascape oil painting of St. Tropez proudly taking up prize position alongside the view, a gift from Lucas after our honeymoon. And most of all, our two beautiful golden retrievers, Sappho and Ariadne, rescued by me from a puppy mill, where they were ruthlessly used as breeding machines. I was thrilled to welcome them to our family, not only because they needed to be rescued from hell, but because of their gentle nature with children, their sense of fun, their loyalty with their family, their pack. *Us.* Lucas and me. Me and Lucas. And now our baby on the way. And these girls sense things: the baby's heart beating to my own, producing in me a fathomless love I never knew possible—the kind that seeps into the marrow of your bones. These dogs are as excited as I am. I want with all my heart and soul to make things work.

I slide my gaze to the French doors. They open onto the deck with a view to the ocean. I love this old wooden house and couldn't wish for anything different. How many homes have a view like this? Except, right this minute, a dark cloud is drifting into my line of vision, like a warning sign. It has come out of nowhere, settling itself in the great expanse of blue, September sky. Tinged with pink and now spreading and dispersing itself.

*Pink sky in the morning, sailor's warning.*

My headache looms back. Negative thoughts crowd in,

clambering in on themselves, trying to gain footing. I try to think back, try to piece together everything that has made up our marriage until now and the person I am. Or at least, the person I believe myself to be. A girl who came from a small town, raised by a single mom, and a dad who left when I was three years old. A person who weathered bullies at school; a person who came from humble beginnings, took three jobs to get herself through college and made things work. A person who knows her own strength.

This is who I am.

Or who I was until my husband started messing with my mind and made me second-guess myself. Is he capable of change?

I guess I'll soon find out.

# SIX

"Honey," Lucas says, coming into the bedroom. He is back from work. I have done nothing all day except think. Deliberate. I am still in my pajamas, stuffing my pregnant self with ice cream when he finds me in bed watching my favorite show, *Go Ask Bobbie*.

He kisses me hello. A chaste kiss on my forehead. "You smell of lily of the valley," I say.

"Your sense of smell has gone haywire since you got pregnant," he responds, and laughs. "It's the ice cream you're smelling, babe, not me." He shrugs off his jacket and shirt as he makes his way to the bathroom. "I'm going to hit the shower."

"Why are you back so late?" I shout after him, shoveling another spoon of Ben & Jerry's Cookie Dough into my mouth.

But he ignores my question, turns his head at the doorway, winks at me and says, "Missed you, babe."

My mind begins to whir with possibilities about where he has been, but, thinking of my baby, I try to block out my negative inner banter.

I spent time in a psychiatric institution after my miscarriage three years ago. I had done everything right, and the doctors assured me it wasn't my fault. I had taken folic acid religiously, avoided alcohol, done just enough—but not too much—exercise, gotten plenty of sleep, et cetera. Yet one morning I woke up bleeding, and at the hospital the ultrasound showed the baby had no heartbeat. I was devastated. I had to go through with an operation under anesthetic the following day, a D & C. It was so final. I suppose somewhere in the back of my mind I had thought that if the baby could feel the power of my love, the warmth and protection of my womb, he or she might miraculously come back to life. "Can't you give it a few more days?" I asked the surgeon. "Just in case?" She looked at me with such pity in her eyes but didn't utter a word. Simply shook her head. Later, she told me how these unexplained miscarriages happen to a lot of women, that I was not alone and I could try again after six months. "After your cervix has had time to heal," she said. I imagined Lucas and I would try again immediately, that we could replace the pregnancy with another and put our bad luck behind us, but it wasn't going to work out that way otherwise my health would have been in danger. When it was over and I was back on my feet, it felt like sacrilege taking the contraceptive pills the doctors had prescribed. I was tempted to flush them down the toilet, try to get pregnant straight away, but they had told me my body needed time to heal first. The whole experience sent me into a spiral of depression and confusion. It broke things.

Our marriage, you see, had been precipitated by the pregnancy. Lucas was in a panic. His parents—being super conservative—made it clear there was no way I could "run around pregnant" without a ring on my finger. I was in no rush, but Lucas was adamant we get married. When he introduced me to Jack and Barbara for the first time, I understood what his problem was. They had controlled him for so long, he had forgotten his own inner strength, his ability to make decisions for himself. They were cold, formal, impeccably dressed. His mother wore a tight chignon scraped close to her head, paired with a Chanel suit and so much Botox freezing up her forehead, I wondered if it had leaked down into her heart. His father, a hotshot attorney, with clients ranging from football legends to A-list movie stars, made me uneasy with his machine-gun questions about my past and my education, which, of course, paled beside Lucas's. I felt, when we sized each other up that first time at Maestro's, that I was being interviewed for a job.

"You were raised in the Wyoming countryside, Lucas told us." Jack lifted a brow as if to tell me how dubious being a country girl was.

"That's right," I replied with pride.

"We don't believe in... well, 'living in sin,'" Barbara chimed in, veering the subject in a new direction. "We need to fix this immediately."

"Fix what?" Were they inviting me to dinner to discuss terminating my pregnancy? I shuddered.

"The wedding," she clarified, "needs to go ahead ASAP."

"Oh, we don't need to get married just because I'm—"

"I've managed to snap up a last-minute cancellation, thank *goodness*, at the Hotel Bel-Air in three weeks' time. What a stroke of luck! Normally there's at least a year-long waiting list."

"Three *weeks*?" I looked over at Lucas, who was nodding in agreement.

Jack took a sip of his wine. "But of course, we'll need you to sign a prenup."

"A prenup?" I echoed. This conversation was getting more surreal by the second. I turned to Lucas. *Say something!*

But Lucas only held my hand, his lips unmoving.

"A prenuptial agreement," Barbara explained as if I didn't know what it was.

"To protect Lucas's inheritance," Jack added. "In fact, I have it right here." He tapped his briefcase. "No point wasting time. After all, I'm an attorney. I mean, if you'd like some time to think it over, but in all honesty, Ava, if you love Lucas—"

"Which we know you do," Barbara cut in.

Lucas still remained mute, just squeezed my hand a little tighter to show solidarity.

"I... this is all so fast," I protested. "I need some time to think, I—"

"Wait, you don't want to marry me? Is that it?" Lucas broke in, his brow heavy with hurt.

"Of course I do, but I hadn't imagined it would be so soon."

When you have three people homing in on you, you're pregnant, and you're madly in love, what do you do? I felt so under pressure, so pressganged. Did Lucas know his parents were going to suggest marriage today? To ask me to sign a prenup?

Lucas, seeing my distress, cleared his throat. "Mom, Dad, this is all a bit—"

"I'll read it over tonight," I said.

I was in love with Lucas, so really, this silly prenup made no difference to me. I earned my own way, had a good job, a prenup wasn't going to change anything. Lucas was committing to me and the baby, and that was more important than anything.

I wanted to prove that I was marrying for love, not money, so I signed that prenuptial agreement the next morning. Of course I did. I loved Lucas, we were going to have a baby, so what was the big deal?

The prenup stated that if Lucas and I divorced, I would leave the marriage with no claims whatsoever to Lucas's earnings, inheritance, or property, future or otherwise. I should have gotten my own lawyer to look it over, to negotiate. After all, they were the ones pushing for the marriage in the first place. But I was in love. I didn't want to make waves or start our life together on a negative footing, so I waived the right to an attorney. I was convinced we would never get divorced. Why worry about a prenup getting in the way? And I earned my own money, so why should I care? Lucas's dad had it wrapped up very neatly; the easiest thing was to sign.

But when I suffered that miscarriage, just a few weeks after the wedding... well, I'm not dumb, I read between the lines. I could sense the distaste pucker on Jack Fox's lips, like I'd tricked Lucas into marrying me by "getting knocked up." I believe Jack Fox felt like he had the last laugh when I lost my baby, because at least he knew his money—the legacy he'd one day hand down to his son—was safe. He was convinced I'd lope off back to where I came from, to my "po-dunk dive in Wyoming." But I wasn't going anywhere. Why would I when I was—and still am—in love with my husband?

Ever since then, Jack has been itching for our marriage to go wrong, for one of us to file for divorce. Lucas's parents think I am from "the wrong side of the tracks." They think I am "poor white trash." They don't understand the value of being raised by a single mom, of fighting your way out of a corner. He wanted an East Coast princess for his son, not a woman like me: a "cowgirl hick" from Wyoming who knows how to ride bareback and shoot a bullseye. I'm proud of my roots.

A little bit of grit and determination go a long way.

Lucas comes back to the bedroom after his shower, a towel slung around his waist. As always, my eyes are drawn to his tan, muscular body. When he browses through his closet to pick out a fresh shirt, his back to me, I notice a scratch on his shoulder. A tiger's swipe, fresh. Raw. I did not dig my nails into his back. In fact, we haven't made love for two weeks. If I ask him, he'll have an excuse at the ready the way he always does. He'll tell me it was his surfboard or some such thing, and then I'll second-guess myself and feel paranoid.

As well as eating for two, I need to *think* for two. Whatever suspicions I may have about what my husband is up to, our baby needs two parents, a loving home, and all the opportunities I was denied as a child. Plus, leaving is not an option. I know what's at stake. He would fight for custody, and he'd probably win. Sure, I could walk out the door right now, but where would that get me? Into a huge mess with a court battle, that's what. And more importantly, how would it benefit my child? Besides, I am in no condition to make radical decisions right now, especially when I don't even trust my own judgment. Because there is always the possibility that I could be wrong.

This is my predicament. I am a seesaw. So many emotions are battling against each other inside my head. A head that has been so confused lately can I even have faith in its assertations? Plus, there's the love issue that tends to get in the middle of things when you're married. I *love* my husband, I do. I don't want to wind up alone. When I made a commitment to marriage, I believed it was forever.

For now, anyway, I will let things ride.

I'll ferret out exactly what he's been up to in my own time.

I have my ways.

# SEVEN

The next morning, enjoying another delicious breakfast in bed, thanks to Lucas, I ruminate about the diamond-hoop earring I found in the bedroom two months ago. When I discovered that tell-tale piece of jewelry, Lucas denied all knowledge of its source. Of course he did. He laughed my suspicions away. Told me I was crazy, that he had given me those earrings last Christmas. "Don't you *remember*?" he quizzed, scrunching up his face like I was losing my marbles.

"No," I replied. "I've never seen that earring before." I stressed the word ear*ring*, as in a singular item. "You gave me a saddle. So I could go horseback riding more often." I wondered, at the time, if the saddle had been Lucas's attempt to get me out of town more often.

"Honeeeeey," he cajoled, adding one of his happy-go-lucky chuckles as he spoke, "I gave you those expensive earrings as *well* as the saddle! I cannot believe you've forgotten! Quite honestly that's insulting." I noticed the addition of "expensive" to his plea of innocence. A way to pull on the guilt-factor strings. I'm a practical kind of woman. I don't like unnecessary, flashy spending. I can buy a pair of rhinestone earrings or second-hand, never-even-worn Jimmy Choos from The Real-Real, and who's to know the difference? I certainly can't differentiate between fake and genuine. It's not what you wear, but how you wear it. I like a bargain, not to be taken for a ride—except by a horse. Buying me expensive earrings is not the best way to my heart.

The very next day after that conversation, Lucas produced a photo. A real, paper photo, framed in a real silver frame and sitting on his office desk, of me wearing the earrings. "See?" he said gleefully. "Remember how I told you how beautiful you looked that night?"

I did remember that night. I wore a red dress and we had gone dancing. But I wasn't wearing those earrings. At least...

Not that I could recall.

It was then I decided to set up a camera in our bedroom. Because either I was going crazy or I had the beginnings of early Alzheimer's.

Or... my husband was lying.

I feed the last morsels of Provence-honeyed toast to my dogs and drain my coffee.

Once I hear the click of the front door and Lucas's electric Lexus purr out of the driveway, I set to work. On the ceiling of our room is the "smoke detector" I installed, which Lucas has not noticed until today; it is a reminder that I need to check the recordings. Oh, for the joys and wonders of shopping online. Nobody has to know your business, and as long as you delete your browser history and change your passwords at regular intervals, who will ever know?

I stand on the bed, but the dummy smoke detector is out of my reach. It is connected to an app on my phone so I don't actually have to dislodge it from its position, since all of the videos will be stored on my phone, with times and dates, and easily located. But I took the extra precaution of inserting an SD card, and that is what I am after.

The dogs get excited when they see me pushing the bed aside and grabbing a stepladder from the utility closet in the kitchen. I shouldn't be exerting so much energy, shouldn't be moving furniture around in my pregnant state, but this mission cannot wait. The strange thing is that I had pretty much forgotten about this camera. Until today when Lucas noticed the "smoke detector" for the first time.

What am I expecting to find? Lucas making passionate love to another woman? In *our* bed? The thought makes the honey lurch up my throat, my heart pound. His blue eyes fixed on another woman's breasts, the curve of her neck, her breath hot against his lips? I push the vivid images out of my head and step away from the ladder. *Why am I doing this?* What good will it do? I have our child growing inside me and I do not want a divorce, I do not want to repeat history—to struggle as a single mom the way my mother did. Or fight over child custody and end up in some nasty battle where the kid is used as a weapon. Or worse, have my baby taken away from me altogether with scanty visiting rights.

The dogs' barking snaps me back to the present. In this moment of time things are still whole. Things are great. I am married and pregnant and I live in a beautiful home. I am provided for, and the fact I lost my job has not affected my lifestyle one bit. I don't take my good fortune lightly. I watch the news. I give to charities, to little girls who long to go to school, to people who have to walk miles to get clean water to drink. To women who have nowhere to turn because they have no legal rights. I am well aware of how good I have it and how lucky I am. Expecting absolute perfection in a marriage is foolhardy. Why would I want to jeopardize any of this? My marriage—to a gorgeous, good-looking attorney who brings me breakfast in bed, no less—is intact.

I dig my phone out of my pocket, swiping back through to our @thefoxyfoxes Insta photos, flicking through those "vacation" pictures again, as I attempt to make sense of the recent past and glaring present. And now I wonder... I can't help it... is my mind playing tricks on me? Is it possible, just possible, that I've got it all wrong? That Lucas and I *were* on vacation, and somehow my brain has turned the facts upside down?

# EIGHT

When I get back home from walking the dogs, Lucas's car is in the driveway. My stomach dips. The bed is still pushed to one side of the room. He'll wonder what I've been doing moving furniture around. It will draw attention to the dummy smoke detector and, although being a handyman is not his forte—I'm the one who changes the lightbulbs—he may have inspected it himself. Uh-oh. What if he's seen that the smoke detector is not a smoke detector at all, but a camera? The last thing I need is an argument. Already I regret nosing around, trying to catch him out, stirring up trouble when I should concentrate on staying healthy, taking my vitamins, enjoying my good fortune, and seeing this pregnancy through. I need to focus on my future, and that of my baby...

As I am chiding myself, a woman breezes out of our front door. What the hell? I had forgotten to put the burglar alarm on before I left for the hike. The dogs race up to her, tails wagging. By the way they greet her and jump about, they know this woman. I can't make sense of it. She waves at me. My mind is still blank. A short, tartan skirt. Long, milk-pale legs leading to a pair of clunky, flowery Dr. Martens on her feet. Hair in a high ponytail. Her short top rides up her stomach and reveals... a bellybutton piercing? Then I realize who it is: Jasmine, Lucas's assistant. We've met just once, when I swung by the office one time.

She waves again. "Hi, Ava!"

"Jasmine? What are you doing here?" I wait for Lucas to emerge, but she shuts the door behind her. Keys clink in her hand. "Where's Lucas?" I ask, bewildered.

"At the office. Good news, he won the Japanese account. Guess we'll all be celebrating!"

*We?*

"Why are you here? And how come you have keys to our house?"

"Didn't Lucas let you know? I dropped off your dry cleaning and brought you some groceries. Lucas told me you needed a hand, that you often forget to do the shopping." Her tone is matter-of-fact, unapologetic, and maddeningly upbeat.

*Forget to do the shopping?* That "forget" word again so easily brandished about by him. And now he is telling other people that I'm forgetful? How dare he!

"And you drive his car?"

She shrugs like it's no big deal. "Sometimes, yeah, when I need to do errands for him."

"What other stuff do you do?" I stand there, motionless. My question comes out a little accusatory. It's not Jasmine's fault she's here with keys to my house. Not Jasmine's fault she's driving around in my husband's fancy car. She's his employee, she'll do what she's told.

"Oh, this and that." Her accent sounds East Coast. New York maybe? She's young. In her very early twenties. She's got a neo-grunge look going on, but is undeniably cute. Even—I would say—extremely attractive. She doesn't look like she belongs in a law firm at all. I wonder what my father-in-law makes of her dress code? I can't see him approving.

"What kind of work are you expected to perform, what are your skill sets?" I probe again.

Lucas's assistant should be wearing sensible pumps, a skirt that reaches below her knees, not someone who has a belly-button piecing. And then it dawns on me. The lone "earring" under my bed? The one Jasmine is wearing is similar in style to the one I discovered. I swat that thought away like an annoying fly. No way. Not possible. She is so not his style. But then... why has he employed a person dressed like this in the first place? She isn't law firm material. Why did he hire her? Looking at her is making me think of the ring he has taken to wearing on his pinkie finger that he told me he had bought online. A chunky silver skull with turquoise stones for eyes. Not his usual style. A gift? From her?

Her big eyes meet mine. All guile and innocence. Too much so. "This and that. You know, spreadsheets, typing up reports, answering the phone."

"At the *reception* desk?" I ask with suspicion. I have never seen her at the front desk. Not a serious look for the firm.

"Oh, no. Olga's still the receptionist."

"So you don't go to meetings?"

"Nuh-uh, I work more behind the scenes. Making graphs, dictations, Photoshop, stuff like that."

*Behind the scenes. Photoshop?* Manipulating images is surely the last thing a legal entity should—or needs to—be doing.

"What do you photoshop?" I ask, my eyes narrowing.

Jasmine turns puce-red like a rash is clambering up her neck and onto her face. She pretends she hasn't heard my question, looks at her phone as if suddenly realizing what time it is and says, "Great seeing you, Ava. I gotta go. Take care." At that, she zaps Lucas's car open with the key fob and jumps into his car, as if her long legs are scuttling to keep up with her torso. As she powers off, the tires squeal a little in her rush to get away from me.

I mull over what I just heard and something unsettling clicks into place.

*Me wearing earrings I had never seen before in that photo. Me on vacation in a place I don't recognize.* Photoshop? Adding earrings to a picture must be pretty easy if you're skilled at Photoshop. If I'm right, my husband has some nerve thinking he can get away with this. Is he trying to drive me back into another psychiatric institution? I whip out my phone and swipe through our Instagram page to look at her handiwork. Either Jasmine is great at what she does, or I am crazy.

Either way, it is in this moment that I know one thing for sure: I need to see with my own eyes whatever is on that spy camera I set up.

No more wallowing in denial.

# NINE

It doesn't matter how incredible a woman might be, there is always a man out there who will cheat on her. Even goddesses are cheated on and tricked. Like Ariadne, or real-life, latter-day goddesses like Marilyn Monroe. Not that I am a goddess. I'm just an ordinary, everyday woman, but still. It's not all about looks. My point is that very rarely is it the woman's fault, and however good a man has it, however lucky they are, some will always want more. More to feed their ego. More because they are greedy. More because... they can. I have only been faithful and true to my husband, and yet, clearly, he can't keep it in his pants.

Some men are wired that way.

I deserve better than this.

Yes, I've had my suspicions all along, but seeing Jasmine swan into my home in her short skirt, right before my eyes, is the closest thing of proof to date. I storm into the house, my sweet golden girls following, oblivious of the rage that bubbles inside me. I give them each a treat, fill their water bowls, their slurping tongues and happy faces calming me somewhat in the knowledge that there *is* good in the world, and sweetness, and pure unadulterated love. Sadly, it usually only comes in the form of dogs. Dogs really are God's greatest gift to mankind.

I stride back to the bedroom with the ladder and get focused on the task at hand. My phone rings. I glance at the screen. Lucas. No doubt calling to let me know the good news about the Japanese account and what a brilliant, clever guy he is. Now is not the time.

I spend the next hour going through the recordings. Most are very dull. Us moving around the room, getting ready for bed. Sometimes laughing, chatting, or making love, other times bickering. The dummy detector was placed right above the bed in a birds-eye view. Anything that happened away from the bed is just a soundtrack, since the camera does not have wide-lensed peripheral vision. It was fixed and couldn't film at an angle. But that doesn't seem to matter as there is nothing there that gives me any clue as to a stranger's voice or an unknown visitor anyway. Simply our everyday life pattering along. Jasmine is not splayed out on our bed, naked, making passionate love to my husband. Nobody is making passionate love to my husband except me. The dogs feature a lot, sneaking on and off the bed, especially when they think nobody's around. I pay specific attention to the dates when I have been away from home, on jobs when I have been on location shooting a movie or series. Nothing interesting comes up.

Being a film and television script supervisor, sometimes the hours are inordinately long, so there were days and evenings when I was away a lot. But I'm not one to mind because time flies by when you are part of a great working crew and when you watch actors make magic before your eyes. My job involves making sure scenes and dialogue flow with flawless continuity so that all the details remain consistent from shot to shot and scene to scene. When exactly an actor clasps his hands or runs his fingers through his hair, or at which precise moment in the dialogue she curtsies or raises her teacup to drink. What lens was used for the shot? What filter? This needs to be consistent so in the editing room they cut it together smoothly without any hiccups and have all the information they need if they have to do a pickup shot further down the line. Vehicles that don't go from dirty to clean to dirty again. Tattoos that stay in the same place, this is all part of my job as script supervisor.

When filming, scenes are shot out of order, and my job is to make sure nobody notices. I act as a conduit between production and post-production. Filming is slow. Sometimes it takes a whole day to film two minutes' worth of movie. For instance, if there's a clock on the wall that says 12:15, you'd better make sure the clock's time moves correctly, according to how much time has passed in any given scene, even if filming that scene has taken the whole day. Burning candles in a scene is also a big challenge. You don't want a moviegoer getting pulled out of the story by some dumb mistake. Because scenes are shot out of sequence, you have to be aware of everything and note all details down, and share those notes—hundreds of pages of them—with the editor, director, and the production office. Someone wearing glasses. Or a watch, or jewelry. Which finger is a ring on? The way an actor's hair is parted. It had better not change mid-scene after they've had a lunch break. Or the length of a cigarette. Or the amount of food on a plate. How much does someone eat or smoke in that scene? The stain on some clothing. The way a scarf hangs around a character's neck at that moment in film time. People notice everything. If a member of the audience sees a book that was written in 1998 show up in a TV show that is supposedly meant to take place in 1997, you can bet someone will notice. I am an indispensable tool for the director, the producer, the actors, the editor, makeup, hair, and props, and every department who values correct and proper continuity for the movie or TV show, so that all the puzzle pieces can be slotted back into place without anyone noticing they were ever out of order to begin with. I need an eagle eye and always have to plan ahead.

That is why Lucas must be deluded to think he can spin circles around me and hope I won't notice.

I notice everything.

I continue watching the recordings, yawning as I go. Pretty dull stuff, actually. I am only half paying attention when a new recording has me pausing the frame more than once. The woman sprawled out on the bed is motionless. The motion-detect camera has been alerted because Sappho comes to sniff her, to check if she is still alive. She is wearing a man's robe and she looks as if she has recently showered because her dark hair is slick and wet. The robe belongs to Lucas. A batik print from Thailand. I know, because I bought it for him as a gift. I pause the frame. There are two bottles of liquor. Empty. One, a bottle of Mount Gay rum on the bedside table, and, cockeyed on the comforter, resting by the tips of this woman's fingers, is an empty bottle of scotch. Ooh, nasty... mixing drinks like that. If that weren't enough to knock a person out cold, there is a vial of pills. Also empty. One pill has found its way into a fold of the bedding; otherwise, one would assume this woman has downed all the medication. Her fingers twitch. She is alive. There is vomit on the bed that has spilled out of her mouth.

I zoom in, unable to process the image because it feels so surreal. So unbelievable. It can't be. But it is.

That woman is me.

# TEN

What follows next is even harder to comprehend. Lucas comes into the frame.

"Oh, shit, hell, what do I do?" He is muttering to himself, pacing up and down the bedroom. At one point he grabs my wrist but doesn't seem to know how to find my pulse. He puts his ear to my chest as if listening for a heartbeat. Turning around in circles, he fumbles for his phone, dropping it and then picking it up again, his fingers no more solid than melted butter. It looks as if he is about to dial 911, but instead selects a number he must often call on auto, since he presses only once. "Dad?"

"Son." Jack's voice is on speaker. Lucas puts all his calls on speaker, hates having the phone close to his ear; he is convinced we are all going to end up with brain tumors.

"Damn it, Dad, I need your help."

"Don't cuss, Lucas. What can I do for you?" Jack's voice is cool, unemotional, but ever so slightly irritated. As if helping his son is a bother to him, an inconvenience.

"Ava is... Ava, she's—"

"What, son. What has she done?"

I am already accused. Not, *Is she okay?* Or, *What happened to her?* But *What has she done?* My father-in-law is a real piece of work.

"She's taken an overdose. There's pills and booze everywhere. She vomited."

"She's alive?"

"Yes! Thank God. Should I call 911?"

*Duh. Of course you should call 911, dummy! I am your wife! What is wrong with you!* I watch on, horrified.

"No!" Jack's voice is a bark. "Do not, in heaven's sake, call 911. Roll her over, massage her back, get all the vomit out, let her sleep it off."

"But Dad!"

"You want a scandal? You want everyone to know what she's gone and done?"

"But—"

"You asked for my help, Lucas. This is what I am suggesting. Do whatever you want, but be aware of the consequences."

*The consequences? I am lying there on my deathbed and the consequences are that I am, in all likelihood, about to die!*

But the chilled tone of Jack's voice is clearly wreaking havoc on Lucas's psyche. The "consequences" are that he will be axed out of the business, that he will not inherit Fox & Co. That Fox & Co. will never become Fox & Fox. Lucas paces up and down, his hands raking through his hair, sweat dripping from his brow. When I zoom in, I see tears in his eyes. But these tears are not enough to propel him to dial the emergency services.

Jack goes on. "Ava's an attention seeker, Lucas. If she really wanted to die, she'd have put a bullet through her head. If you pander to her, she'll try this again, you know that, don't you, son?"

*What a cruel bastard...* Watching this makes my legs feel like

Jell-O. Like my body cannot support me, like I'm falling with nobody to catch me. This shows how ruthless Lucas is. I am his wife and he simply doesn't care. Am I expendable?

I watch on.

Lucas says, "Dad, I—"

"Night, Lucas. You married the woman. Deal with it." The phone goes dead.

"Honey, I'm home!" For a second I think this is coming from the video, but a split second later, Lucas bursts into the bedroom, a grin on his face, his suit crumpled. I stuff the SD card into my jeans pocket and solemnly hand him my phone, the recording still on the screen. I am trembling.

"Congratulations on winning the account, Fox & Fox. You know, Fox & Fox is perfect for you and your father. Just perfect, considering how cunning foxes are reputed to be." My tone is a notch more arctic than I want it to be.

"What's wrong, honey? You *pissed* at me for some reason? Sorry I didn't have time to tell you about Jasmine coming over. I thought it would be a nice surprise for her to do the grocery shopping, I thought—"

"It's not about Jasmine."

"What has gotten into you?"

"Watch the video. It speaks for itself. And for you. I already knew what an asshole your father is, but I had no idea you could be this cruel, this detached. This is not the man I married. You've turned into some kind of monster. To think I imagined us being a happy family. To think I imagined us having a baby... together. Why didn't I walk when I had the chance? Why did I..." My voice breaks into a sob. I have no words left. This man—my husband—left me to die. *Who is he?*

Lucas's jaw is slack, his eyes incredulous. He genuinely has no idea what I am talking about. He thought, because I never brought it up, that he had gotten away with this, that I had blacked out that night and had forgotten everything. It feels good to have some proof in my hands.

I fix my gaze on his fake, puppy-dog eyes. "You wanted me dead? Is that it?"

"What?"

"Watch the video, Lucas. It's all here. A couple of months ago I set up a dummy smoke detector above the bed. The camera never lies."

"A *spy* camera? Why? Why would you even do something like that?"

"Excuse me? I set it up because I didn't trust you! And what I found was even worse than I imagined! I was right not to trust you because it looks like you wanted me dead!"

"That's crazy. I love you. I would never harm you, you know that!"

"You left me sprawled out on that bed after taking pills and drinking booze and you didn't call 911!"

"I was trying to protect you!"

"How is it protecting me to *not* call an ambulance?"

"I... I *wanted* to!"

"Oh, please. Nobody was holding a gun to your head. You followed your daddy's instructions because you're weak! Pathetic! You can't think for yourself! I am done! Done with this marriage. Done with you and your cruel-hearted daddy. Done with you gaslighting me!"

"*Gaslighting* you?"

"The vacation photos. You think I'm an idiot? I know what Jasmine's skills are, besides the obvious. She has been photo-shopping pictures of me!"

"Jasmine?"

"You're crazy to think I wouldn't catch on."

His concerned face and creased brow melt all of a sudden into an easy smile. The same smile that got me saying yes to our first date. "Okay, I lied, so sue me. Told you we'd been on vacation. It was a joke! I was messing with you and you took it seriously! Babe, I was fooling with you!"

I stand there in stunned silence. Is he seriously going to pull that on me? Turn it around, try and make me forget? Lucas has a clever way of always winning an argument. Of twisting things and making *me* look like the one who's in the wrong. Making himself turn out to be the good guy. If you play a joke on someone, you don't let that joke fester. You say "Joke!" You let the person know you're kidding straight away. Maybe my hormones are robbing me of a sense of humor, but I don't think so. No, Lucas wanted me to truly believe him, believe his big lie.

"It's not a funny joke," I mutter.

"Ava! I was playing around! Wanted to see what your reaction would be. Sweetheart, believe me, I was fooling around, you know how these silly games work. You need to lighten up!"

"What would you have done if I'd died that day?" I retort, my mind back on that hideous video showing what I did.

"You want to know the truth? The real truth?"

"I would *love* to know the truth."

"Okay." He takes both my hands, brings them to his lips and kisses my fingers. Then he sandwiches my hands in his and places them on my belly. His message is clear. *We are a family*.

"Ava. You tried to kill yourself. When you woke up, you had no memory of what had passed. It was better that way. You needed time to recuperate. I needed to take time off work to look after you. So, yeah, I pretended we'd been on vacation to account for the days we were... you know, dealing with your problem."

"What you did was insane!"

"No, babe, what *you* did was insane."

My breath catches in my throat, stopping me from uttering a word. I'm speechless. I literally can't think of anything more to say because I am so floored by what he did. But then what I did was equally shocking. How can I judge him? When what I did was so wrong, so reckless. I feel horribly ashamed. I try to forgive myself for the desperation I must have been feeling at the time. The black hole I was in. Is that how I felt? That I had no choice? That it was my only way out? I feel so sad for myself looking back on it now. I want to reach out to that desperate child inside me who did something so deplorable. Pull her out of herself. All I can do though is move forward, learn from it, and be the strongest version of who I am now. I have a baby to think of now. Something I didn't have then. I am a new person. Stronger. Wiser.

I notice Lucas trying to delete the video on my phone.

"Give me my phone."

"No. This. Did. Not. Happen," he says, emphasizing each word.

I snatch my phone from him. All the videos are still there. "I have it backed up on an SD card. It happened. Sadly, it happened."

He holds out his hand. "Give it to me."

"It's in a safety deposit box," I lie.

"Well, we can go get it and destroy it. You want anyone to see this? You want people to know you tried to kill yourself, is that it? You want your future child to see this one day?"

"I haven't thought that far ahead," I tell him, shaken by all that has passed, by the person I have turned out to be, the things I have done, the lengths I have gone to out of sheer despair. "I'm as shocked as you are about this. I hooked up that nanny-cam, not really thinking, not—"

"Exactly, you were not thinking, Ava!"

"Why didn't you call a doctor? Why didn't you call 911?"

"Because your suicide attempt would've been on record and the authorities might've said you're unfit to be a mother and take your baby away. Don't you see, sweetheart? I did this for you. To *protect* you. You want social services meddling in our lives? Hell, they might put you under observation and force you to give the baby up for adoption. I did this for you. For us."

"Lucas! I wasn't pregnant at that point! The video was six weeks ago. What you're saying is completely crazy!" I stick my phone into the back pocket of my jeans.

"But we were trying for a baby and I thought you might already be pregnant. Don't you remember you thought you might be? You'd missed a period. You'd even taken a home pregnancy test, remember?"

He has my head spinning, doing mental math. "No! That's not true. I got pregnant a month later."

"But we didn't know that at the time, did we? At that moment, we thought you might be pregnant."

My mind is doing gymnastics, trying to think back. If I had been pregnant, I would not have drunk even one glass of wine, let alone two bottles of booze. He, as usual, is trying to bamboozle me, spin my thoughts like yarn, tangle me into confusion.

"Ava. You were in a state. When people fall into depression there's no rhyme or reason for their actions."

I shake my head. Press the heels of my hands onto my closed eyelids. This is all too much. How did I get myself into this mess? "Something must have made me do it. Something bad." My voice is whisper quiet.

He curls his fingers around my wrists, takes my hands away and kisses me. Small kisses all over my face, pressing his soft lips onto my swollen eyes. "All I want is for you to be happy," he breathes into me. "For *us* to be happy. To start afresh. We're a family!"

"We *were* a family. But you know what you did." It is all coming back to me in a rush.

His gaze is wide. Guileless. But I can see right through him, like transparent water. He is lying. Lying is his default setting.

"What are you saying, honey? What did I do? Whatever it is, tell me!" he says through his kisses.

I don't answer him.

But I will force him to watch what he did—or didn't do—make him pay for his crime.

# ELEVEN

The next morning, when Lucas leaves, tail between his legs after I made him sit through the recording of that night, I feign a headache and stay in bed until I hear the door close and his car leave the driveway. Today he is taking the dogs with him on a run. He and his dad do power runs together every Saturday, with the dogs in tow. They talk business, man to man. I dread the topic. It is bound to be me. Not so much the suicide attempt itself, but the fact I have proof of what a monster Jack Fox is and what a weak shithead my husband is. If Lucas is smart, he will not broach the subject of the smoke detector camera with Jack. But Lucas isn't that smart and he won't be able to resist. Somehow the subject will come up because Lucas can't make decisions without his father's blessing. He will be itching for Jack's opinion of what to do, of how to play me and win me over.

Last night, Lucas was all charm. He tried everything to cajole me into giving up that SD card. By which time I had snuck it out of my jeans pocket and slipped it behind a frame of one of our wedding photos. An ironic little hiding place. Our wedding—shotgun though it was—was beautiful. And I have to commend Barbara for organizing such a splash in such a short space of time at the stunning Hotel Bel-Air. Champagne flowed and the flower arrangements in pink and white looked like a movie set. Swans gliding around on Swan Lake, set amidst the tropical gardens with little bridges and stone fountains in an idyllic fairy-tale setting. There were a lot of guests, most of them on Lucas's side. Barbara was all smiles and grace. I could hear her telling her friends how we had been dating for nearly two years. Lie! How I was a "movie producer" and knew "absolutely everyone who's everyone in Hollywood." She clearly thought being a script supervisor was not glamorous enough. No mention was made of my then-pregnancy that my wedding gown cleverly hid... heaven forbid. Nobody asked why my movie-star friends were not at the wedding. Barbara has a way of wrapping her sentences up in Saran Wrap. Tight and impenetrable. People don't dare dispute anything she has to say.

I have to give her her due though; our wedding was amazing and giddy-making. It resulted in a lot of fancy gifts, too, most of which we never use. Our home is a treasure trove of kitchen gadgets and coffee machines. China plates and gold flatware. Turkish rugs and crystal glasses. On occasion, since I lost my job, it has occurred to me to start a props company with all our still-shiny wedding booty. We were all over each other on our wedding day, Lucas and I, into *each other*, not all the trimmings, so those gifts meant very little to us.

Standing on the deck outside the bedroom, I hear someone calling my name. It's my neighbor Jill. I lean over and see her in her running gear, jogging in place on the beach below.

"I can't believe you guys know Claudia Spector!" she calls up breathlessly. She jogs up the steps, moves in closer and leans on the gate.

"Claudia Spector, the actress?" I ask.

Claudia Spector is an A-list movie star of the hit TV show *Go Ask Bobbie*. She plays Bobbie, a kick-ass yet vulnerable woman fresh out of prison, who has served time for a crime she never committed, and she is hell-bent on finding out who framed her. If she were a new client of Lucas's, I'd be sure to know. I get a running commentary about his problems at work and clients pretty much every evening.

Jill is grinning from ear to ear. "Oh, my *God*! I spotted Lucas having dinner with her a couple days ago. Is she a *client* of his?"

I freeze my lips into a grin and grit my teeth. *Dinner?* A trio of seagulls fly overhead, screeching as they go, punctuating how I feel in this moment. Something smells fishy to me, and it's not the sea air. "Yeah, can you believe it?" I fib. "She's their new client. I mean, they're still talking stuff over, but how cool is that?" I am desperate to ask her more. Which restaurant? What time, exactly? But I can't let on I don't know. It's too humiliating. I need to hear it from Lucas's lips.

Jill grins back at me. "*Go Ask Bobbie*'s my favorite show!"

"Me too!"

"I know! I know how much you love her, too."

A few months back I was interviewed by a women's magazine, one of those "a typical day in the life of" an everyday working woman. The makeup I use, my favorite haunts, the book I was reading, my favorite vacation spots, TV show, that kind of thing. I cited *Go Ask Bobbie* as my favorite show, and Claudia my favorite actor. How her talent for creating such diverse characters blows me away.

"So have you *met* her yet?" Jill gushes.

"Just in passing," I lie. I rewind to two nights earlier. Was that when Lucas came home late or when he told me he had an important meeting?

"They sure looked intimate together," Jill elaborates. "They must be close. I mean, she must really *trust* your husband. Their heads were kind of locked together, like they were sharing a secret."

My smile is still frozen in place. "It's his job to, you know, gain clients' confidence."

She wipes beads of sweat from her brow. "You're so cool, Ava, so matter-of-fact, the way you don't get jealous. But I guess, well, considering it's Claudia *Spector*..."

"Yeah, pretty amazing," I say, my heart hammering a thousand miles an hour. I make my excuses to Jill about needing to fix the dogs' breakfast even though they're out on a run with Lucas right now, and I head back inside the house.

While watching from the window to check Jill is out of sight, I observe some surfers in the water, black figures in wetsuits hunched over their boards, waiting for an offshore breeze to blow against the top of the wave, creating the perfect breaker to ride. The hours and hours I have spent watching Lucas surf, and now this?

Instead of calling him and asking what is going on with Claudia Spector—because why bother when you know you'll be fed a lie—I call my father-in-law directly and congratulate him on their new A-list client.

Jack laughs. "Claudia Spector? The *gay* actress?"

I flinch at the way Jack throws out that word, like there's something wrong with her being gay. *Our dog Sappho likes girls too*, I want to say, but I let his comment ride.

"No," Jack says, confirming my suspicions. "That Claudia woman has never crossed paths with our firm, I'd know if she had."

Remembering how Lucas was hovering by his closet the other night, shuffling stuff around (sporting that tigerish scratch mark on his shoulder, no less) I make a beeline for it, meticulously searching through every article of his clothing. His shirts are arranged by color and shade and rival Gatsby's, neatly organized and crisply ironed by our housekeeper, who comes once a week. His suit jackets, too, are impeccably ordered by color and style. It's like there are two Lucases: one the laid-back surfer dude, and the other, the cool, stylish professional. There is the Lucas I adore: loving, kind, funny, and sweet, and the Lucas I fear, the manipulator, the liar, the man who will do anything to get what he wants.

I search, my fingers groping and walking through every jacket pocket, and in every pair of pants, trying not to jumble things up, hoping to find some clue, like a phone number or a note.

I strike gold. Better than any clue, I come across pure evidence.

A burner phone.

It is stuffed into the toe of one of his lesser-worn dress shoes —but it takes me an hour to locate the right cable to charge it, which is hidden, almost invisibly, under a black woolen sweater. It's an old flip phone from a couple of decades back, so not technically a "burner" but ancient enough so all it does is receive and make calls and send messages. No apps. No tricks. It takes a while for me to work it out. Its simplicity seems wildly complicated in this day and age.

There are dozens of messages to and from Claudia Spector herself.

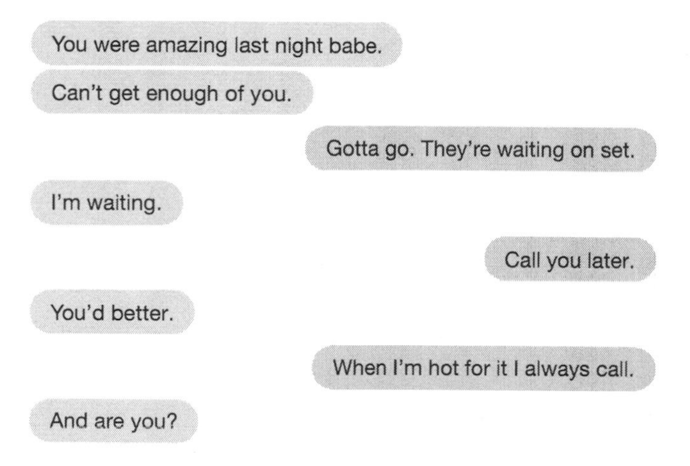

Am I what?

Hot for it?

You'll find out tonite

The first thing I do is throw up. It happens so quickly I don't have time to make it to the bathroom, so I grab the offending shoe and upchuck inside it. I wipe my sicky mouth on one of his pristine dress shirts, which gives me a momentary thrill. Morning sickness mixed with flabbergasted shock. Filled by a numbness filling my entire body, a buzzy floaty feeling rendering me speechless and in such a state of disbelief, all I can do is collapse back on the floor. I sit, burner phone in my shaky, sweaty hand, without moving a muscle. What makes this discovery even more soul-destroying is that I love *Go Ask Bobbie* so much. Claudia Spector has always felt almost like a sister to me, like I know her intimately, like we are almost the same person we have so much in common, especially our single-mom backgrounds. When I first arrived in LA, in the days when Ellen DeGeneres had her talk show, Ellen interviewed her and I was in the audience; a friend of mine had gotten me a ticket. Claudia was so gracious and charming, and funny too. Her acting skills are up there with Meryl Streep's, I have always looked up to her.

Now I feel—illogically—betrayed by *her* almost as much as Lucas.

How can this have happened? Why *her* of all people, and why did she choose Lucas? He's just a guy. A lawyer. He's not a movie star, he's not a rock star. She could get anyone! Besides, Jack's right—she does have a reputation for being gay. She was even engaged to Crystal Cormac, another actress. The affair makes my intestines coil into sailor's knots. What if she is in love with Lucas? She will win. I am an ant next to her, a soaring eagle. This is so out of my control. So beyond anything I can even manage to fathom. Claudia Spector!

Claudia freaking Spector!!

I am way out of my league.

I feel a storm brew inside me. It starts in the pit of my belly and spills through my veins, in turn heating my blood then chilling it to ice. As I picture Lucas and Claudia kissing, sweat gathers on my brow, behind my knees, under my arms. Her perfect body, her perfect hair, those plush lips, the high feline cheekbones, those rounded gray eyes, lashes dark and thick, her quirky, crooked smile. The pert breasts, her figure like a model. Long legs. One of those movie stars whose imperfections make them perfect all round. One of those movie stars we all want to be, if only we dared, if only we knew how. If only we'd had a lucky break.

And she fell for my *husband*?

I check the dates. These messages started in May, four months ago! How rich that he accused me of having an affair when all I had done was put on heels and makeup for his benefit and *he* was the guilty one all along! What a cruel trick.

He needs to be brought back down to earth with a bang.

# TWELVE

Not only do I have the spy-camera video, I have the flip phone evidence. I think I might give Jack a call and get his take on it all. He will not be happy. I imagine his face, puckered, red and furious, yet trying to stay calm and emotionless, with his usual detached demeanor. But he won't be able to hold in his ire, because he will not be the one in control. Who will he be angrier with? Me? Or Lucas? And Barbara will be simpering in the corner, worrying about what her country club friends might think, the ones she plays bridge with. Wanting to bite her nails but resisting because a perfect manicure is part of her signature look.

I arrange to meet Lucas at Nobu. I will give him the news about my latest discovery. Just after we've ordered.

Lucas arrives at Nobu, a fusion restaurant that combines the minimalist, sleek architecture of a wooden Japanese inn with the rustic elegance of the Malibu coastline. With his suit jacket discarded, Lucas's look is more casual than usual, now he has officially been handed over the firm, just last week. Since winning that Japanese account he so cosseted, he is the new managing partner of Fox & Fox, and it shows in the unhurried lines of his face. He is smiling. A flash of white against his tan. He can do what he likes. Dress as he likes. It must feel good to be in control for once, to not have to pander to his father. Although, I wonder if he has truly broken free? Time will tell. Today he looks the part of a successful person who runs the show.

After what I have to tell him, perhaps his new-found cockiness will be taken down a couple of notches.

I have a table outside, a patio booth that looks onto the ocean, perfect for observing the golden hues of the setting sun.

He orders a cocktail named Monkey Business, and I think how apt that is. I ask for a non-alcoholic cocktail. I give him a chance to come clean. I ask him if he has any new clients. He tells me no.

"No fabulous movie stars?" I check. The question is a possible one. They do represent actors.

"No, babe. I wish."

I want to slap him, but we chat and even hold hands, listening to the shush of the lapping waves, talking about names for our baby. Silly, really, as it's such a long way off. I do worry about jinxing things, but I can't live in fear. The idea of being a mother is the only thing holding me together right now.

He grazes his teeth over his lower lip and gazes lingeringly into my eyes. "Wow, you look beautiful tonight, Ava."

An ironic smile plays on my lips, wondering if he said those very same words to Claudia, and what she's like in bed. Just because someone is as beautiful as she is doesn't necessarily mean they know how to move well.

"I remember when we met," he goes on. "And you were wearing all black. Tight black jeans and a tight black T-shirt. And your dark eyes looked almost black, like pools of liquid dark chocolate, and I thought, damn, *that* woman... I need to get to know that woman."

"And I saw you staring at me. I smiled and walked away."

*Let him pursue me*, I had thought, as I looked over the sea of diaphanous gowns and tuxedoes, at the partygoers who had made such an effort with their attire, at the tummy-tucked women with chandelier earrings in Louboutin heels swaying to the beat of soft jazz coming from the live band. I weaved my way through the throng, Lucas's eyes trailing after me. Even then I knew he was a man who liked a chase. I suppose I should have seen it coming. But you don't. You think—or hope—you're special. That you're the only one. That you can tame a womanizer like Lucas.

"You walked away! Linked your arm with—who was that person, that director?—and just walked off. I thought you were a new actress in town."

"Actor, not actress," I snip, letting my anger get the best of me. "Nobody says actress these days, unless they're talking about the Academy Award Best Actress category."

"Whatever." He takes a sip of his cocktail, his eyes landing on my cleavage before moving his gaze back up to my face. "I thought you must've been, like, dating Leonardo DiCaprio or something. You piqued my interest because you didn't seem to give a damn."

*Peaked your interest*, I think with a wry smile, knowing how his actions are guided by one particular part of his anatomy. The night of that party, with Lucas imagining me as an actor, makes me remember why I came to Los Angeles in the first place. I cannot deny that I had high hopes of forging a career in TV and film. I took acting classes to hone my craft, spent a fortune on a renowned coach, and silly money on professional headshots. Though by the time I met Lucas at that party, I had long forgotten those girlish dreams and had become very successful as a script supervisor, which was far more rewarding in the end, actually earning me a steady income without having to wait tables. I had only ever landed one acting role: in a commercial for diapers, as a young mom. Not quite the part I had envisioned, but it did pay a few bills. I got into my job as a script supervisor by sheer luck, replacing someone on maternity leave, and it grew from there. By word of mouth, I gained a reputation of being super observant, of being a good team player, of never ever showing up late for work.

"I'm glad I'm not an actor," I tell Lucas now. But it brings me back to my sharp reality; I have lost the job I loved so much, I have no savings left, and all that remains is a husband who is cheating on me, gaslighting me, and apparently indifferent to whether I'm alive or dead. Yet despite all this very soiled laundry list, deep down inside, I still love the shmuck. But I need to be strong.

He must see a sad look in my eye and be reading my mind because he takes my hand and kisses it. "Honey, don't worry about losing your job. Maybe it's serendipity. You need to stay home anyway, take it easy. We don't want to lose the baby this time around. If you were running about on set working your ass off it'd be dangerous for your health. Things happen for a reason."

For a millisecond, I wonder if Lucas orchestrated my getting fired, but I push that thought away. No, it was bad luck. The love and concern in his gaze appear so genuine, my next sentence is hard to form. But I eventually say, "We need to talk."

He laughs. "We *are* talking."

"We need to talk about..." I turn my head and look around me, taking in my surroundings. The wooded deck, the natural palettes of teak, bronze, and limestone. For a second, I imagine Claudia is present at a nearby table. Certainly, this place is frequented by stars, not least Robert De Niro, who was an original investor and founder of the Nobu chain. I swallow and finish my sentence. "About Claudia." For a microsecond—literally no more—a flash of horror crosses his face, but the easy smile is still there, albeit the tell of a tic of a tiny muscle in his jaw. He doesn't reply, just crumples his eyes, his brows knotting, and claws his hands through his thick mane of blond hair. His Lucas-like tells, signaling to me that I have caught him out.

"Claudia Spector," I clarify.

"I know you love that TV show she's in."

"Not as much as you love *her*."

He does the crumpled look again. The *you-are-crazy* look.

I cut to the chase. "I found your old flip phone. Found the messages between the two of you."

He still, amazingly, plays dumb. "I don't know what—"

"Please, Lucas. Don't insult me. The messages are proof. There's no way you can wriggle out of it."

He gives me the boyish, naughty, *I'm-busted* smile. His eyes slide over to the beach, the hum of the crashing waves a backdrop to his lies. "Honey, it was one night. It meant nothing. Nothing at all. I was star-struck. I mean, you understand, right? You're a big fan of hers. I said yes. She pursued me, like, seriously set her sights on me. I'm a guy, I folded. I'm sorry, but it was only one time, I swear."

"Bull." I lift my chopsticks to my mouth, savoring the black cod with miso as it melts on my tongue, hoping, somehow, the sublime silky flavor can take away a little of the pain. It does help. But no, the hurt is still festering.

"Sweetheart, it was just physical. It meant nothing. My heart belongs to you and no one else, I swear." Lucas spears a fork into his Jidori chicken, raises a morsel to his mouth and chews.

"The messages go on for a whole lot longer than one day and a night," I say in a cool tone. I have learned with Lucas that raising my voice gets me nowhere. If we were at home, he may have left the house by now. Would be taking the dogs out for a night walk while he honed his lie, polished his response. Maybe even calling his daddy for advice. That's why I picked a public place.

He swallows his mouthful of food. "So what do you want me to say?"

"Is the truth so hard for you?"

He lifts his hands in a surrender position. "She hooked me in, I can't explain."

"So it was all her fault? Is that it? She was Eve who tempted you with the apple, and you were poor, innocent Adam who took a bite?" *The Bible has a lot to answer for*, I think.

"You have no idea what Claudia's like." He is the victim now. Of course he is.

"When did the relationship start?" I fire out.

He flinches and drains the last of his Monkey Business cocktail. "I can't remember."

"I'll tell you, to refresh your memory. It was four months ago. Three months before the night you found me, when you decided *not* to call 911. If I'd died that night, you would've been free to carry on your romance with Claudia without me getting in the way." I know the dates because of the flip phone I found. He can't wriggle out of this.

"No! That's crazy!" His words are loud. Some chic Asian diners, next to our table, and dressed in elegant black and beige, turn around. Lucas looks shamed. He hates scenes. He whispers, "Babe. I love you. Please forgive me, it was a mistake, I never meant to hurt you. I'm scum, I'm sorry."

That is one of Lucas's lines: *Men are scum. Women are psycho.* Omitting to explain how when "women are psycho" it's because of the scummy way their partners behave.

"Look, I swear on my life it's over with Claudia. I haven't even seen her or heard from her in, like, six weeks. It's over. All I want is for us to be happy. I promise I won't stray again. Please forgive me. I love you more than life itself." There are tears in his eyes. Why, I wonder, did Lucas not pursue acting? He's a master. Golden Globe material. His lips are quivering now. A tear rolls down his cheek. "Please, Ava. I screwed up. Please give me a second chance." And now his hand is reaching under the table, resting on my thigh. This is one of the key elements of our relationship, I cannot deny. Make-up sex. Arguments followed by mind-blowing orgasms. Another reason I picked a restaurant to thrash this out. So he can't get his way with me.

Tears chase each other down my cheeks. "You left me to die," I accuse. "I could have *died*."

I picture the scene. Me, sprawled out on the bed, two bottles of liquor and a vial of pills. Anybody witnessing that would see how desperate I was, how I had hit rock bottom. A woman who tries to take her own life must feel she has nothing left to lose. Had he had sex with Claudia that day? The day his wife had given up? Did he care *at all*?

Maybe. But what's far worse is that he carried on his affair afterward.

The man has no heart. Not only is he a cheater, but a cruel, conniving bastard.

Will karma get him in the end?

# THIRTEEN

"I want a divorce," I announce coolly to Lucas over dessert. Nobu is filling up with diners, the setting sun is casting a golden glow across Lucas's face, lighting his hair up so it glints like an angel's halo. Irony staring me right in the face.

He splutters, his second cocktail spraying over his pale blue shirt. He dunks his napkin into a glass of water and dabs at the stains. "Are you nuts? We're having a baby!"

"*I'm* having a baby," I correct. "This baby is mine."

"Hey! The baby's mine too! No way are you taking my child from me! This is a joke, right? You're teasing me."

"No, I'm perfectly serious."

"Where the hell did this come from? What have I done?" Lucas has a way of sounding so innocent. How does he do it?

"Did you not hear me earlier, Lucas? You think you can have your cake and eat it too, don't you? That you can have an affair with"—I whisper her name; I don't want our fellow diners to hear—"*Claudia*, and carry on with me as if nothing has happened? Like you didn't break my heart, my trust, my faith in myself? My faith in humankind, actually. Do you have any idea what it feels like? When the person you married, made vows with, discards you for some star?"

"She may be a star, but *you're* a comet."

His charm is not going to work this time. "I'm *serious*, Lucas! This is no joke."

His brows crease in seeming agony. "I never 'discarded' you! I said I was sorry, honey, and I mean it. A thousand times over, I mean it. What more d'you *want* from me?"

It's funny, I think, how people assume that because they are apologizing, that will be enough. It is only enough if they can put themselves into your shoes and really *feel* what it's like for you. Properly empathize. If they don't quite get it, get what they have done and *feel* it for themselves, an apology is nothing more than words.

My eyes fix themselves on his, unmoved. "I've already spoken to my aunt. She has a room made up for me. I'll be moving there next week."

"To Montana?"

"To Montana."

"No, Ava. No way! No way am I going to let you live in goddam Montana."

"You have no choice," I tell him.

"This is crazy! Have you thought this through?"

I sink my spoon into my chocolate harumaki and push some into my mouth. I nod. The flavors meld together on my tongue.

"How will you survive?"

I swallow. Taste the sweet tang of the fruit mixed with dark chocolate and everything seems okay in this instant. Chocolate can do that for a woman. "I used to horseback ride for a living, remember? I can get a job at any ranch there. I can wait tables. I can be a receptionist. I could work at a clothing store. There are a number of things I'm qualified to do."

His jaw goes slack. He runs his hand over his face and groans. "This is insane. No wife of mine is doing menial work."

I want to laugh. Even with the weekly visits from our housekeeper, I am kept busy. Lucas doesn't seem to mind all the "menial" stuff I do for him. Picking up his dirty socks, for starters.

"I have to do what I have to do," I say simply. "I signed a prenup and I can manage alone and make my way."

Lucas's eyes narrow. "So you're going to punish me because of the prenup?"

"This is not about the prenup, Lucas, this is about you and your extra-marital affairs. It's also about your lies, your lack of loyalty and empathy. That video is proof of who you are inside and what you're capable of. I could go on."

"All right already about the video! I said I was sorry. And it's an ex-affair! It is *over*! Why can you not get that into your head? I love you! All I can think about is our future! The baby's future. We are—"

"A family," I cut in sarcastically.

"Exactly! How can you do this to me? To us?"

I want to laugh. Again, all this is my fault. He is somehow the victim. "You went a step too far, honey. You have to learn to accept responsibility for your actions. You had free choice, you chose a certain path, and now you have to live with the consequences. Ever heard of *cause and effect*?"

"This cannot seriously be happening."

I take out my purse and fumble around for my wallet. This meal is going to be astronomically expensive but will be worth every dime. Not only because of the delicious food, but because it will contribute to my personal mental well-being: to be able to prove my autonomy to myself as well as to Lucas. Show Lucas how I can look after myself financially. Let him see with his own eyes how I can do without him.

His face stiffens in panic. "What are you doing?"

"Getting my wallet to pay the check. Something I'll be doing from now on."

He chuckles nervously. He always picks up the check. "Don't be ridiculous."

"I'm not. I'm going to be a single mom, and I need to get accustomed to paying for myself, that's all."

"Since when haven't I paid?"

I raise a brow. "I need to get used to being self-sufficient. There won't be anybody picking up my checks when I'm in Montana, or wherever I may end up living. A couple of friends have also offered me a room, to get myself on my feet here in LA, so that's another possibility. But I need to think of what's best for the baby."

He raises his hands in exasperation. "You're not going anywhere. This is crazy!"

"I'm a free woman. This is not Iran or Afghanistan. I'll be moving out and starting my life anew, and you and I will be getting a divorce."

"I don't want you to go! *Please*, Ava."

"My mind's made up."

"My parents will—"

"Your parents will be delighted."

"No, they will not! My mom, she's... she's over the moon about the baby on the way. She wants to be a grandmother. Montana's over a thousand miles away. A thousand goddamn miles! You can't do this, Ava. I won't let you! I need you at home where you belong." His voice is hoarse from trying to keep himself from shouting.

*At home, where you belong*. Ha! No more pairing Lucas's socks. What a relief. How wonderful to not have to deal with a man's socks. How liberating! Not only washing socks and pairing socks but picking dirty socks up off the floor. Bending down, finding them under beds, couches, behind cushions, stuffed into shoes, strewn into balls around the room, even sometimes in the kitchen or outside in the yard. Or in one of the dogs' beds. You never know where a lone sock could be lurking, or downright hiding, like they have a brain of their own, some hidden agenda. Maybe you'll find it months later. Maybe you might never find it at all. He—and I bet I speak for most men, not just Lucas—will never search for this stinky sock though. Oh, no. The lone sock that has vanished somewhere. It will be up to me to hunt it down.

Or simply leave it right where it is.

And that is what I feel like doing.

*We,* I muse philosophically, *are like socks. Even if we start out as a perfect pair, some day we will end up single.*

A low moan leaks from Lucas's throat like he is physically in pain. He rakes his hands through his thick blond hair. "I can't believe this is happening."

"Get over it, honey. You can't stop me. I will never forget about the recording. How you and your father behaved. What you both did was monstrous. Leaving me there to possibly die? Who *does* that kind of thing?" I pause, letting the truth of my accusation sink in.

Lucas hangs his head in shame, not answering.

I continue. "Even if I'd been a stranger, that kind of action—or inaction—is unforgivable. But to do that to your own wife? To your daughter-in-law? What was *wrong* with you both? Neither of you are normal, you know that, right? Do you have beating hearts under those puffed-up chests of yours? Sometimes I wonder. Sometimes I ask myself if aliens dropped you both off on planet Earth and forgot to come get you. I need to confront Jack about what he did, actually. Let him know what I think of him. I bet your mom would love to know what kind of man her husband is when the chips are down."

Lucas comes back to life. "Don't you dare!"

"Oh, I dare. Watch me." I know what Lucas is terrified of. He fears I may upload that video on YouTube, exposing him and Jack as ruthless monsters. I wouldn't do that... yet, never say never. A woman scorned...

He groans again. "Jesus. This whole thing has gotten out of control."

"Don't cuss," I reprimand, playing the part of his father and relishing it.

"Babe, stop this nonsense, *please*. What can I do to stop you?"

I shake my head. "Nothing. Now that my mind's made up, the doing part will be easy."

"This is... this is not what I want." He tears his hand through his hair again.

"You having sex with another woman was not what I wanted, but there you go," I retort. "We can't always get what we want in life." I call the waiter over. "Would you bring me the check, please." It feels good to be in control.

So very good.

The car ride home is silent. Lucas is genuinely stunned. Finally, his lifestyle has caught up with him and he is incredulous. He cannot believe the strength I am showing, my spirit of independence trumping everything. That feeble, broken woman is behind me. This, he is unable to compute. Even *I* am amazed by the well of strength I find inside me.

"The irony is that I am now managing partner of my own law firm," he tells me in a quiet, shell-shocked voice. "You choose this moment to leave me? *Now*, when I'm finally financially solvent, now that I am in control of the business? When I can offer you the world?"

"We all make our choices," I say in response, "and we need to be accountable for them." I yawn, close my eyes, stretch my legs, sinking further into the car seat while I let him navigate the road. My tone is bored and gives off the impression that I don't give a damn. I *do* give a damn. I am terrified. But I know my husband and how his mind works. I put my hand on my stomach. Lucas notices. His eyes sharpen.

He says in an icy voice, one hand slackly on the wheel, "You'd never leave me, because you wouldn't want to risk it."

"Risk what?"

"Losing custody of your child."

I say nothing, but my new-found confidence is rattled. With his father's powerful contacts, with both he and Lucas being attorneys, I know they'd be able to mount a case against me as an unfit mother. Lucas would lie to get his way, and his parents would support him.

I don't let him know he has gotten to me though, and choose to end the evening on an even stronger, more final note. I move into the guest room, where I will spend the night. Of all the things I have done and said so far, this will hammer it home.

The following morning, I find him outside the threshold of the locked guestroom door, curled up in a sleeping bag. Lucas does drama so well. As I step over his body, I notice that skull ring is no longer on his finger. Good. That's a start. He looks up at me, bleary-eyed, exhausted, dark circles under his eyes, his hair damp with sweat.

"We need to talk," he says seriously.

"About what?"

"About our future. About our baby's future."

I feel a chill run from my scalp to my toes. I knew leaving him wouldn't be so simple.

# FOURTEEN

My husband is all about making deals. He was born into a deal. The deal was that his father made the money while his mother stayed home, ran a perfect house, made sure she too was perfect—nails, hair, skin, teeth, attire, behavior—and that, by all appearances to the outside world, nothing was astray. Lucas's part was to go to school, then college, and score straight As. To excel at sports, be popular, and *swim with the sharks*.

This is what Lucas has now proposed, and this is what I am mulling over at this minute:

He wants:

1. The SD card so he can destroy it.
2. For me to sign a non-disclosure agreement about everything that happened in that recording. Including not ever mentioning it again, even to him, and especially not to his parents.
3. For me to stay in our marriage for at least three more years. Living with him in the marital home, spending nights in our marital bed, all household

and other expenses paid by him, no need to work or find a job.

In return, he will replace the prenup with a newly signed marriage contract that states—according to California law—that in the event of divorce, we will split his assets fifty-fifty. And a clause: in case of death, our child will inherit everything in trust, with me as guardian until the child is twenty-one. If there is no child, I will inherit half of his assets, his parents the other half.

He has made it clear that if I oppose any of the above, he will fight me "with full-on ammunition" for full custody of our child.

He swears the affair with Claudia Spector is done and dusted. I have spent sleepless nights going over and over everything, assessing my situation, asking myself what I should do. It's hard when you love someone who doesn't deserve your love. But when you are pregnant with their child it's even harder.

But the biggest clincher of all is his threat about filing for full custody of our child.

What choice do I have? I would love for this marriage to work, if possible. He swears he has changed. He has admitted what he did was horrendous. Can we make a fresh start? *Do* people change? Whatever the answer is, my baby is my top priority. I cannot risk losing my child.

"You know what I've been planning, Ava?" he asks. We are walking on the beach, the dogs bounding ahead of us, fetching sticks. An inexhaustible game that can stretch on all day. My arm is aching. But, for the first time in ages, I am content. Relieved, at least, to have made a decision. In life, you have to move forward. If you hold on to the old, especially the grudges and the pain, all you will be doing is attracting more of the same.

I look up at him, his face lit up by a burst of sunrays. How is it that Lucas gets to look so innocent and full of light when he has so much darkness inside? "No, what?" I say.

"To sell Fox & Fox to the highest bidder. Do what Dad threatened to do with me all along."

"That would kill him."

"He doesn't need to know."

"He'd find out, wouldn't he?"

"Maybe, by which time it would be too late."

I marvel at Lucas's new-found independence and resolve. Not only to give his all to our marriage, but to release the one thing he had been clinging on to: his obsession about pleasing his father. It's a positive sign. I didn't think my husband had it in him. To go against his dad, to pay him back for years of psychological bullying. Or maybe it's not a case of payback at all, but simply taking the reins, calling his own shots for once. I respect him for that. He has lived his entire life under the shadow of his shrewd, adroit father. He must be desperate to break free.

"I'd be a very rich man," he adds.

"Then why does it bother you about your dad seeing the recording?" I ask, confused. "If you don't care what he thinks?"

"It's for Mom's sake. It would break her. Believe it or not, he finds it hard to keep secrets from her. They've been together so long she can kind of read his mind. The truth might out in the end."

"True. But she knows what kind of man Jack is, who she married."

"She does, deep down inside, yeah. But that video... it's like, so in your face. I watched it all the way through, you know. It's pure proof. It's ugly. Puts both of us in a really ugly light. Especially me. Sweetheart, I'm so sorry for what I did. For what I didn't do. Will you ever forgive me?" He stops walking, turns so he is facing me and holds me gently by the shoulders, so I have all his attention. His gaze is full of remorse, his eyes watery. Brushing a salty strand of hair away from my cheek, he lets his fingers rest on my face and peruses it as if he is seeing me for the first time. But unlike the actual first time, when he spotted me at that party and was hot for me, the way he sees me in this moment is in a different light. There is love in his eyes. Appreciation. Respect. He takes his phone out of his shorts pocket and takes a snap of me.

"If I didn't forgive you," I reply, "I wouldn't be here now."

He holds my hand. I feel the possibilities ahead of us, feel them flicker in the warmth of his fingers he intertwines with mine. We could be happy, Lucas and I. We can play at being in love, like it was at the beginning when the world seemed to be just us. Before that prenup cast doubt on our relationship. We have a child coming. It would be selfish of me to rob him or her of a full-time relationship with their dad. I know what it's like not to have had a father in my life. It wasn't just a financial struggle for my mother, it was a psychological drain on her which trickled down to me. Not having that support, another person in the home to shoulder the responsibility, to help raise a kid. Not being able to share the events of the day as a family. Always a one-to-one relationship, so no matter how close you are, there always feels like there is a missing element.

And here Lucas is now, offering to make this huge change, to start afresh, to destroy that prenup in exchange for destroying the recording. And that's something to cling on to, even if the main thing hanging over my head is his threat that he'd take my child away from me. It's a no-brainer, really. He's right in that I don't want any of my children—or anyone—to come across that horrendous scene. As he says, things have a way of coming out, of being discovered. *Truth will out in the end.* It puts me in a bad light. What would they think of me? How would I explain it? Actually, I would be doing *myself* more than anyone a favor, by wiping it out of my life. Pretending it never happened.

I'm pretty sure I'll take the deal. What choice do I have?

# FIFTEEN

Barbara calls me the following day. She invites me to lunch at the Polo Lounge at the Beverly Hills Hotel, a famous hub of Los Angeles power dining, where movie stars have business meetings with their agents, where million-dollar deals are made over a truffle lobster risotto or an egg-white frittata. This is a first. Barbara has never invited just me, alone. Should I be fearful? I wonder if she intends to reprimand me about the destruction of the prenup, accuse me of being a gold digger or for being a bad influence on Lucas about something—anything. I am wary when I accept her invitation.

But she is all smiles. She even kisses me hello on my cheek—another first.

We are seated at a booth, the famous green and white candy stripe ceiling making me feel like I am at a fairground and I am still a kid and Mommy is in control.

"My treat," Barbara begins. "Just us girls today. Fun, don't you think? Men always spoil the dynamic, in a way. You know, you can really be yourself when men aren't around."

I have never seen this side of Barbara. All girlie conspiratorial mingling with buzzy warmth. She is dressed in a pink Chanel suit, hanging off her skinny, Nancy-Reagan frame, her hairstyle freshly primped and colored. I can smell hairspray and the whiff of Joy as she breezes into the restaurant. Barbara is a paradox. She is lavish, but she is also a spendthrift. She prides herself on being frugal when it counts. She still drives the same car she has had for years, a birthday gift from Jack, a 2002 Oldsmobile, which is now almost a classic. She keeps her shoes and suits for years, which lend her a vintage quality and style. She is a strange bird. A character who baffles me. She has always kept me at arm's length, but today her attitude has done a one-eighty. Why? I can only assume it is because of my pregnancy, which we announced to them recently.

"Giada De Laurentiis was spotted here, just the other day!" she whispers, widening her eyes.

I respond with a blank look.

"You know, the food chef? I watch her show."

I nod. "Cool."

I am not that impressed by famous people. Except Meryl Streep, or Leonardo DiCaprio and, once upon a time, Claudia Spector. But that's because they are such great actors. A star for the sake of being a star doesn't do it for me. I meet stars all the time with my job. They are just people. Often you pass them by without even realizing who they are. Often, they are far shorter than they appear on screen. Sometimes, kind of plain in the flesh. It's amazing how some actors have such a rapport with the camera they can create magic and transform their persona into something rare and special.

With an uncharacteristic smile sweeping across her powdery face, her brows plucked into symmetrical Roman arches, Barbara is arranging a host of shopping bags on the banquette. Dolce & Gabbana, Armani, Calvin Klein, and various expensive kids' stores. She notices me eyeing the bags.

Beaming at me, she says effusively, "I couldn't resist. So sue me! I went shopping. I wanted to wait so we could go together but... well, I hope you like what I've chosen." She fishes out a bag and watches me with a grin while I pull out an acid-yellow cashmere sweater, in large.

"Something cozy to watch TV in," she says. "For around the house. Don't do your gardening in it though!"

I stroke its baby softness. "It's exquisite, thank you so much, Barbara."

"Large, to give plenty of room for the baby to grow. I don't like clothing designed specifically for pregnancy. Just buy large is what I say. Check out the Dolce & Gabbana bag."

The waiter comes over, rattles off the specials and takes our order. I choose a crab cake to start, but Barbara intercepts.

"No, I'm sorry, but we won't take the crab cake. No, honey, no shellfish for you!"

"You're right, I hadn't thought."

Barbara taps her jeweled fingers on the snowy tablecloth. Her long nails—perfect manicured talons in pink—make ski runs in the white cotton fabric. "She'll take a McCarthy salad followed by a chicken parmesan—and make sure it's nicely browned—and I'll have just the McCarthy salad. A Perrier water, for my daughter-in-law, please, and a Kir Royale for me. Breadsticks for her to nibble on while we wait. No butter. Thank you." She dismisses the waiter with a backward wave of her hand, the gigantesque emerald and diamond ring on her wedding finger catching all the light in the room. "Now, where were we, honey?" *Honey*. This is new, too.

"Ah yes." She extracts a rectangular box out of the Dolce & Gabbana bag. "Those dull aviator sunglasses you go around in, Ava. You need something more fun. More glamorous. Something more feminine." I open the box to find a winged, fifties-style pair of impossibly large shades, in red. So not my style.

I laugh. "They're wild," I say.

"They're fashionable," she corrects. "And elegant."

I go through all the bags, one by one. The money she has spent on these gifts is eye-watering. None of it to my taste. Even the baby blankets are strangely unalluring. But so *expensive*, which makes it worse. Not that she has left the receipts in the bags, in case I'd like to change any of the items for something different. No. She doesn't even hint at that suggestion. Her choice is my choice as far as she is concerned. But luxury and quality cannot be mistaken. This must have cost two months' worth of my old salary. The whole thing makes me feel very awkward.

"You're beyond generous, Barbara. I'm blown away by all these gifts." Both of those statements are true. All the time Lucas and I have been married, I fantasized about Barbara reaching out to me. But the reality is something else. More lunches like this with my mother-in-law? I'm not so sure.

She fiddles with a humongous dome earring, set with a giant pearl in the center, which hides the entirety of her lobe. "I've enrolled the baby in three private nursery schools."

"How? The baby hasn't been born yet."

"Don't worry, I'll cover all the costs of enrollment fees. You have to be so careful these days with all this non-binary this and non-binary that, you know, confusing children about what sex they are. Telling boys they can wear pink if they like. Taking their toy guns away. I don't want my grandson being fed a load of nonsense by pedophile types. We need to make sure we pick the right schools. Private is the way to go."

"I think you're jumping the gun a little, Barbara." I become aware of my play on the gun word after it leaves my mouth. "I mean, I don't even know how I feel about early education, maybe I want to stay home with the baby, maybe—"

She takes my hand. "We need to make these decisions together, my dear. I'm here for you, Ava, and the baby. And I'm sorry I haven't been very attentive to your needs, but here I am now."

*Yes, here you are now.*

"We can be a team, make plans together. Spend *time* together. As a family. It'll be so much fun!" She wraps her fuchsia-pink lips around a breadstick and snaps it in two.

I force my mouth into a smile. "Can't wait."

# SIXTEEN

My neighbor Jill runs by later that day and calls out to me. If only she knew the mayhem she caused. I'm on the deck, tending to my raised flowerbeds, wearing the acid-yellow sweater, funnily enough. The one Barbara told me not to wear while gardening. There's a cool offshore breeze. I'm planting things that need little or no water. Climate change is real, especially in California.

She jogs up the steps. "So what's new?" she asks, panting, her slim arms looping over the picket fence of the deck. We chat about small things. I invite her in but she insists she needs to get going. Usually that means at least twenty minutes of gossip.

I observe Jill and wonder if I am looking at my future. She looks amazing for her age. She is fifty-nine and with a figure any mid-thirty-year-old would be proud of. But she knows that's not enough in this town. Her husband is "in the business." He's a TV producer. Jill, like me, is not from California. And although Malibu is not Hollywood, nor even Los Angeles —it is a separate county altogether—the Hollywood values spill into it. People care about looks. Particularly, looking youthful. Youth and beauty triumph over wisdom, over experience, over everything. Money worship and success follow smartly behind. I have noticed something interesting. Those born and bred here—Angelenos—can handle it. But those of us who come into this cut-throat world from outside find it much harder to assimilate. You have to be made of iron to thrive in Hollywood, to not let it get you down. Or become a surfer and care about nothing but the waves. It is a disingenuous place, Los Angeles. It tricks you. Even its name, *The Angels*, leads you to believe that by living here you are blessed, protected. The perfect weather, the impossibly blue sky, the palm trees reaching up to the heavens, the smiles on everyone's faces: all of this makes you presume that life could not get any better. But there's an insidious worm that eats away at your soul. You never feel enough. When women are gorgeous everywhere you look and everyone has their eye out for a better deal, a better house, a better car, better love, it is hard to stay grounded. You have to muster up all your confidence, all the faith you have in yourself, to not feel expendable.

Especially if your husband has a wandering eye.

"You know, Ava," Jill says. "I don't give a damn anymore. If my husband wants to put it around town, that's fine by me. Even better. I've passed menopause—men-oh-pause... get it? And I don't care if I ever have sex again. I mean, most of my friends are on HRT—of course you're too young to think about that yet—but me, I don't see the benefits of taking hormones. I mean, women are getting testosterone implants, like pellets inserted under their skin? To jiz up their sex drive. Call me dull, but that's not for me. I don't want sex getting in the way of things. Sex is what gets you into trouble in the first place, that's for sure. Sex is what makes you make bad decisions. I mean, when I think of some of the guys I slept with in my youth... worse, some of the men I obsessed over, it makes me cringe. Guys who were nothing! Total jerks! And I was crazy about them! Being in lust makes you crazy and jealous and do dumb things."

Jill looks around to make sure nobody is listening to her monologue. Being outside it's pretty safe to say that nobody can hear. She lowers her voice anyway. "William and I both pretend. I pretend I don't notice, and he pretends he's still in love with me. In fact, the more I turn a blind eye, the more I'm rewarded. The gifts I get from his guilt! I call them 'guilt packages.' He gets to screw around to his heart's content and play the bigshot producer, and I get great vacations, a beautiful home, to hang out with my kids, and have a stress-free life, all bills paid and then some. And let's face it, William's not exactly known for his good looks. Not anymore. Those women are welcome to his paunch, quite frankly. I don't know why more women don't follow my lead. You know my favorite song? 'The Great Pretender.'"

Jill makes me laugh, but she has a point. I struggle to believe I will end up like her in twenty-five years' time. Maybe I *am* looking at my future self. Today, I do something uncharacteristic of me. I share a secret with her.

"Lucas was having an affair," I reveal.

"No way! But you're, like, the perfect couple!"

I think of how we must look to the outside world, especially through our Instagram feed. Lucas loves playing the family man. Photos of us kissing, us and the dogs on the beach, hashtag, living the dream, hashtag, grateful. I sigh. "That's what I thought, too."

She tilts her head, her eyes quizzical. "Wait a minute... not with..."

I nod.

Jill can't contain her grin. "Seriously?"

"I found a burner phone. With messages to and from Claudia herself."

"No way!" Jill is still grinning. Fame overtakes everything.

As if the fact that Claudia Spector and I were sharing the same man validates me. Makes me hot property. Extra special.

"Wow!" she gushes.

"I know," I say.

"Have you confronted Lucas?"

"Yes. I even threatened him with divorce."

"And?"

"He says it's ended."

"Oh, yeah?" Her tone is laced with sarcasm. "What makes you think that?"

"Because the messages have stopped. And he swore to me that Claudia would never come between us again, that she was gone from his life for good."

She lifts a russet brow. Jill's hairdresser does her brows to match her hair color, which changes every few months. "The messages on that particular flip phone have stopped, but that doesn't mean..." She doesn't finish. Jill's no fool. In fact, all women who have anything to do with showbusiness in Hollywood gain extra brain cells—the street-smart kind—while living in La-La Land. We gain eyes in the back of our heads, an extra dose of intuition, a sixth sense. Notably when it comes to relationships. "Have you searched high and low?" she quizzes. "I mean, if he knows you're onto him, he'll be extra careful."

"I trust him," I tell her, hearing the wish in my voice.

Her mouth shifts into a smirk as if to say, *Are you kidding me?*

"You think I shouldn't?"

"Depends. If you give a damn or not."

I shrug. "I do. I do give a damn."

"Well, then," she says. "Let me know if I can be of assistance. We girls are in this together. Until we take over the world, that is. Which will happen someday, I'm pretty sure."

I laugh. "Are you sure you don't want to come in? Have a drink. Got booze, got soft drinks. Got snacks."

"No, I'm good. I'm picking up Norah from LAX later. I need to get going." Norah is nineteen and has been doing an exchange program at a college in New Zealand for the last year. Jill is determined that her daughter finds work elsewhere, even if it means living away from home. "This town is poison," Jill has often said. Everyone refers to Los Angeles and its vicinity as "this town" even though the sprawl of it goes on for nearly five hundred square miles, even though it incorporates dozens of distinct areas and even counties.

"Let me know if you find anything incriminating," Jill says, jogging in place, in preparation for her continued run.

I nod. "I will."

She powers off, Ariadne and Sappho barking after her, miffed they have not been invited to go on her run, and it feels good, actually, to have a confidante, someone whom I can talk to about this, who understands and won't judge me. People think you're weak to want to hold on to your husband.

They have no idea the strength it takes.

Love is not sensible. And sometimes it is unkind. But if we were to give up and not forgive, we'd be giving up on the key element of life. At least, this is what I tell myself.

I'm not going to go through Lucas's belongings again. I don't want to be that person digging around, paranoid, jealous and insecure. I'm going to enjoy my marriage, enjoy Lucas, have fun being in love again even if it's half pretend.

I know what I'm doing.

At least I think I do.

# SEVENTEEN

Everything is play-pretend perfect.

For a while.

Lucas and I do fun excursions like a drive-in movie, and a day out in the desert at Joshua Tree. We also spend plenty of time at home, particularly on our backyard deck, watching the ocean. Our deck is set high on stilts above the sand, with a view to the ocean and steps down to the beach. We have raised beds of lavender, and climbing jasmine, cactus, and wild grasses. Out here we catch the buzz of passing bees, the shrill of cicadas, the flutter of butterflies. We watch sunsets together and listen to the crashing waves in the evenings, go on long walks, sometimes by our house and sometimes we take the car and set off to the mountains. There are places in Malibu where you won't see a soul for miles, canyon upon arid canyon, where mountain lions roam, and buckwheat and needlegrass and sage scrub bleed into the endless view, the colors changing by the hour. People assume incorrectly that Malibu is synonymous with the stretch of land hugging the coastline, but Malibu reaches far into the mountains, too. Ariadne and Sappho love these hikes. They even wear special doggie backpacks, designed with pouches so they can carry their own water.

These passing days have been special. Each minute is the making of a memory, a moment in time. Each second becoming the past, a past you kiss goodbye to as you plan the future, which, once present, quickly becomes the past. Time. It's a funny thing. We live so little in the true present. It's an art, isn't it? To live in the present? To not anticipate the future, to not wallow in the past, but seize the moment as it is. The now.

And it is in one of these "now" moments when I am watching the news, and the past is hurled in front of me, and my future looms ahead of me, and the present screams at me, all fusing together in a whirl, in an instant, as time seems to freeze before my eyes.

"Academy Award winner Claudia Spector is missing," the newscaster pronounces in a grave tone. "The star and Golden Globe winner of Netflix's blockbuster series *Go Ask Bobbie*, and Oscar winner for Best Actress for the 2018 movie *Champions*, has been officially missing since Tuesday, when she did not show up for work for the second day running. The actress is currently filming *Cat's Cradle*. Ms. Spector was once engaged to fellow actress Crystal Cormac, but the couple broke up only a month before they were due to tie the knot. Spector's agent, Helena Ronstein, told reporters that Ms. Spector is never late on set and never misses work, that she is a consummate professional. This is the first time in her career that she has not shown up for work, and those close to her say this is uncharacteristic and they are extremely worried. 'Spector failed to return home and has not been seen or heard from since,' police said in a statement. 'Friends, family, and colleagues fear for her safety.'

"Anyone with information is urged to call LAPD detectives at 213-996-1800; 877-LAPD-247; or Crime Stoppers at 800-222-TIPS."

I zap the TV off. I can't bear to hear any more. What has

happened is terrifying. I imagine myself in her shoes, and shudder, a chill racing through my body, to my scalp, goosebumping my flesh all over. Lucas breezes back into the living room as if nothing monumental has happened, sweaty from an evening run with the dogs. I move my glass of orange juice from the coffee table seconds before Sappho's tail has a chance to swipe it crashing onto the floor. It takes me a while to digest what I have seen on TV. The reality. The shock of it. My husband was having an affair with Claudia Spector, and now she has disappeared... This moment in time feels surreal, almost otherworldly, like our lives are suspended in midair. This moment is humongous. This moment will dictate the rest of my life.

"Claudia Spector is missing," I tell Lucas in a somber voice, my heart thwacking against my ribs as I spell out the words. I need to see his reaction. Need to see the expression in his eyes. See how guilty he looks.

He regards me hazily, not taking in what I've said, just wipes sweat from his brow. "It's beautiful outside this evening, babe. Did you see the sunset? It's totally technicolor. So beautiful, you should catch it before it's gone."

*Did he hear what I said?* "Lucas, when did you last see Claudia?" I quiz.

He passes the back of his hand across his brow. "I can't even remember. She told me she was leaving town for a couple of days, and I... well, I wanted to end things anyway. Our relationship... no, it wasn't even that. It was more like a... a 'situationship,' and it meant nothing, nothing. Honey, why do you want to dig all this up? It's over with Claudia. I don't even want to go there. Please don't go on." He plunks himself on the couch in front of the TV and reaches for the remote. The dogs trot over to me, panting, their nails clicking along the floor.

As I lose my hands in the softness of their ears, more words want to scramble from my lips about Claudia, about where she could be, question Lucas about what he knows. I want to ask him when he last saw her—the exact date—where they were. But I don't say anything more because I am flummoxed as to how to react and what to think, and more importantly, I don't want to dissect his ex-affair and live with all the details. Go to sleep with the details, wash my hair with the details, sip my coffee with the details. What good would that do me? I can't bear to fight about the past. There is nothing I can do to change it. I'm trapped here and I just have to accept that for now. I am pragmatic that way. I try to find solutions, not wallow around in recrimination. Finger-pointing won't get us anywhere, nor will wallowing.

I wish my husband had made different choices, and that I too had made different choices. But that's the haunting thing about the past; you can't change a damn thing.

That doesn't stop me from speculating now, though.

"Claudia Spector is missing," I say to the dogs, once Lucas is out of the room. "Where do you think she went? You guys have any idea?" It occurs to me that they might. Lucas takes them all over the place; they love car rides, and it's true when I come to think of it; he has been going out for long runs a lot lately, especially in the last few weeks. Runs not in our neighborhood—Runyon Canyon, for example—runs that involve taking the car. The dogs are great the way they always come when they're called. We often allow them to be off the leash because they never stray, never go chasing after wild animals. Rescue dogs are often loyal in that respect. I haven't joined Lucas on these runs, especially when he's taken the car and the dogs with him. Running while pregnant is a risk I am not willing to take. Did the dogs hang out with Claudia, get to know her well? She might have petted them, might have given them treats. I know she likes dogs because there's that famous Annie Leibovitz portrait of Claudia and her black Labrador kissing in profile. Ariadne and Sappho visiting her house in the hills is something I don't like to think about.

And then an unbidden and somewhat whacky thought slips into my mind: dogs are often witnesses to wrongdoings but stay loyal to their owners; they don't care. I wonder what they have seen? What they know? But no, that's crazy. Lucas may have been unfaithful, may have cheated on me, but I tell myself he is innocent in this. He doesn't have it in him to actively harm another person—does he? Yet he does. He left me practically for dead, didn't he? My instinct tells me to watch out. Am I in danger? When a man is on the edge, as he clearly is, I need eyes in the back of my head. To be prepared for anything. I want to know more backstory concerning Claudia according to him. I am itching for details.

If only the dogs could talk.

I promised myself I wouldn't go rootling around through Lucas's personal belongings. I am pregnant. I do not need the stress, the strain. Everything has been so harmonious between us lately. Do I really want to stir things up?

# EIGHTEEN

I lie in the tub, frothing over with orange blossom bubble bath, reading an old *Vanity Fair*. One I have kept because of the piece about Claudia. It doesn't matter how well I feel I know her, I never tire of lapping up more, and rereading old articles about the star. Her past, her upbringing resonates with me. And I guess I feel like she's someone I could have been if I'd had all the luck in the world, the way she did. *I* could have been that person plucked from obscurity and made into a star if I'd gotten my lucky break, if my acting classes had morphed into something more. If I hadn't been a realist and snapped up the opportunity of being a script supervisor instead. I guess I didn't have guts like her to follow my dream through. We all fantasize about being in these stars' shoes, don't we? We all play the "what if" game, right?

Maybe that's why we gorge on these celebrity stories. Why we hunt for clues that make us feel a little bit like them. Why we rejoice when they have a zit or cellulite or a bad relationship, or some kind of failure that proves they are just as human as we are and that we have something in common. Claudia is one in a million. No, one in ten million. Yet something makes me believe I could have been her.

I gaze at a double-page spread of her, lying horizontally on a fluffy white rug. Dressed in a chartreuse silk negligee, she is looking up into space. Romantic. Dreamy. Her blond hair cascades over her shoulders in gentle waves, her haircut almost as famous as Jennifer Aniston's was in the *Friends* years. She is exquisite. A quote reads:

> "I'm not gay and I'm not straight, I'm just myself."
>
> Claudia Spector has the seal of Hollywood royalty stamped upon her. With her *Go Ask Bobbie* TV stardom, her engagement to fellow actress Crystal Cormac, not to mention a flourishing film and theater career—which has earned her a Tony Award and an Oscar for Best Actress—the star feels like she is just getting started.

"I feel like I have so much more to give," the caption quote on the page reads. "The awards are proof that people see me as an artist, not just a celebrity."

I turn the page. Another gorgeous photo, this time Claudia standing. She is wearing a black, one-piece bathing suit, with a swimming pool in the background, her signature long legs muscular and worked out.

On the adjacent page, the article begins.

> The car climbs higher and higher, a vertiginous ascent around hairpin bends on the road that leads to Claudia Spector's hidden Hollywood home, where she has lived for the past five years. At the top, I reach an imposing wrought iron gate, the only sign there is a house behind this hideaway in the hills. I have been given a code to open the gate, a code that is apparently only for guests, which changes every few

days: a way to monitor who comes and goes. Security is paramount to such a star, whose life was once threatened by a stalker who ended up behind bars. From the summit, the view to the sprawling city of Los Angeles below is breathtakingly beautiful, reaching all the way to the Pacific Ocean. Behind these anonymous gates, the house is not flashy, but eclectically tasteful. The French Normandy revival-style abode, with canyon views and landscaping, is so well hidden, only her friends know she lives here. Palm trees sway in the breeze, wind chimes tinkle. The scent of jasmine is unmistakable. Orange and lemon trees adorn the property. Claudia is wearing a faded pink T-shirt and camouflage pants and is barefoot. Her honey-colored hair is pulled back into a messy ponytail. Fit and slender, she looks younger than her thirty-four years.

She gives me a tour, letting me know that she appreciates the artistic history of eclectic Laurel Canyon, where musicians like Joni Mitchell and Jim Morrison once lived. Her house is grand, yet feels cozy and lived in. Modern art adorns the walls ("I'm somewhat of a collector.") There is a wet bar that looks as if it has been transplanted from a chic French bistro, replete with an array of the finest wines. Giving me a journey through the house, Spector leads me to a formal living room with antique, hardwood flooring that was sourced from a real Normandy chateau. A Carrara marble fireplace dominates one end, surrounded by classic wooden paneling on the walls. With floor-to-ceiling windows overlooking the estate, the rooms, effortlessly leading from one to the other, feel bright and airy, with large white couches in nearly every room. It is no secret that Spector is considered a recluse and guards her privacy fiercely. The fact that she has agreed to this interview is testament to how her latest relationship has changed her. "I'm a more carefree spirit since meeting Crystal."

Since Spector's engagement to Crystal Cormac, the press can't get enough of the couple's same-sex relationship. Has Spector always been gay?

"I don't think about pigeonholing relationships or genders," Spector says. "You fall in love with a person, simple as that. We kept our engagement out of the press for several months at first. It was our secret, and it was so great to be able to have that precious time to ourselves. Both being actors, we treasure being together alone. Filming takes up a lot of time, not just actual time but head-space time, if you know what I mean. Huddling here, cooking up a simple pasta or steak and fries, you know, it was very special."

The two actors met while filming Long Gone. Because they were on location in Mexico, shooting in an arid desert where nobody lived and with no press around, the couple were able to retain anonymity.

"We weren't friends at the beginning. I like to totally immerse myself in a role, and because we're enemies in the film, I kind of kept in character." She laughs. "Crystal called me out on it after a particularly grueling day of filming, and quoted Sir Laurence Olivier when he said to Dustin Hoffman… you know, when Dustin Hoffman got a little too method about his role in Marathon Man, when he hadn't slept for seventy-two hours because he wanted to make the scene more realistic? Well, Crystal quoted him, saying, 'Why don't you just try acting, it's easier.' After that the ice broke, and Crystal and I bonded. She's such a great actor, but she knows not to bring it home with her. I learned a lot from her. She explained to me that not only did I have to exercise a character, but I needed to exorcise that character too at the end of the day. I tend to take acting too seriously. She's my barometer, my sanity."

Claudia Spector arrived as just another penniless actor in Hollywood when she was eighteen, after leaving her home in

> Nevada. Her father, "a boozer and a deadbeat," left Spector's mother when she was just three years old. "It was devastating for my mom," the actor tells me, her eyes misty. "He cleaned out the family bank account, left my mother to raise us three kids alone. He never gave her a dime, never came back to visit us."
>
> Yet this same man, Jimmy Spector, sold his story, and a negative exposé about his daughter after she became a star. Spector sued the paper for defamation. "It broke me," she says. "But also gave me strength to carry on working. Work is very important to me. I have been working since I was a teenager, earning my way, supporting myself and my mom."

I fill up my bath with a fresh dash of hot water, marveling how similar our stories are. I have read all this before, but love taking it in all again. We have lived the same truths, she and I. No father in our lives. We were both three years old when our fathers split. We have so much in common. Our mothers broken. Left to raise their kids alone with no financial help, no moral support. I never got to grow into adolescence. It was like my body outgrew the frightened child inside me. Just like Claudia.

I turn the page.

The photo of her on this page is black and white. A close-up. Wisps of windblown hair, impossibly white teeth peeking out from heart-shaped, glossy lips.

There is a caption on top of the picture, very witty, referring to Claudia's awards and her relationship status:

> "The only male figures in my life right now are Tony and Oscar."

I ask if she believes her father had an impact on how she feels about love relationships, if her union with Cormac was, in some way, influenced by her past.

"Maybe. Maybe I have trust issues. And I do suffer from a sense of inadequacy. But I don't think that has necessarily had anything to do with my relationships but more with a continual internal battle with my self-esteem. I may just as easily have fallen in love with a man. Crystal happens to be a woman. I am not a poster child for gay rights—although I believe in them wholeheartedly—I am simply one person in love with another person."

I reread that line. Like she says, she could just as easily love a man as a woman.

Lucas.

I skip to another paragraph, where she is talking about work.

"I'll never stop acting. Never. But I don't want to do the same old, same old. I want to push my limits, stretch myself with exciting, fulfilling roles. Take creative, bold decisions in choosing parts. Because, crazy as it sounds, I always think whatever job I'm doing could be my last. I guess I suffer from impostor syndrome. I'm riddled with insecurities. I think most actors are, despite whatever success or fame they may have achieved." She shoots me a wry smile. "You never forget your past. Never forget going hungry. Never forget how blessed you are to have a job and food on the table."

True, I think. So very true.

I devour the rest of the article.

Spector is as famous for her roles as she is for her online presence and the foundation she started for young women in need. I ask her about the internet forum and website she began several years ago, GenerationWhy.com, where girls can discuss their problems.

"I think it helps when they see their role model is just a regular person, you know? There's nothing special about being a celebrity, it's just a job at the end of the day. I still feel like a teenager inside, still insecure of myself. It started out as a safe space for them to discuss relationships, family, weight issues, gender identity, mental health, and so on, although, lately, there's been a fair amount of trolling and bullying, which is the exact opposite of what it stands for. Social media is a great way to connect, but it can lead to people having low self-esteem. We're living in a strange age that's incredible in one way and hard to come to terms with in another. I'm just someone trying my best, but you know"—she rolls her eyes—"I don't have the answers, I feel like a failure half the time."

With her philanthropic efforts, and lustrous career, Spector has nothing to apologize for. With fifteen movies under her belt, success on Broadway, racking up not just coveted Tony, Oscar, and Golden Globe Awards, for *A Streetcar Named Desire*, *Champions*, and *Go Ask Bobbie*, but adding to that a stunning six Academy Award nominations for *The Last Girl*, *Sara*, *Over the Moon*, *Happy Times*, *Nineteen*, and *The Night That Followed*, she is clearly here to stay and grace us with more stunning performances.

I ask her what her aspirations are for the future, apart from the much talked about wedding to Cormac.

"I'd love to work in Europe one day. Do an arthouse movie. I love French and Spanish films. I'm very happy with how my career has turned out so far though, and feel incredibly blessed. I'm so proud of what we achieved with *Go Ask Bobbie*. My agent begged me not to do TV. But TV is the new film. Gone are the days that television is considered a lesser medium, an inferior platform. So, to answer your question, I'd like to do more TV, for sure. Every role is fascinating to me, even when I had my first walk-on part with no lines when I was twenty. I'll keep on working forever. As long as I'm getting offered jobs, I'll be in this business till I die."

Her last line sends a shockwave through me. I set the magazine down, pull the plug and let those words infiltrate my thoughts.

"Till I die..."

# NINETEEN

I am at Ralphs, the grocery store, cruising the aisles with my shopping cart. I am on a specific food mission. It is midnight. How cool is it that I can shop so late? Not being born and raised here I still can't get over the client-friendly shopping hours that are possible in Malibu. I couldn't sleep, raided the fridge at home but wasn't satisfied. I had a sudden craving for certain foods that could not wait until tomorrow, so here I am. I'm no stranger to odd combinations now and then. Like dipping cookies in milkshakes or honey on pizza or chocolate on bread. But pregnancy cravings are a whole other monster. It is licorice I am after this time, and soft pretzels dipped in hot sauce. And pomegranates. And mangos. If I don't score some mangos tonight, I don't know what I'll do.

I left Lucas sleeping soundly in bed. If he wakes up, which I doubt he will as he is such a heavy sleeper, he'll assume I'm in the kitchen. It's not the first time I have sneaked out at night. It's too much bother to tell him where I'm going, and either he'll insist on coming with me and it will take him forever to get ready, or he'll try and persuade me to stay home and we'll end up in an argument. My mangos are non-negotiable, I didn't want to risk it. The dogs are in the car, windows cracked. It's easier to bring them along, and safer, because sometimes they bark with excitement when I return home, and I so do not want Lucas to wake up and for me to have to explain.

I love shopping at night. No traffic to get here, which is such a plus. Hardly anybody is around. Unlike Ralphs on Sunset where some people go to spot rock stars (it has actually been nicknamed Rock & Roll Ralphs), Ralphs here in Malibu is very low key at this time of night. I find all the things I have come for, minus hunting down the hot sauce, which suddenly makes me retch even imagining it. What was I thinking? I go to the checkout counter to pay, grab some gum, and that's when I see it, splashed across the front page of the *National Enquirer*:

CLAUDIA SPECTOR FEARED MURDERED IN HER OWN HOME!

I glance at the first line of the article, which reads:

Crime scene investigators have found signs of a struggle at Claudia Spector's Hollywood Hills home. Her cell phone, passport, and credit cards discovered by police suggest Claudia Spector never left home despite her sudden disappearance.

I grab the paper, look behind me to see if anyone is watching. Why I feel so self-conscious, I can't explain. Nobody, apart from myself, is in the checkout line. The teller, a young woman chewing gum, yawns and rings up my groceries. Debating whether I should buy it or not, I finally chuck the paper on the conveyor belt, adding it to my pile at the last minute. I pay, roll it under my arm, eager to read the contents of the article in the car. Everyone says you can't trust these types of tabloids—it's all nonsense—but I happen to know that their journalists get their hands on the scoop long before anyone else because they pay high sums of money for info, and often their stories wind up being true, because the serious papers corroborate the same stories weeks later. Not things like *Aliens Land on the Moon*, but celebrity gossip, crime news, and investigative reporting. Nonsense or not, I need to see what it says.

Safe in my car, dogs snoozing in the back, I read the rest of the article while gorging on licorice, my tongue sticky and black.

> Claudia Spector has been missing for nearly a week. Detectives are investigating how an A-list movie star has simply vanished. She was filming a new TV series, *Cat's Cradle*, and when she did not show up for work, wasn't answering her phone calls or messages as usual, work colleagues and family reported her missing. Her housekeeper, Juana Juarez, found her smashed cell phone on the couch along with what appears to be all her credit and debit cards, and passport, as well as a broken lamp and side table. Unfortunately, the actress's home surveillance cameras were switched off at the time.
>
> "We don't know if she is alive," her mother, Ashley Spector, said. "Why wouldn't she get in touch, otherwise? Why would she leave her cell phone behind? And her credit cards and passport?"
>
> Her family confirms that Claudia was not suffering from depression, had no plans to travel, and there is no reason whatsoever for her disappearance. Crime scene tape surrounds Ms. Spector's lavish Hollywood Hills home. There was no sign of forced entry, which rules out burglary. Police fear that someone close to the actress with access to her home, or someone she invited in, may have harmed her. The police are treating her Hollywood home as a crime scene. Under UV lighting, investigators have found traces of blood. As well as blood, a broken Tiffany heart necklace was found

> on the floor of her living room. The police searched her house for drugs and drug residue, but none were found, which rules out drug-related motives for her disappearance.
>
> Claudia was engaged to actress Crystal Cormac, but they broke off all wedding plans and parted ways. She was not dating anybody in particular in more recent months, but police are urging anyone who might be able to shed light on her disappearance to come forward as soon as possible.

When I pull out of the parking lot at Ralphs, I could swear I spot Barbara's Oldsmobile at the other end of the lot, too far away to read the plates, too far away to see who the figure is in the driver's seat. The car screeches off. Is she *spying* on me? On behalf of her son? And if so, why? I shake my head. That would be absurd. She goes to bed early. She would never be shopping at midnight. And what would she be doing in our neighborhood anyway, when they live in Beverly Hills? It's just that her Oldsmobile is pretty unique; there are so few models of that car anymore, and it looked like the same color too. Brown. *No*, I tell myself again. *I'm being crazy. There is no way that was Barbara. The licorice sugar rush has gone to your head, Ava.*

Once back home, I find Lucas still asleep in bed as if no time has passed at all. It's amazing what you can get away with when you're blond, I think. He always looks so virtuous. So angelic. I swear, sometimes, when the light is shining a certain way on his flaxen hair, there appears to be a halo around his head. All those secrets he was keeping from me. His betrayal with Claudia. None of this shows on his face. Like Dorian Gray, I think. When someone has lied to you, can you ever trust them again? Yet we lie to ourselves every day, don't we? We are all guilty of fooling ourselves. Does that mean we lose trust in our own selves too? Possibly.

Because right now, I don't know who or what to believe.

Least of all myself.

# TWENTY

A week passes, and an old colleague calls, asking me to help out on a movie for HBO. The head script supervisor is sick, and they are over their heads apparently. I snap up the opportunity immediately, even though, in all honesty, I've become accustomed—worryingly quickly—to my new lady-of-leisure status. The first time in my adult life I have been jobless.

Even though I've not yet agreed to Lucas's terms concerning the prenup and am still in possession of that recording, I feel the warmth and relief of financial security because he has been trying to convince me that I never have to work again. As long as I don't try to take our baby away, anyway... Yet I love what I do: the creative energy, the excitement. This job is only temporary—maybe just a few days—I can't turn it down.

I drop off the dogs at the doggie daycare—a place in Topanga Canyon they adore. This way I don't feel guilty about leaving them in the house or worry about what time Lucas makes it home after work.

In LA, it's hard to avoid major traffic jams these days, so you need to plan shortcuts and be prepared for your car to serve as an office as well as a means to get from A to B. Waze is my best friend. My phone is set up, hands-free, I have Wi-Fi, a printer, pens, paper, notebooks, and even a fax, all in my car, an old roomy Toyota Prius station wagon, not unlike the old toy car my dad gave me. I am not the only one who uses her car as an office. I met an actor the other day who told me she "prays for traffic jams" so she can learn her lines and get all her phone calls done. She has makeup and several changes of clothing in her car, which also serves as her wardrobe. I too have a pair of heels ready, and a chic sports jacket, in case I end up in some impromptu meeting with a director or producer.

The studio sent me the script and call sheet for the day, and I am on it, already mapping out the story beats, tracking timelines, props, and wardrobe, what needs to be done, and inconsistencies to watch out for. Not easy coming in mid-shoot, especially where continuity is concerned. As is normal, we are shooting out of sequence. Two scenes. One scene takes place right at the beginning of the movie, another at the end. The same actors, the same setting, yet three years has lapsed in movie time. Part of my job, along with hair and makeup and costume, is to make sure it looks like there has been a genuine three-year gap in time.

I am meticulous. I have my pet peeves: actors who swing giant, packed-to-the-brim suitcases like they are feathers. To stop them doing so—because it is not my job to give direction on their performance—I weigh the suitcase down. I have seen this mistake a thousand times while watching TV, and it drives me nuts. I could go on: glugging down a "hot" drink when it is obviously anything but. "Vomiting" when there is no vomit or retching on the actor's part, just coughing. When you vomit in real life, you vomit, you don't cough. I make sure props has Campbell's Cream of Chicken Soup on hand. I go over and above what I am required to do, but I am persnickety and my eye for detail honed sharp. On occasion, I have been accused of treading on my colleagues' toes, but overall, I think my tips and efforts are valued and appreciated by my peers.

In this business, we start the day early. Lucas was still asleep when I left. I managed to steal out of the house without the girls making too much hullabaloo, in order to get to the set on time after dropping them off. Being such a good customer, and because I am friends with the owner, the doggie daycare people make a special concession for me to do early, five a.m. drop-offs. The place is like an all-inclusive resort for dogs and as expensive as a human hotel. But they love it so much and it has been a godsend. They get to socialize with other dogs, romp around the spacious grounds on a hillside, and sometimes they get training classes from the staff, who are super caring.

My cell rings. Lucas. I hesitate. I left him a note in the kitchen, but he probably hasn't made it that far and has woken up to an empty space beside him in bed, wondering where I am.

"Hi, honey."

"And you are... where?" he demands. His voice is groggy.

"I left you a note."

"You sound distant. Are you in your *car*?"

"About to drop off the dogs. On the way to work." I fill him in with the details. I can tell by the stretches of silence he is *not* happy.

"I suggested getting rid of that prenup for a reason," he snipes. "The main reason is so you do *not* have to work."

*That's not true*, I think. *The main reason is so you get that recording*. "It's just for a few days." My tone is chirpy. Upbeat. "I'm filling in for someone who's off sick, is all."

"Why are you doing this, Ava? I thought we had a deal."

*A deal*. There is always a deal with him. "We still have the prenup in place, so I'm covering my bases."

"I have been more than generous! You do not *need* to work!"

"I know, honey, but still. I'm just being cautious."

There is silence. I concentrate on my driving, maneuvering

the sharp bends of Topanga Canyon. The dogs are wagging their tails in anticipation. They recognize this road. More leaden silence from Lucas. To check he is still on the line, I come up with, "Anyway, you work, so why can't I?"

"It's different. I'm not pregnant."

Lucas is always going on about "us" being pregnant. About how "we" are having a baby. Yet I suppose when it comes down to it, he knows it will be me doing the work. "Honey," I cajole in a cheery voice, "it's no big deal. You know I love my work. I need to get out of the house once in a while."

"If you're that unhappy at home I'll buy us a bigger house."

I laugh. "Don't be ridiculous. I love our house." I do. I adore our house.

Our two-bedroom, cabin-style home is testament to the days when Malibu signified a cool, laid-back vibe, when people lived next to the ocean because of the way of life, the fresh breeze of briny air, the sound of crashing waves, not because of the snotty, real estate price tag. Our place is pretty funky compared to most of our neighbors', and I love it. I do not hanker after a bigger, swankier, fishbowl home. Though I love hanging out there more than anything, I don't want to stay home all day twiddling my fingers while pregnant. I need to get out, to get away from Lucas and those four walls. Plus, I love the ambiance at work. The camaraderie. Being part of a crew buzzing with creative dynamism, all of us producing something magical. People talk about how important doctors and nurses are for humankind, and it's true. But what would the world do without art and entertainment? Without TV or movies, or music, or books? I love what I do. I get a kick out of knowing that I'm helping to give people a means to escape when they come home from a grueling day of work. I think artists save lives in other, more subtle ways. In a day-to-day way. I feel proud to be a cog in that wheel of creativity.

"I love our house," I tell Lucas. I am at the top of Topanga now. I put on my blinker and swing a left on Old Topanga Canyon Road.

His reply is all business. "I'll have the new marriage contract ready when you get home. I'm getting rid of the old prenup. And remember, I want that recording, Ava. The SD card. In my hands by the end of today."

"Fine," I say. "It's your call, but remember that—"

"My other phone's ringing," he cuts in. "Call you back later."

His other phone? That was a slip-up. What other phone? If it had been the house phone, he would have said, *the* other phone's ringing. And anyway, neither of us uses the landline anymore.

The flip phone? Last I checked, it was in his shoe.

Does he have another cell phone, specifically for work? That would make sense, I guess.

I promised myself to not dig around. *Leave it,* I tell myself, as I park the car at the daycare center and let the dogs out.

*Leave your marriage alone and do not spoil things. You don't have a choice.*

Yet I ask myself, *What is Lucas up to now?*

I need to find out.

# TWENTY-ONE

Getting involved in a project halfway through and subbing for someone else is tough, but I hunker down to work, concentrate a hundred percent and put my brain into gear, armed with my clipboard and pen. I read through reams of notes and old call sheets to get myself up to date. We are in a studio which has been dressed to look like a Victorian conservatory, lush with plants and creepers, some real, some fake—members of the props team constantly spraying water here and there, and moving things around. It is a period drama, hoping to attract the same audience who watch *Bridgerton*. The set is busy: gaffers, makeup artists, set designers, costume designers, everyone concentrating to the maximum on their particular task. It feels great to be back in the thick of it, but also daunting. I don't want to screw up so I keep my head down, chat a lot less than I usually do but make sure I clock everyone's names and jobs. Some of the people here I have worked with before. Others, I have no idea who they are. After ten takes of a particularly difficult shot, when one of the actors needs to trip over a chair, smack into the arms of their adversary (who they will also, in that instant, realize they are smitten by), the director calls "cut" and for us to "take five." I am bushed; we have been going for hours without a break, so I jump at the chance to grab a coffee and snack. As I'm stuffing a muffin into my mouth, I hear a familiar voice.

"Ava! Is that you?"

I turn around. It's Sunny. I met Sunny on one of my very first jobs. We spent two weeks on location in Upstate New York and had a blast working on a thriller together. She took me under her wing and taught me so much. I laugh when I hear her voice. Sunny is the kind of person who will always bring a smile to your face, hence her nickname. Her real name is Sunita.

"Sunny! The light of my life." I grin. "Haven't seen you in a work environment for a while."

She flings her arms around me and squeezes me in an embrace. "They told me you were here! Can't stay long, I'm shooting next door, but so great to see you back at work."

The funny thing about being on location and working on movies is that you become like family very quickly. Filming can be intense. You get to know the core of who people are, at their best and worst. You may not work with these members of crew for ages, maybe even ever again, but that closeness will always be there even if you don't reconnect for years. The bond is *there*. Like an old school friend. You don't need to go through the motions of explaining or making excuses as to why you haven't called. It is like plugging in a cable to an electric socket. Instant, you can pick up where you left off. The relationship is and always will be.

"I was going to call you, actually," she says, hooking her arm through mine. She is dressed in a black bomber jacket, jeans, and a T-shirt. Sensible worker clothes, as am I. Sunny is from London but has lived in LA for twenty years and is married to a man who works as an animator at Disney. If you get invited to a barbecue at Sunny's, you may come across dozens of her relatives at any one time. She's as British as you get, with a south

London accent, but her parents are Asian, born in Gujarat, India, so her extended family is very spread out. They wanted her to marry a nice Indian boy, but she refused, point-blank, to even have a cup of tea with any of her parents' arranged choices and met Daniel in a bar on Sunset when she was on vacation. She never went home. At first her family were horrified by her choice: a "pasty-faced farm boy from Iowa," but now they love Daniel, appreciate her "love match" and come and visit Sunny whenever they can.

We catch up on gossip and work-related stuff. We chat about my pregnancy, and she tells me that she never wants kids, but that she and Daniel are planning on getting a dog, because lately he's been working from home a lot.

Then she says in a conspiratorial voice, "Did you hear about Roger?"

"Director Roger or actor Roger?"

"Director. He fell off a cliff and died."

Roger is—or should I say, was—a director famous for his temper. He was incredibly unpleasant to Sunny. Though we admitted it wasn't racial prejudice because he behaved that way across the board, he was capable of even making extras cry. She and I did a toilet paper commercial with him one time and vowed never to work with the guy again.

"They were filming in Devon, by a cliff overlooking the sea," she tells me, pulling me into a corner, away from the bustle of the craft-service table laden with tea, coffee, and cakes. "On a commercial. He was yelling at someone through a loudspeaker, took a step back, stumbled, and toppled over the cliff, I kid you not." And before I have a chance to say a word or even react, she adds, "So much bloody drama in our business! First Roger, now Claudia Spector."

My heart plummets into my stomach. I take a deep, calming breath to steady my nerves. "They haven't found her?"

Sunny lowers her voice so others can't hear. "Nope. But

apparently, she was last seen in public with some guy. Having dinner at Chez Suzette in Beverly Hills, kissing and canoodling, all over each other, and then they drove off together."

"In the same car?"

"Yup."

"A real relationship then." In Los Angeles even couples use separate cars most of the time, because getting stuck without wheels is not like in most cities where you can catch an Uber, a subway, or train, or bus. I mean, yeah, Sandra Bullock did ride that bus, but if you catch a bus in LA, it usually means you're broke, or you have a crazy amount of time on your hands. And if you get an Uber, wow! How much money do you have to burn? Unlike London or Paris or New York, Los Angeles is so spread out, so humongous, everyone is wedded to their car, because life without a car is almost impossible. Two people in one car means carpool, family, best friends, or love.

"Do you know where they were going?" I ask.

"West on Sunset, they said."

"*Who* said? Is this in the news?"

"Not yet."

"Why not if it's common knowledge?"

Sunny raises a brow and twists a lock of her thick black hair between her fingers. "It's not, because someone"—and she dips her voice to an even lower whisper—"is protecting someone."

"What do you mean?"

"Rumor has it—through the grapevine on set—it was Jason Junot and he's such a good client of Chez Suzette the management doesn't want a scandal and is denying he was even at the restaurant that night. Weirdly, nobody took any photos."

"Why are they denying having a movie star in their restaurant? Isn't any publicity good publicity?"

"Not when people are thinking she might be dead."

I don't know whether to feel relieved or panicked. Lucas is a dead ringer for Jason Junot, an A-list actor who, of late, has been dating just about everyone who's anyone. They have that same rumpled blond hair, long dark lashes, same height and build. Even dress in a sharp, similar way. It's uncanny how alike they look.

"Probably because all the famous people who eat there are stars in their own right and the management has a reputation for banning social media influencers and paparazzi," I offer. The last thing I'm going to mention is my husband, or the affair he was having with Claudia, or the fact he has often had girls come up to him asking for his autograph, mistaking him for Jason Junot.

"Do you think the truth will come out?" I ask Sunny quietly, my heart hammering. I hear the assistant director, like an echo, calling everyone back to the set.

"We'll have to finish this conversation later. Promise you'll call? We have a *lot* to discuss!" Sunny kisses me on both cheeks and begins to slink away, aware she's not meant to be lurking around in the middle of someone else's shoot.

A PA's voice looms into my earshot, and I snap back to attention. "Quiet on set, please, going for a take."

"Bye, Sunny," I mouth in silence, miming a telephone, as she slips out of the studio. "Call me."

"Sound rolling..." the PA calls out.

"And... action!" the director booms.

Silence. One of the actors takes a step. Apart from the pounding in my ears and the blood rush to my head—caused by everything I have heard about Claudia—you could hear a feather flutter to the ground. The actor delivers his lines.

# TWENTY-TWO

"What the hell time do you call this." No question, just a furious proclamation that somehow manages to escape the thin line that is Lucas's sullen lips. Ironic for him to accuse me, when he has come back late so many times. He is sitting on the couch, TV remote in his hand, sound turned down. Which shows he hasn't actually been watching TV, but stewing over how late I am and how irritated he is. The look in his eyes fills me with dread.

Earlier, he picked up the dogs himself. I got a series of furious messages about the value of his time. Why do some men so often feel their time holds so much more value than ours? Or is that a sexist statement on my part? Maybe that is simply my perspective from personal experience, and there are magnanimous husbands and boyfriends out there who genuinely believe their partners' time is equal in worth.

I smile at him benignly. "Sorry, honey, you know how filming is."

He holds out a contract and makes a show of ripping it in two. *The prenup.* "You have the SD card?" he snaps.

"I do," I say. *It's still lodged behind our wedding photo.* I make a show of putting my hand in my pocket.

He reaches out. "Give it to me."

"Okay, calm down. I need to go to the bathroom first. Wash my hands, freshen up."

"Don't be long."

My gaze trails around the living room. "You said you picked up the dogs? Where are they?"

"With Jill, on a run."

"This late?"

"I'm sure she won't be long."

In the bedroom, I extract the SD card from the back of the photo frame and stick it in my jeans pocket. Go to the bathroom, where I stay for a while, going over in my head the logistics of our deal concerning a new marriage contract that gives me fifty-fifty to Lucas's assets. This is normal in the state of California, unless otherwise stipulated in a prenup, like the one he has just shredded in half. A no-brainer, right? Any woman would spring at the chance—especially if she doesn't have much of a choice to leave anyway. But Claudia Spector looms in my mind, her last name, *Spector*, actually perfect, given the ominous circumstances of her disappearance. Lucas thinks he has gotten off scot-free, that I have forgiven him completely for what he did. That his generosity overrides everything. That because he has professed his rekindled love for me, he is off the hook. Most women wouldn't think twice about the offer. Having that ugly scene on the SD card does me no favors. I will be glad to be rid of it. Never think of it again. But Lucas has stipulated conditions in this new marriage contract he wants me to sign. To stay in the marriage for at least another three years, to share the marital bed with him. I know what he's banking on. If I stay for another three years in our marriage, our child will be old enough to have fallen in love with his or her dad and it will be harder for me to leave the marriage, knowing I have a little one's soul at stake. If I leave when the baby is too young to understand, it will be easier for the both of us. The three-year thing does pin me down. As for the marital-bed part, he assumes that because he's such a great lay and makes me come every time, my gaga brain, pumping out dopamine or whatever, will forgive his transgressions. I know how his mind works. Yet all I can think of is Claudia Spector. She is *gone*. I have proof that he had an affair with her! Plus, he admitted it. Does Lucas have any idea that Claudia was last seen—in public anyway—with a blond man of his appearance, a man they are mistaking for Jason Junot?

Mistaking him, for now.

The truth will out in the end. It usually does.

Let's face it, whichever way you look at it, I am in danger. I am playing with fire.

Our marital conundrum is interrupted by Jill bringing the dogs back from their run. She texts me when she is outside our house. I open the sliding doors to the deck, take in the salty air and the soothing sound of crashing waves, and close them behind me. As I open up the back gate to let the trio in, Sappho and Ariadne bound, slobbering, up the steps and through the gate, tails wagging thrillingly, their faces showing how delighted they are with themselves and life in general. So simple to be a golden retriever. How lucky they are. But then I remember their horrendous past, how they were used and abused as breeding machines, and my heart both breaks and melts for them all over again, as it does several times a day. I greet them with gusto, praising them for how wonderful they are, and invite Jill in for a drink. She is sweaty from the run and shakes her head, no. The dogs go straight to their water bowls, trailing sand everywhere, shaking off droplets of water from their jowls. I look behind me, at the house, to see if Lucas is observing us from the glass doors. He isn't.

Shielding my eyes from the sun, I say, "Jill, you're an angel, thanks so much. Was it Lucas's idea or yours to come by for the dogs?"

She unzips her windbreaker, opens it up to let in a gust of cooler air. "It's always my idea, you know that. Actually, I wanted to come by anyway. Lucas told me you were at work. Ava, that's great news! You found a new job? That's what you were praying for, isn't it?"

"Just for a few days. Filling in for someone on sick leave."

She glances at the house and says, "Rather you than me. I hate working. Maybe it's because I've never found anything I'm good at."

"Everyone's good at something," I say.

She shrugs. "Look, Ava, I wanted to tell you something. In private. William told me that—" Jill carries on talking but the crash of a wave and the lowering of her voice muffles out the rest of her sentence. "You think that's possible?"

"What did you say? Sorry, I didn't hear."

"You think it could have been..."—and she points to the house—"having dinner with her at Chez Suzette? I mean, they look so alike, don't you think? Jason Junot is furious, apparently. Has put out an official statement via his attorney that he does not even know Claudia Spector and he was definitely, categorically, not having dinner with her at Chez Suzette. William says it's going to be in the papers tomorrow."

"William knows Jason Junot?"

Jill knots her brows like I'm being dumb, like I should know. "Yeah, you know William's the producer of *Deep Water*?"

Seven brown pelicans fly overhead. I observe them with interest, counting them as they go, welcoming the distraction. Usually they are around early morning. This is why I live here. For the nature, the surf, the smell of the ocean. I don't care about the trappings of Hollywood and its insidious gossip. My thoughts bend back to Claudia and her dinner partner, the possibilities of what will happen next, too life-changing to take on board. I cannot lose all this... my home, my view, my life, these pelicans. My baby.

"Of course, that's right, how could I forget?" I reply absent-mindedly.

And now I regret letting Jill into my secret. In the light of the early evening, I see her for what she is. Not a true friend, but a fun, gossipy neighbor, a woman who looks out for herself, married to a man she is no longer in love with. Nothing wrong with that, and I am not one to judge, but why did I tell her my innermost secret about Lucas having an affair with Claudia? It was a reckless thing to do. This is no joke. What may unfurl is no joke at all. She is being kind. She is giving me the heads-up and I should be grateful, but she is also, by the eager tone of her voice, grilling me, trying to extract more information from me. I need to consider where my loyalties lie. It has not escaped my attention that in the last twenty-four hours two friends of mine have come through with information about Claudia Spector. The woman is on everyone's mind, her name on everyone's lips. And Lucas was having an affair with her! I should never have told Jill about the burner phone. What was I thinking?

"Thanks so much for taking the dogs with you," I say, by way of wrapping up our conversation. I can't say more, can't talk about this anymore, without incriminating my husband.

"Sure," she says. "Take care, Ava." There is a flicker of something in Jill's voice that tells me that things have changed between us. Not just on my part, but hers too. The "take care" feels like she is disassociating herself from me. Like knowing me could be dangerous for her, like I could be contagious.

I know how this town works.

Jill, I am sure, will want to keep her distance from me, after what has been—or is surely about to be—revealed about Lucas's date with Claudia. It's probably a good thing if she stays clear of me.

I need to be careful. Keep my mouth shut.

# TWENTY-THREE

The next day at work, nobody is talking about anything other than Claudia Spector and her love life. In Claudia's case, surely it was "falling in lust," at least, that's how Lucas made it out to be. A sexual relationship without love. But there is still no proof that Lucas was the blond man. I avoided asking him that question last night, perhaps because I didn't want to see his expression. See for myself. Be reminded, once more, how he betrayed me, sneaked around behind my back, lied to me.

There are several articles in the papers, both online and in the tabloids, with Jason Junot formally denying dating or even knowing Claudia Spector. "We met once, for a New York second," it reads, quoting the actor. "Many, many years ago, at an audition, before she was such a big star. I am a fan of her work and would love to have dinner with her one day, but can assure you that it was not me at Chez Suzette on a date with her."

On a break, I call Lucas. I do not dare text him. Dare not mention Claudia's name. I go outside so nobody can listen to my call. Later, after I finish work today, Lucas and I have arranged to meet at the law firm of one of his colleagues. To sign the new marriage contract, with two witnesses present.

"You've read the papers?" I ask him on the phone. "Nobody is talking about anything else. It was you, wasn't it? You having dinner with her?"

He clears his throat. "Ava, I—"

"Wasn't it?"

A long pause. "Yes."

"Oh, God. What now?"

"I don't know. But I swear, I swear to God, on my baby's life, I swear to God I had nothing to do with—"

"It'll come out," I assure him. "It's only a matter of time. You know that, don't you?"

"Oh, *God*." He sounds as if he is about to burst out crying. I can hear the misery in his voice like an animal in pain. "Please, Ava, believe me when I tell you I had nothing, *nothing* to do with it."

"With what?"

"With her... going missing."

I don't reply.

"Please believe me, baby, *please*!"

"Have you told your dad? Conferred with him?" I don't know why I say this. It's a little twist of the knife I can't resist.

"No," he replies, and lets out a tiny whimper.

"You should. You may need to lawyer up."

"Oh, God. I wish I'd never met the woman." And when I don't say anything in response, he says, "Baby, please don't leave me!"

"I need to think about this."

"Please! You were going to sign our new deal."

"I was, but things have changed."

"We're having a baby. I love you. Without you, I'm nothing. My life won't be worth living."

*True. But you should have thought about that before. When you had it all and went and spoiled everything by having an affair!* I don't say this though. Just remain silent. I know he needs me. With me by his side, things will look so much better for him. A wife leaving her husband in the middle of a scandal does not look good at all. Makes him look guiltier. Politicians know that, in particular. He needs me to be the trusting, loyal wife.

"What are you going to do?" His voice is a whine now. A child in time-out who has had every last toy snatched away from him, who feels that whatever he did, the punishment is unjust. "Baby, please. *Help* me."

"Lucas, I don't know how."

"You're still coming, right? To meet me at Neil's? To sign? We're a team, baby. If you leave me..."

"Well, I don't know. I have work again. Looks like they may offer me another job, a full-time job. To be honest, that old prenup doesn't bother me. I need to keep my options open."

"Baby, please, don't let me down *now*! You don't need to work! I need to know you're with me, on my side."

"I don't know, Lucas. You always want to do a *deal*. Like force me to stay in the house for three years. Saying if you die, all the money will go in trust to the baby. It's so untrusting. You don't trust me, so why should I trust you? Think about it. How is that fair? At least with the old prenup it's clear. I can walk any time. It's cut and dry. I have my freedom intact and you get to keep all your money." I am winging it here. I know he'd fight me tooth and nail for my baby, but I need to seem carefree or he'll home in on my Achilles' heel and trip me up.

A beat of silence. I can see he is weighing things up in his mind. I am waiting for him to remind me of how he'll fight me in court, bring up my past. But he surprises me. Coldly and with a touch of suspicion, he says, "What do you want from me?"

"Nothing," I reply. "I'm not asking a thing. That's my point. I'm working again. The director's talking about a TV series in a couple of months. Could be permanent, maybe not even freelance but on a wage, you know, with benefits and even maternity leave. Things are looking up." The fact that Lucas ripped that prenup in two does not mean it doesn't still exist in the eyes of the law. Not until a new contract takes its place or it is legally nullified.

"Fifty-fifty, no conditions, no clauses," he bursts out. "And if I get hit by a bus, you get it all."

I don't speak. This new deal shows how desperate he is. Even if his reasons are entirely selfish and suspect, it warms me that he is so eager to hold on to our marriage.

"Did you hear me?"

I nod. "I did."

"And?"

I consider what he has said. This is huge for him. It tugs at my heart. I can't help it. "How can I trust you won't have another affair?"

"I think I've learned my lesson by now, don't you?"

*One would think so. But...*

"Ava?"

"I'll meet you at Neil's. But I'm not promising anything."

"Please, sweetheart."

"I've got to go, they're getting ready for another take." I end the call.

I will let him wallow around in his proverbial bed he made for himself, all day. Let him really *think* about the consequences of what he's done. And then I will sign. My baby needs a father. A home. And more importantly...

He's still my husband, with a lot of balls in his court, legally speaking.

I am ninety-five percent sure I will sign that new marriage contract.

Because the crazy thing is... despite it all, despite everything he has done, I do love the life we have together, for the most part. And we both know I don't really have a choice, anyway...

# TWENTY-FOUR

Lucas, despite it all, is worthy of my love, by the way.

After my miscarriage three years ago, I was not only devasted about losing the baby, but I was fearful I'd lose Lucas too. Everybody talks about post-natal depression, but having a miscarriage—especially one which ends with invasive, non-elective surgery—is often brushed aside. I had to go under general anesthesia. A gown. A hairnet. An oxygen mask. An IV. I had a baby growing inside my womb one day, and the next, it was literally sucked and scraped out of me, leaving me in a void. Empty, and emptied, both physically and emotionally.

You are told, in the nicest possible way, that you need to get on with your life and move forward. I fell into a vortex of despondency and cataclysmic depression in the weeks that followed, and for the first time in my life started taking medication. I had kept away from everything up until that point, hardly even popping a Tylenol for a headache. My mother had been dependent on prescription drugs, even before the cancer took hold, and they say addiction is inherited, so I had always been wary.

Lucas was amazing when I came out of the hospital. A part

of me feared he'd want us to be over. We had married because I was pregnant, and now it was just me and I had nothing to offer but myself; how would he feel? In the car, on the way back from the hospital, he had a stash of juice and cookies and ginger ale waiting for me. A blanket. A bunch of yellow roses. Yellow to cheer me up, because red was romantic and this was not a romantic occasion. I sat in the passenger seat, my face glum, my mind a wreck, wondering why. *Why did I lose my baby? Why me?*

"Sweetheart," he said, reaching his hand over to capture my lifeless, pale palm. "It's okay. I married you for *you*. The baby was just... look, I would've wanted to marry you anyway." *Had he read my mind?*

I turned my head to him, taking him in. His handsome face, his lithe surfer body. A California boy. All I could think about, and all I had thought about for weeks, was what the baby would look like. Would it inherit Lucas's amazing blue eyes? His thick mop of golden hair? Who would teach our child to read? Him or me? But now I was forced to put all those questions into a *would've should've* past. There was the self-recrimination too. *What did I do wrong? Why did I miscarry? What did I eat? Was it the pineapples? Was it when I went running on the beach? Was it when I took that hot bath? That massage at the spa? Had my own anxiety of being unexpectedly pregnant caused the fetus to die?* A noose of sadness was hanging heavy round my neck.

My eyes lifted from Lucas and strayed down to my little belly pouch. Empty, but not flat enough for me to forget. I'd need to go to the gym to tone up, but I couldn't face it. I couldn't even imagine how I'd get out of bed each morning, let alone muster up energy and get physical.

"Ava." He squeezed my hand. "I mean it. I don't want to be with anyone else. We're a team. It's no big deal, we'll get through this. I love you."

His words were a balm to my psyche. Somewhat. Although

telling me it was "no big deal" was not what I wanted to hear. Was it true he loved me? When you fall into a pit of sadness, nothing anyone says can snap you out of it. I tried chanting positive mantras to myself, in silence, rolling them over and over in my mind. Tried to turn any negative inner banter around the other way, switching words like *What did you do wrong, Ava?* into *Well done, great job, Ava!* Breathing in deeply, slowly, then out, all out... I tried every cure, every technique to get myself back on track.

It *was* a big deal. It will be a big deal forever. You can't undo a momentous event like that. I wondered what had happened to the fetus. Stem-cell research for Parkinson's and degenerative diseases? At least that would be something. Or had they simply thrown it away like trash? Now in the car, I regretted not asking the doctors if I could keep it, to give it a burial. To recognize my baby as a human being and not just debris from a medical intervention. Why had I not organized that? The hospital would have probably discouraged it, if not given me a straight-out *no*. But I should have at least asked. I hadn't been thinking. I had wanted to get it over with. Now I wished I could rewind time.

After a weekend of rest, I went back to work. An automaton. I went through the motions of everything I was skilled at, smiling and being professional, wondering what the point was, what the point was of anything at all. Then I collapsed at work from fatigue. It wasn't fatigue, it turned out, but a broken heart. That's what the therapist said. People always associate a broken heart with lost love from a partner, but hearts can break in many ways.

Losing that baby made me lose my identity. I spent a couple of weeks in a psychiatric ward. That sounds so scary, but it was really just a lot of therapy and soul searching. Learning to forgive myself for... I didn't know what, really. Finally, though, I was able to talk about what happened without feeling like I was dragging others down with my problems. It was such a relief.

When I was well enough to come home, Lucas gave me a hundred percent of himself. He organized a surprise second "wedding" on a remote beach for us. Nothing official, but still a ceremony, with garlands of flowers, Hawaiian style. He invited a group of close friends and even caterers, who organized a grand picnic for us. Champagne mimosas, finger sandwiches, Belgian chocolates. People's dogs and children came. It was bikinis and sarongs and frisbees. His best friend, Lionel, dressed up as a priest and we renewed our vows. We danced. Lucas committed himself to me all over again. I felt a new spark of hope and excitement about life for the first time since losing our baby.

"Till death do us part," he promised me. I promised him the same.

So, you see, whatever Lucas has or hasn't done, we are bonded.

Probably for life.

# TWENTY-FIVE

We celebrate after the signing of our new marriage contract. Drinks at The Roger Room.

A mistake.

So many people stare at Lucas. Scrunching up their watchful eyes in an *is it, or isn't it* sort of way. They have seen the story about Jason Junot and Claudia Spector on the news. Read about it online and in the papers. For the most part, as they examine Lucas now, feature for feature, they know he isn't Jason Junot. But one woman rushes up unashamedly to the bar with a pen and drinks napkin, about to ask for an autograph. She stops short of flinging her arms around him. She giggles. "Shoot, I'm sorry, I thought you were someone else."

"Stop wearing suits," I whisper to him.

"Old habits die hard."

Lucas's father insisted he wear a suit to work. But now Lucas is managing partner, he can wear anything he likes. The part Jason Junot plays in the show *Deep Water* also happens to be a lawyer. A lawyer sleuth who solves murders. And he favors suits.

"Change your dress code." I sip my virgin margarita, letting the salty rim sting my lips. "And maybe you should even cut your hair." For the moment, the fuss has died down and the staring has stopped; it seems customers realize Lucas is just a regular guy. But then I notice a man, standing at the end of the bar in the shadows, who can't take his eyes off my husband.

"Let's get out of here," I urge him. "Besides, the dogs will wonder where we are."

It isn't long before the situation shifts into a new gear.

It starts off with a photo that goes viral on Instagram and Facebook. From a fan page of Claudia Spector's.

A photo of Claudia and Lucas touching foreheads, a little grainy, but clear that the man in the picture is not Jason Junot. It was taken at Chez Suzette, the last time Claudia was seen in a public setting.

The media picks up on the photo and it is everywhere.

Nobody has come forward to the police with any sightings of Claudia. At least, no sightings the police are taking seriously, it seems. They are probably dealing with a load of crazies. Fans and wannabe Claudia Spectors. John Hinckley types, maybe—Claudia has had her share of stalkers in the past. Whatever, as far as the media is concerned, the mystery man in the photo was the last person to see her alive.

Lucas.

Right now, the general public doesn't know who Lucas is, but it won't be long, surely? With the way social media is, things spread faster than a Santa Ana fire. Everyone has an opinion. Twitter, Instagram, TikTok. It won't be long before he's exposed.

The first time I lay eyes on the photo myself, an intense sadness seeps through me, rendering me almost numb. I curl up on the floor in a fetal position, nose buried into Sappho's golden mane, and bawl my eyes out. All my energy is sucked out of me. I feel hollow. Sapped. As if I have lost huge amounts of blood or been tapped like a maple tree. It brings back similar feelings after the D & C at the hospital. A sense of hopelessness. Emptiness. Loss. A realization that I will lose Lucas. Then I tell myself, *No, no. This is not me, not who I am*. I cannot surrender so easily. Losing a baby is one thing, but this? I can control my emotions this time, I can surpass this. A little flame from somewhere deep in my solar plexus begins to flare. A healthy whoosh of anger and righteousness sets a fire alight in my belly, thinking of my new baby, my new pregnancy. I will not let anything rob me of this second chance. I will not allow anxiety or fear to get me down. I will not lose sight of who I am, and refuse to let anyone take away my strength, my self-respect, my dignity. And above all, my happiness.

I deserve to be happy. I do.

I will allow myself the luxury of a little contemplation. And time.

I don't go to work the next day. I am too occupied staring at the glassy ocean, ignoring my phone, which rings nonstop, so I turn it off. I want to slip away from the boundaries of real life, switch myself off too, at least for a while, to remember what it was like before. Before Claudia Spector entered our lives. I sit all day in a hazy stupor, watching the light drain from the sky, little by little, feeling the cooling of the day's sun, fixing my eyes on the blue seam of the horizon.

The dogs sit by me, also in quiet meditation. No waggy tails smashing anything in their path. No jumping up. Ariadne rests her head on my lap, gazing up at me. As if she knows some huge bubble is about to burst and their lives could change.

It is only a matter of time before it hits the news and Lucas is formally identified. The minute the media finds out our address and who Lucas is, there will be no peace, no privacy. There are some crazy Claudia fans out there. A lot of people are obsessed with her. She has a huge following. They will not take kindly to anyone who may have harmed her.

I am not surprised when, at around six thirty that evening,

two detectives are at the door. They tell me their names and show me their badges.

That's when Lucas calls his father.

I invite them in. I am polite. Ariadne and Sappho not so much; they instantly make a beeline for the detectives' legs and crotches, fascinated by such a medley of unknown, sniff-worthy odors. I pull them away. "Excuse our dogs," I tell the lady cop. "They get a little too friendly sometimes." My laugh seems highly inappropriate judging by the woman's reaction. Given our dogs' backgrounds and that they came to us as adults, we have been pretty lax about their manners and training. We want to make up some of the happiness they lost; so, yes, I admit it, they are spoiled.

The detective nods, with a clipped, professional smile, which demonstrates very clearly how they are not here on a social call. Her hair is pinned up neatly at the back of her head, face devoid of makeup. Being used to seeing actors dressed as lady cops on the TV shows I have worked on, she looks scarily authentic, which, of course, she is. Authentic. A real live detective in my living room. The other detective—a man—is burly, in a T-shirt and cargo pants. Both wear sturdy, black, lace-up boots. Neither is wearing an official uniform. If this is supposed to make people feel more at ease, the opposite is true. They introduce themselves, but I am so nervous, their names go in one ear and out the other.

"Can I get you guys a coffee?" I offer.

She shakes her head. "No, thank you."

"Water? Soda? Tea?" I am trying too hard. I put my hands in my pockets to stop them from shaking. I can't believe how jittery I feel. I sense a manic Joker smile fixed on my mouth.

"No. Thank you, though." The guy cop folds his arms. His body language is not a good sign. "We want to ask a few questions to help with the investigation."

*Investigation.* The word alone sends a shiver skittering up my spine. "Sure," I say. I hear my husband wrapping up his call to Jack. He is outside on the deck in the back. That won't look good, will it? Insisting on having his attorney present, right off the bat? I wonder if Lucas will hire a criminal lawyer, since criminal law is not Jack's expertise. They have friends and colleagues; they know the best in the business.

"You're maybe aware that the actress Claudia Spector has been officially missing for over a week now?" the guy cop says.

I nod. "Yes, I saw it on the news."

He continues to talk, his voice an echo, far away. Blood is pulsating in my ears; I can't even take on board most of what he is saying, my nerves are so frayed. They know all about us. That I am a script supervisor, Lucas an attorney. They ask me if I know Claudia Spector personally. I am about to answer when Lucas strides into the living room.

He introduces himself in a cordial, easy manner, and assures them, "No. My wife has never met Claudia Spector. If you would like to talk to me, I can come down to the station with my attorney present."

Lucas is so relaxed when he says this, I am stunned. Cool, professional. Being a lawyer, he is unfazed in stressful situations and used to maintaining a good front. He does not discuss the photo of himself and Claudia. He neither denies anything nor admits anything. Just sees the detectives to the door, promising that he, or his attorney, will be in touch tomorrow morning. I guess he needs time to get a story together with Jack's help, to make sure he doesn't incriminate himself. But he already *is* incriminated. He can't wriggle out of this one. What story will he come up with? Photos do not lie. It looks like he was the last person to be with Claudia Spector before she disappeared. Even if I tell myself over and over that's not the case, he can't prove otherwise. Nobody else is coming forward. No family member, no friend, no work colleague. Nor her agent. What will Lucas tell them? Half of me doesn't even want to know.

The idea of my husband murdering a woman is repugnant to me. I cannot let myself entertain those disgusting thoughts. What will happen next? Will they get an arrest warrant together? A warrant to search our house, Lucas's car? Whose car did he and Claudia drive off in when they left the restaurant? I want to ask him. His? Hers? And more importantly, where—I am dying to quiz him—did they go? To Claudia's house, by any chance? All these things are on the tip of my tongue, but I don't inquire, I am too overwhelmed. Too stunned by the breakneck speed of everything that is unraveling. And most of all, too in denial that my own husband, a man I put my trust in and the father of my baby, could possibly be dangerous. People would think me crazy to even be in the same house as him.

*Am* I in danger? More than I already feared?

I say, "Honey, oh my God, what are you going to do?" Things are bad enough for him, I don't want to make even more drama by grilling him myself about the details of *that* night. I just want my husband back, for things to be the way they once were. If only. I don't need to conjure up any more images than are already festering in my head. My wishes are impossible though. As they say, that ship has sailed.

A muscle on Lucas's jaw tics. He holds up his chin as if claiming what is left of his pride. "I'm not going to deny that it was me having dinner with Claudia or that we went back to her place after dinner. I am not going to deny that we made... we had sex. I'm so sorry, honey, that it has led to this. I have already begged for your forgiveness, but I don't want you to be involved. You deserve better."

He was about to say "we made love," wasn't he? His slip-up wounds me. Like a thousand needles in the heart. I have to believe his relationship with Claudia was about sex, nothing more. I have to tell myself that, over and over again. I cannot think of his lips in the crook of her neck, or on her breasts, or on her mouth. No, no, no. I need to remind myself that he renewed our vows on that beach, that he chose and still chooses to be with *me*.

"You made out you'd finished the affair long before that," I point out.

He bows his head. Looks down at his feet. "I didn't want to hurt you, Ava, I'm sorry. I'll say it again... sorry, sorry, sorry, and I will spend the rest of my days telling you how I regret what I did. Babe, I messed up. I won't deny it. I'm *sorry*." He takes a step toward me and gets down on his knees. Taking my hand in his, he kisses it, then rests both of our hands, laying one on top of the other, on my stomach. The message is clear; he is milking my emotions.

*You are having my child.* Or rather, *We are having a baby.*

*He made mistakes. We need to move on. I need to forgive him.* But it's too late to turn back the clock. My pitter-patter voice, full of love and sympathy, blathers on, telling me that kindness and forgiveness are everything, while another, more insistent voice booms, *He lied to you, Ava. He gaslighted you. Tricked you. Left you for as good as dead after your suicide attempt. You cannot trust a word he says. He was in love with Claudia, of course he was. Love can lead to acts of passion. Acts of passion can lead to anything, even violence. Violence can lead to...*

*No, stop, Ava.* I refuse to go there. Refuse to get sucked into that abyss of no return. There's no point. I'm stuck either way.

He is still on his knees. He has his arms around my legs like a child. "Ava, I love you so much."

The last time he was on his knees, or one knee, at least, was when he proposed to me. Even though his parents had pretty much instructed him to marry me, at least he proposed in style and made it seem as if it was his idea all along, which I appreciated. It made me feel wanted and that our marriage was more than just about the baby. The baby I ended up losing.

It was cute. I was lying on the sand soaking up some rays and Lucas was surfing. He's good. Never been a professional surfer, but those born and bred along this coast have surfing in their DNA. I'd been watching him, impressed by his moves. He came out of the water, untied the leash from his ankle, then holding his board shook his sun-streaked head, droplets of water falling like shiny crystals to the sand. Setting the board down, he pulled a ring out of his pocket. It was the most surprising thing ever. Impressive. It was risky to carry a diamond solitaire ring into the ocean. Needless to say, he hadn't wiped out or fallen... just cruised atop the surf all the way to the shore. If it was meant to impress me, it did. That's when he knelt on the sand and asked me to marry him. I was so happy that day. We were sun-kissed and golden and had our future ahead of us. It felt perfect. It was perfect.

I observe him now, remembering those vows we made. *In sickness and in health. Till death do us part.* But now the "death do us part" has a whole new meaning. If Lucas gets accused of her death, what then? Is this what will part us?

He is trembling. Still clinging to me. My heart goes out to him. At times like this you have to make a choice.

Walk or stay.

We may have lost our first child, but now we have another chance.

"I'm here for you, honey," I tell him, taking his hand in mine. "I'm here to support you, to stand by your side."

Sometimes you know you're doing a dangerous thing, but you do it anyway, right?

It's fight or flight. When your only option is fight...

# TWENTY-SIX

That night, my dream wraps me up and spits me out into a sweaty turmoil. My mother yelling at me:

*You will never find love in this world, Ava. Because you have no idea, no goddamn idea at all, what it's like to be a parent. And I hope you never will, for your sake. Hope you never have a kid, because you know what? Kids suck it all outta you, drain you of everything you've got. You are a leech, my girl, nothing more than a leech. You're the biggest mistake of my life.*

I sit up in bed, sweat beading on the small of my back, prickling under my arms. This woman in my dream used to be my reality. That was who she was. A person who was meant to love her child more than anything in the world, twisting that love into one big sad burden, even apparent hatred. More images float into my mind. Me, standing on a chair and pulling out cans of tomatoes from the kitchen cabinet, trying to find something to eat. Bringing Mom an instant coffee when she's conked out on the floor, unconscious. Me walking three miles to school while she sleeps, my stomach rumbling, no lunch box in my hand like the other kids, but with a lipstick I stole from her purse, which

I'll trade for food. Me, telling Mrs. Clifton that I bumped into a lamppost and all the kids laughing at my clichéd lie.

I shrug off the covers, get up, leave Lucas sleeping, and go downstairs to the kitchen to get a cool glass of water, vowing I will love my child like Earth's orbit around the sun.

Sappho pads behind me. I glug down two glasses of iced water, hardly stopping for breath. I lie on the rug with Sappho and bury my face into the softness of her fur, tears spilling down my blotched face, trickling into my nose and lips. Lips I graze into the silky folds behind my beautiful dog's ears, the smoothest most delicate part of her. She knows me so well... Sappho knows that it wasn't a nightmare as well as I do. No dream, I hate to admit, but a memory wound into a tight ball, buried somewhere in the depths of my psyche, in a place I had hoped wouldn't unspool. But your body and mind hold on to every scarred old wound, don't they? Especially the invisible ones. Your subconscious needs to let things out in the end. I have been reading stuff lately that tells us that many of our habits, fears, and memories are predisposed, generated from our ancestors, carried in our DNA. That we are born with them and bear them from generation to generation, like it or not. To protect us, supposedly. So we can run from the clutches of a lion, learn not to stick our hands into flames... that sort of thing.

*No*, I say to myself. *My mother is dead now. I do not want to unearth the negative. Concentrate on the happy times, Ava.*

I worshipped my mother as a little girl... my beautiful mother. I would lean up against her in the back of the car and smell her hair. Rosemary and lavender. But I cannot kid myself. The "happy times" was either then, before my father left us when I turned three, or when I was grown-up, when she had lost her power, when she was ill, when she needed me and had nobody else. Far from punishing her for years of mental abuse and neglect, or pushing her away, I embraced her new helplessness. I could love her freely and pretend she loved me back. Need has a way of making cruel people kind.

Need will out in the end.

And this is the tricky part. How can you differentiate between love and need? It's a fine line. A baby needs her mom. When does need become love? To what degree are the two entwined? I am thinking of Lucas as I ponder this.

He sure needs me now.

I crawl back into bed, nestling myself beside him, basking in the warmth of him as his sleepy arm enfolds me and pulls me tight against him. I feel the comforting rise and fall of his familiar, muscular chest, the rhythm of his breathing. Sliding my leg through his, I nuzzle my head in the nook of his neck, inhaling his sunny, salty, Malibu scent. At dawn he went surfing. It is his meditation, his therapy. It's as if I can taste the waves on him, still, the thrill of the ride. I want to cling to him, never let him go.

Something tells me, though, it might already be too late.

By the time I awake, Lucas is already out of the house. There is a note in the kitchen, with fresh coffee and a stack of homemade pancakes for me to heat up.

*Didn't want to wake Sleeping Beauty.*
*Will be back home when I can.*
*Love you so much.*
*L xxx*

My heart pinches. Even with all this turmoil in his life, he is thinking of me. I don't want to turn on the news, so I don't, but foolishly I let my fingers absentmindedly pick up my phone. An invasive habit we all share nowadays, however much we say we hate social media, hate how our phones have taken over our lives. Apple News is suddenly glaring at me. Claudia Spector's housekeeper has spoken to a variety of news outlets, telling them about my husband, how he and Claudia met, how often he came to her house in Laurel Canyon, and even what they ate. I try not to tap on the stories, to pinch open the photos to make them bigger, but of course I do.

"They looked pretty in love," Juana Juarez says in a video clip, her large brown eyes hazing over with emotion. "Mr. Fox came around here a lot. Nice guy. He often asked me to make his favorite dish, chili con carne. I was so happy to cook for him as he loves my cooking! He told me it was the best recipe he's ever tasted. There's no way he hurt Ms. Spector, he isn't that type of man. He even gave me a gift one time. He's a kind man and he always treated me good. Always treated my employer very good, you know?" She goes on to say how she has been working for Ms. Spector for ten years, that her boss sponsored her to get her green card and that, even though Ms. Spector's house was cordoned off as a crime scene and she herself discovered her broken cell phone and credit cards and passport left behind, her Mercedes was missing and she believes her boss will be coming back, that the Lord would not let her die. "He wouldn't. She is special, you know? So many fans. So many people who love her. I am praying for her return every day." Did she know Mr. Fox was married to another woman? "No, that doesn't sound like it could be the same man," she states. "There must be some kind of mistake. The Mr. Fox I know is a nice guy, he's not a cheater."

*Not a cheater*. Her words break my heart. And such love and loyalty for her employer. Such hope about her returning. The article also states that Claudia has no children or animals, but her mother, brother, and older sister are beside themselves with worry and say, "We need to get to the bottom of this," complaining how long everything is taking, that there must be more evidence and clues. That they don't want to judge, but the police seem to be excruciatingly slow.

Every time I read Lucas's name, my stomach flips in horror.

This is my husband they are talking about. The father of my future child. This is the man I married, the one I was supposed to grow old with.

I call him, but his phone goes straight to voicemail. He is probably down at the police station now. Or maybe he is having a meeting with Jack, going over every minute detail. They do that with clients. Put them through fake interviews and simulate courtroom situations, fire questions at them and rehearse what they are going to say so they are prepared. Jack will be saying things like, *Why didn't you report Claudia missing if you hadn't seen her all week? If this is a woman you were in love with, why didn't you alert her family or friends?* And then Lucas will probably say something like, *We were not in love. It was a casual relationship. In fact, that night at dinner, we broke up. She told me she was leaving town for a while; I didn't think anything of it.*

I have no doubt Lucas will do his usual smooth-talking. But fingerprints do not lie. Blood splatters do not lie. What have they found? The police came to our home.

As these panicky thoughts vie for my attention, my phone rings.

# TWENTY-SEVEN

The name Jack flashes on my phone.

"Jack," I say.

"Ava. Can you come and meet me, please?"

"Is Lucas with you?"

"Not anymore. We spoke earlier."

"Has Lucas been detained by the police?"

"Not yet, and that's why I need you to come and see me."

"But I don't understand. Why—"

"Come to the office. Now." He ends the call. I try calling back to get more information, but Jack doesn't pick up.

In no time I am in my car, racing along the freeway. I arrive at Fox & Fox and am just about to head down to the underground parking when Jack waves at me. He is dressed in a raincoat. There is a light drizzle in the air. Jack's that type of guy: always prepared, always one step ahead, even with the weather. This, though—what has happened to Lucas—must have knocked him for six.

I pull up beside him and he motions for me to open my car door. I flip the lock and he slides in.

"Drive," he commands, without any greeting. He brushes

off a few dog hairs from his coat with a look of disgust on his face.

"Where?"

"You think I care? Anywhere. We need to talk and this is nice and private. Drive anywhere you wish."

I move off slowly.

He covers his face with his hands. "Jesus." This is the first time in the history of forever that I have heard Jack "use the Lord's name in vain" as he himself would say.

"Jack, what's happening?" I shoot a glance at him. He is a gray-haired version of Lucas. Though his features are more chiseled. Harder. His firm jaw tighter, his eyes harsher and without Lucas's gorgeous blue gaze. Yet there is no doubt he is a very handsome man. In great shape too. He runs every day, he does push-ups. Normally, I would feel fearful of him. But I remember he no longer has a hold over me. The prenup is something of the past. Lucas has sold Fox & Fox. Jack is nothing more than my father-in-law.

"Keep your eyes on the road, goddammit," he barks at me. Another first. I have never heard him swear.

I say nothing. I keep my cool. I have never liked this man, never warmed to him, even on the occasions when he is playing nice. I know that reacting to him won't serve me, and especially not Lucas, in any way.

"Lucas needs an alibi," Jack announces, staring at the road ahead.

A silence wars between us. I'm so surprised by what he has just said, I don't reply. This is not the upstanding Jack I know. The ex-marine who stands by truth and honor.

"I can't lie," I reply, almost in a whisper.

"He's your husband."

"Jack, he cheated on me! I'm not the one who got Lucas into this mess."

"He needs you, Ava. I heard what he did. He got rid of the prenup, put all his faith in you, and you owe him one."

I let his words sink in. They annoy me, actually. This man is a bully. I am done with bullies in my life. I respond with, "I don't *owe* Lucas anything. Husbands and wives should not be tallying up what they owe each other. And for the record, dissolving the prenup was his idea, not mine." It feels good to answer back to my father-in-law, to not let him manipulate me.

"Ava. You're not thinking straight." His tone is ominous. A threat? Is he insinuating that he has the power to hurt me?

"Can't someone else give Lucas an alibi? I mean, can't you pay someone?"

Jack glares at me like I'm crazy. I can feel outraged fury emanating from every pore in his body, even though he says nothing. Sitting in the passenger seat, a muscle throbbing in his temple, he rakes his hand through his seal-gray hair. Like father like son, they have the same mannerisms. I have never seen Jack lose it like this, lose his calm collected demeanor.

"Okay," I reply to his silence. "That was a reckless thing to say. But, hey, you want me to lie, so what's the difference between one lie and another?"

"Family. That's what. My son is the father of your baby. He is your *husband*. You know as well as I do that Lucas did not harm that actress. I don't know what the hell is going on, but Lucas is innocent. And we need to prove it."

"Jack, he had an affair."

"Is *that* what's bothering you right now? That your husband had some meaningless affair with some cheap actress? Ava, *please*."

Jack has nailed it. It does bother me that my husband had an affair, of course it does. But he is right. In the big scheme of things, my feelings are not at stake here. "What do you want me to say?"

"That night. The night he went to the restaurant, to Chez

Suzette, where someone took that goddamn photo of him and Claudia Spector. The two of them returned to her house in Laurel Canyon. This is where you need to come in. I need you to say that because Lucas had been drinking, you came to pick him up from the restaurant. You were with him. He cannot have gone to Claudia Spector's house because he was with you, at home, the entire night and the following morning."

I gasp. "But they'll have surveillance cameras in the restaurant parking lot, won't they? They'll know I'm lying!"

"The restaurant does not offer on-site parking. You could have parked anywhere."

"They have valet parking though."

"Nobody is obligated to valet park. You could have parked anywhere."

"What about them driving off together in one car? They were seen."

"If there was proof, there'd be a photo of it in the media by now."

I shake my head. "I don't know, Jack. This whole thing sounds risky."

"It's all we've got. We cannot have Lucas at the scene of the crime that night. We cannot have circumstantial evidence getting in the way."

"They'll find his fingerprints."

"Sure. But not from *that night*."

"There'll be phone records," I reason. "If we didn't talk on the phone, how could we have made arrangements for me to pick him up from the restaurant?"

"Check your phone. You'll find there was a call between you two at 7:26 that evening. A lucky coincidence that works in our favor."

"Wait a minute... you've already worked all this out with Lucas, haven't you?"

Jack doesn't answer. He doesn't need to. Yes, he and Lucas

have already worked this out, down to the last minutiae. And I am being used as his alibi.

I narrow my eyes. The reality finally dawning on me. This is not a request but more like a done deal. "And you've already been down to the police station with Lucas and given the interview?"

"We have."

"And Lucas has already used me as his alibi?" I double-check. "Without consulting me first?"

"There was no time, Ava. We had to think on our feet."

"Thank you. Thank you so very much."

"You *will* be thanking me. I'm doing this for you, as a family. You'll see it's for the best."

"You've landed me in the *shit*." I wait for him to rebuke me for my language, not that he has a leg to stand on today.

He doesn't tick me off. Just says, "You can add in your statement that you were hoping to meet Claudia Spector yourself because you're a fan, so decided to go and pick Lucas up. I figure that gives it extra credibility and something everyone will believe, especially since that little article in the women's magazine Barb showed me that had you gushing about her."

*Little article*. Jack has a way of belittling people. I push back with new reasons not to go through with this. Not that I should even be having this conversation. I should have told him to get out of my car. Should have dumped him on the sidewalk amidst the traffic. "They can examine my phone. They'll know I didn't make that journey to Chez Suzette."

"Good point but easy to circumnavigate. Where were you that night anyway?"

"At home."

"You tell them you left your phone behind. You tell them that, as far as you were aware, it was a business meeting between Lucas and Claudia. You deny he had an affair. You tell them you believe your husband, that he did not cheat on you. That it was nothing more than business."

"What about the housekeeper? She saw Lucas time after time. She's a witness to them having a loving relationship." The words "loving relationship" twist my heart as I say them, but I cannot lie to myself.

Jack clears his throat. "Your word against hers. A maid who isn't even an American citizen. Who do you think people will believe?"

My jaw drops. *This man is something else.* I am so stunned by his snobby, veiled racism, his narrow-minded bigotry, I am momentarily lost for words.

"And the photo of them looking all cozy together at Chez Suzette?" I scramble, after a long pause. "How did you two get around that glaring piece of evidence?"

"Don't worry about our testimony, think about what *you* need to say. You're the trusting wife. I don't care how much evidence piles up against him, you believe Lucas. He is innocent. You love him. It was a business meeting at Chez Suzette. Maybe he was a little... starstruck, you can say, impressed by his new client, maybe he flirted a little, let his emotions get away with him, but they were *not* having an affair."

"But she wasn't his client, you said so yourself!"

"She is now. Claudia Spector was a client of ours. At least, a prospective client. This is the storyline we'll go with."

"Jack, that isn't true. And these people—"

"Trust me, Ava, I have ways of proving all sorts of things." He shifts in the car seat, his long lean legs trying to stretch in comfort.

"You can put the seat back, by the way."

"Remember one thing, Claudia. You need his alibi as much as he needs yours. Or next thing you know, you, the jealous wife, could be under suspicion. And what would happen to your baby then?"

*He wouldn't, would he?* My heart freezes. His threat is real. I can just see Jack hard at work, mounting a case against me.

He carries on talking. "Drive back to the office, please. After you drop me off, call one of the detectives that paid you a visit. Detective Hawkins or Detective Johnson. You have their numbers, right? On one of their business cards? Inform them that you want to come in and give your statement. Keep it simple. Don't elaborate too much. Do not let yourself get derailed or go off tangent. Just do and say everything we have discussed between us. If there's a question they fire at you that scares you, a question you cannot answer, then don't answer it. It is better to keep your mouth shut than get caught out."

"And you'd come with me? Stand by me while I did the interview?"

"No. That wouldn't look good."

"Why not?"

"It'll look a lot better if you go there willingly and speak freely without an attorney, trust me. If you were being detained, that would be a different story, but this will simply be you approaching them, paying them a quick visit to corroborate your husband's story. If you don't, it's just a matter of hours before they'll come knocking on your door again."

I cannot believe I am hearing this from someone who always recommends his clients, and indeed anyone, to have an attorney present at all times when dealing with the law. I smell a rat. But don't know what kind of rat. The kind that sniffs out landmines that saves thousands of lives? Or the kind that lives in sewers?

I am dumbstruck. I say nothing.

"Thank you," Jack adds, giving me a "fatherly" pat on my shoulder.

"I haven't said I'll do it."

"If you don't, your life won't be worth living." His voice is a monotone. The lack of emotion in his tone is terrifying.

My eyes meet his for a second. They are calculating and as cold as unpolished beads. They don't have Lucas's blue translucence. Jack's eyes are a sludgy green that reflect nothing back. Give nothing back. They hold no expression whatsoever. I have always maintained that Jack has dead eyes. Soulless.

"What do you mean by saying my life won't be worth living?" I shoot out. "That's a horrible thing to say to anyone."

"I mean, Ava, that your life will be miserable with your husband in jail. Or you in jail, if things get spun a different way. Think of your child. You'll be ruining several lives at once, including your own."

Lucas may not be capable of murder, but this man... this man is capable of anything.

# TWENTY-EIGHT

*What if?* I think. I concoct a scenario in my head. What if it was Jack who...

*No, that's crazy*, but it does flash through my mind. The way he spoke about Claudia Spector as "cheap." What if Jack had known about their affair a while ago? Was guilty of perpetrating the crime himself? And now he wants me to clean up the mess. Very convenient.

I ponder his demands. I had always assumed Jack had a moral code, a sense of ethics. He and Barbara are so upstanding, or so I thought. But this man is a liar. A bully. Just like his son. But at least Lucas does it with bravado, in a charming, "oops, I got busted" type of way. At least he apologizes for it. Begs for forgiveness. But Jack has no compunction, clearly, about being a total fraud. Talk about being a great pretender. It is all about appearances. Does he even care what happens to his son? Or his future grandchild? Genuinely care? Or is it because he cannot bear the Fox name being dragged through the mud? It is pathetic that he was bothered about us having a child out of wedlock, but my lying to police and possibly later, in a court of law, to a jury, doesn't faze his conscience? Fabricating a bullshit story comes so easily to him he is assuming it will be a walk in the park for me. And his cold threat? The man is a monster.

But what choice do I have?

*If you don't, your life won't be worth living.* I roll his menacing words around my head. I thought I'd escaped the clutches of Jack Fox.

I was wrong.

I call Lucas. Again, no reply, straight to voicemail. Is Lucas avoiding me on purpose? He has clearly collaborated on all this with his daddy—every step, including the avoidance of my calls. Timing it so I end up having no options. If I don't go to the police station, the detectives will be at my door again, any minute. They will want to hear my side of the story. *The jealous wife.* Jack has a good point.

I pull my phone and Detective Hawkins' business card from my bag and dial. She is the lady cop. I leave a message letting her know I am on my way to the precinct. Yes, I should have an attorney present, even I know that. But who? Who can I trust at such short notice? You are meant to tell your attorney the truth. I can hardly let my lawyer know I am lying up front. How could they protect me then? I'd get myself into double trouble. I have seen how Lucas, sometimes in the past, has been furious with clients who have lied to him or kept secrets from him. It has put him on the spot. Made his job extremely hard. Shown him up as a fool at times.

And Jack knows this. This is why he has suggested I go in alone.

Thrown to the wolves? No, I am being *fed* to the wolves.

I can just imagine how I will feel at the police station. In the interrogation room—which I know is where they will take me—I will panic when they shut the heavy door behind me. A click when they exit the room will fill me with chilled terror. Maybe they will leave me alone. Leave me, sitting by that table, a million dark possibilities competing for overtime in my brain.

All alone, wondering if they are watching me from their one-way mirror, the one they use for line-ups. They do that, don't they? Leave the suspect/witness/whoever alone so their minds start whirring with paranoia and fear? So that they will talk, blabber their heads off, say things they shouldn't. They leave them to wallow in silence, not caring if they suffer from claustrophobia. It will be the way it is on TV and in the movies: a white oblong box room with no window, a soiled carpet—or not?—a plain table and a couple of chairs. But what movies don't convey is the sickly fear that blocks the person's throat as they try to speak, the dread that takes hold of them in the solar plexus and won't let go. The heart rate thwacking and jackhammering behind their chest, their mind spinning with the worst possible scenarios of what could go wrong.

Everything I say will be recorded. Everything can and will be used as evidence in a court of law. I could be arrested for perverting the course of justice. For wasting their time.

Or worse...

I picture Claudia. How many hours have I spent watching her on TV? How many hours of intimate moments have I spent being with her as she cries and laughs and persuades and shouts and screams? The Oscar-winning, Tony-winning actor who is able to charm and cajole and make everyone believe in her. Love her. Root for her, worship her, even when she is being a bitch. Even when she has done wrong. Charismatic actors can do that. Just her smile, her glittering eyes, the way her gaze looks off to one side and then back at you, holding you in thrall, as you wait for what she will say next. Do next. Waiting, waiting, jaw open. No wonder my husband fell in love with her.

I call the detective again. This time she picks up.

"Mrs. Fox, thank you for calling."

"There's something I need to tell you," I begin. "And I'm not sure why I've left it so late."

I think about the flip phone in Lucas's closet. All those

lovey-dovey messages, plans to meet, plans to have off-the-chart sex, nearly always at Claudia's place. Once, though, they went to Lake Tahoe where they rented a cabin. It's amazing they managed to keep their affair under the radar considering the way the paparazzi followed her around. I rewind more exchanges in my head. Things I remember by rote.

Love your body, it makes me wild.

Call of the wild, that's you babe.

Call me any time.

I do.

See you tonite?

Is that a rhetorical question.

Ha ha.

Why was I so naïve? How did I miss what was going on? He was "staying late at the office." He was "having a bite to eat with a client." When he was "catching the red-eye to New York" he was spending the weekend with her. When sex is the dominating factor in a relationship it overrides reason, it blocks sane judgment. Lust is the most powerful emotion known to man. Or woman. It is uncontrollable. It has toppled nations and changed history. God made it that way so humans would keep reproducing. So our species would survive.

It still doesn't let Lucas off the hook.

Claudia was single; she wasn't cheating on anyone. My husband, though, was another story.

"Mrs. Fox? Are you still there?"

I pull my incensed, furious thoughts back together and remember I am on the phone. "Oh, sorry, Detective, yes, I'm—"

"Can you come to the station—"

"No... I mean, I can't come in today."

"You called *me*, Mrs. Fox. I was assuming you wanted to make a statement? Your husband came by, and we do need to talk to you as well."

I take in a deep breath and force myself to say, "I wanted to let you know that Lucas can't have been at Claudia Spector's house the night after dinner at Chez Suzette because he was with me." *There, I said it. I am such a loyal wife I am lying for my husband.*

"Please, Mrs. Fox, we need you to make an official statement and need you to come in, in person. This is very important. I hope you realize you mustn't delay or things could get complicated."

"I understand."

"Would you like to come—"

"I have to go. I can't talk." I end the call and don't pick up when she calls me back.

I drive home. Fear roils around in my gut, and I can't shake the feeling that my world is spinning out of control. Jack. Lucas. The detectives. Claudia. Myself. My baby.

I need to sort this mess out.

There's something I urgently need to take care of... before it's too late.

# TWENTY-NINE

When I get home, six hours later, Lucas is waiting for me. He is sitting rod-straight on the couch and leaps up when I walk into the room. His five o'clock shadow has grown almost to a beard. He is red-eyed like he hasn't slept. Scruffy.

"I found something," he says, taking a step forward but not embracing me or welcoming me home as he usually does. Lips turned down, eyes glowering, he adds, "Something that turns everything on its head."

My heart misses a beat, or at least it feels that way. *What does he know? What did he find?*

"What did you do to Claudia?" He fixes me hard with an arctic-blue gaze.

"What?!"

"I'm asking you, Ava. What did you do to Claudia?" His voice is quiet. Controlled. This is the Lucas I fear. The cold, calculating man who plans ahead, who zeros in on people's weak spots, gouging out little bits of flesh at a time, and before you realize what has happened you have a huge gaping wound and he comes in like an apex predator for the kill.

I say, "Nothing. What are you saying?"

"I found a book of matches in my jacket pocket in your closet. From Chez Suzette, weirdly enough. On the inside flap is Claudia's address, in your handwriting. How did you get hold of her address? From my phone? Did you break into my phone?"

*Of course I "broke into" your phone, dummy,* I want to say. I know the password, or did until Lucas changed it. You'd think, being a lawyer, he'd come up with a smarter password. His date of birth. Seriously? Math has never been Lucas's strong point, and numbers—any combination of numbers—confuse him. In fact, if Jack hadn't basically bribed Harvard with donations, I'm sure Lucas never would have been accepted to such a prestigious college. Also, if you're having an affair with someone, putting their address in "notes" is not exactly hiding it. Still, I am on my guard. Lucas may be dumb about small things, but he has a killer instinct. His eyes are still on me. Flecks of steel embedded in that aquamarine gaze.

"Okay," I hedge, "so I found out where she lived. So?"

"What did you want her address for? For what purpose?"

I feel like I am in court being cross-examined. "Everybody wants to know where movie stars live, don't they? Curiosity. Oh, and, P.S., I'd found out that this particular movie star was having sex with my husband, so yeah, her address was particularly interesting to me."

"Did you *do* something to Claudia, Ava?"

I am gobsmacked. This is typical of Lucas. Trying to turn this around on me. "Like what?"

His lips are trembling. *An act?* "Did you kill Claudia?"

After three years of marriage, he thinks I'm capable of murder? My eyes swim with tears. I have tried so hard to put the past behind me. I have. I have given Lucas the benefit of the doubt as much as I can. Agreed to stay, for more reasons than one. Yet here he is, accusing *me*? I would never have the strength, either physically or mentally, to do something so final to someone. Take their last breath? I think of the logistics of how I would possibly be able to pull it off, even if I wanted to. It had not even crossed my mind to want Claudia dead at any point. I had simply wanted my husband to end his affair with her. I shake my head, stunned by his accusation. Is he trying to drag me into his mire of lies? "That's crazy."

His eyes hone in one mine. "Yes, it *is* crazy. But you were *acting* pretty crazy. You did a crazy thing, remember? You showed me you were capable of something really nuts." *Is he referring to my suicide attempt?*

"I was desperate, obviously. Driven to feeling like a piece of shit because of the way you were treating me."

"I treated you like gold, Ava! I always have!"

*Is he serious?* My eyes round in amazement. He made me feel like I was less than nothing. Those feelings of inadequacy never leave you. When you have done everything to make your marriage work. When you have loved your husband to oblivion, despite all his faults. His emotional betrayal. His negligence, which could have killed me. That would make anyone suspicious of their husband, a man who is supposed to have your back, supposed to care about your well-being. He didn't call 911 when he had the chance. *He was willing to let me die.* His status with his father and his job were more important than my life! That's not love. How could I ever truly forgive Lucas for that?

*Till death do us part.* Those were the vows he made to me. Oh, the irony. A man who sees his *wife* lying on a bed, full of booze and pills, and does not call the emergency services is capable of anything. Even murder. And he dares accuse *me*?

His eyes tell me everything. The arctic stare that holds no mercy, no remorse.

"Who's playing who, Ava?"

"You! You're playing with my head!"

I cannot believe he's grilling me this way. My eyes bounce

around the oddly silent room. Something is off. Where are Ariadne and Sappho? Panic rises in my chest. Right now, they are the only thing holding me together. "Where are the dogs?"

"I took them to daycare. I figured in the next forty-eight hours one of us is going to get locked up with all this shit going down. I wanted to make sure they, at least, were safe."

*One of us*? Is that a hint? A clue? At least my girls are safe. More than I can say for myself. "You did the right thing with the dogs," is all I say.

Lucas starts pacing around the room, hands raking through his hair.

"You know what I did for you today, by the way?" I let him know. "I called Detective Hawkins and told her I was with you the night Claudia disappeared."

"I guess I should say thanks, though it makes it sound like you're doing me a favor. I can't believe what's happened to Claudia. Are you sure you didn't hurt her?"

This is Lucas's technique. Twisting things so the blame lands on me. "You *know* I could never kill anyone, Lucas, don't be ridiculous, don't make this about me."

"That's right. You couldn't even kill yourself, could you?"

I am stunned into silence. His words prove one thing. This man is colder than ice. "That's a nasty, vicious thing to say. Everything I've *ever* done is because I love you," I shout at him. "Unlike *you*!"

"Oh, so getting rid of the prenup doesn't show love?"

We stand there, both seething. Our trust in one another—or lack of it—recalibrating.

"What have you done with the matchbook?" I ask, trying to keep the tremble from my voice.

"I set light to the part with your handwriting on. You think I want my baby being born in a jail? It's evidence, Ava. Evidence that would put you on the detectives' radar. But, by God, I wanted to keep it and hand it over. But I would never do something so low." He glares at me. "Please tell me the truth, honey, *please*. Because I sure as hell haven't done anything! And they think I fucking killed her!"

His tone is softer now, showing his desperation. But his desperation is dangerous. He would pin this on me if it let him off the hook. I know he would.

I try to keep the edge out of my voice. "If they had proof, they would have arrested you by now," I reason. "All they have is a broken cell phone and a few drops of blood. And a bunch of credit cards she left behind. That proves nothing. They need probable cause. They need evidence she's actually gone."

His voice spirals into a wail. "The woman is missing and clearly isn't coming back! She left her passport behind! You've read the papers! She didn't turn up for work. She's a world-famous movie star! If somebody had seen her, you can be sure they would've posted it on Twitter! She's *gone*!" He's striding around the room. He turns. Like flicking a switch, his fury abates somewhat and he says in a calmer voice, "Sweetheart. Please just tell me if you did something... to hurt her. I won't turn you in. I get it, you were jealous. A crime of passion. If you admit what you did, we can work out a plan. Together. You're going to be the mother of my child. I'm not going to let you rot in jail."

The word "rot" makes me queasy. Just the mention of jail makes me wonder what is truly on his mind. Lucas has wronged me a thousand ways. Is this what he is planning? To mount a case against me with his father, behind my back? Pretend he is protecting me to my face when in fact he is plotting to bring me down? To accuse *me* of murder when he's the one under suspicion?

The ultimate gaslighting technique.

Of which he is a master.

# THIRTY

The doorbell chimes. I don't need to go downstairs to know who it is. My friends would be texting. Jack and Barbara always organize visits weeks in advance and never stop by without telling us first. I know it will be the detectives wanting to interview me. To take me to the station, for me to give my statement. It's strange that there's no barking to announce their arrival, that the dogs are not here at home but at daycare. It feels eerie actually.

I hear the front door creak open. It needs oil.

"Mr. Fox? We have a search warrant?" Hawkins. Her tone is tentative, polite.

I hear Lucas's voice. "Excuse me?"

"We have a search warrant. Signed by the judge. Here it is."

Lucas answers, "Well, I suppose I have no choice. I won't stand in your way. But please try not to make a mess of things."

"We need to look around. If you could show us, please, where you keep your shoes, that would speed things up a little. The more you cooperate, the sooner we'll get the job done. Is there anyone else in the house?"

"My wife."

"Where is she?"

"Upstairs, in the bedroom."

"We'll need her to come downstairs."

Lucas calls out to me.

I make my way down. I had pretended to Lucas that I needed to lie down for a while. But I am still fully clothed. As I am heading out of the bedroom, I cross paths with them. The same two detectives, Hawkins and the burly guy cop, plus a woman in a CSI jacket, armed with boxes and specimen bags.

Their big boots on my carpet. Their unwelcome presence. I can't say I am anything but horrified. "Excuse me," I say, brushing past them. There is no point in niceties now. They have a job to do. Offering them a cup of coffee is not going to make any difference. I am not going to play nice, smile at them, or even say hello.

At the bottom of the stairs, there is another officer, in uniform, waiting for me.

She pinions me with her stark, no-nonsense gaze. "Mrs. Fox? I need you and your husband to stay in one place while my colleagues search the premises."

*The premises? This is my home!*

She pats us down, asking me to put my hands in the air. The same drill you have to go through at the airport. Then she turns her attention to the couch, slipping her hands behind all the nooks and crannies, and slaps the cushions too. She is clearly making sure that there are no weapons hidden anywhere. Satisfied, she instructs us, "If you two could sit down here, please."

It's an unnerving feeling to have your home taken over by strangers, telling you what to do. I feel violated, knowing they are putting their grubby hands all over our personal possessions. I am aware, from what Lucas has told me in the past with some of his cases, when they have a warrant signed by a judge, they can pretty much do what they want. The "premises" is lawfully theirs while they are here. This lady cop, who has not introduced herself, is young. She does not smile. She stands near us, at first scanning her serious eyes over both of us in turn and then looks off into the middle distance as if giving us a modicum of privacy. I turn my attention to my hands and see they are shaking uncontrollably. They look like alcoholic's hands—the hands of my mother.

Lucas holds his head down. I tentatively touch his knee. Despite our fight, his accusations, despite it all, he is still my husband. We are bonded in this moment. Us against them.

"They want my shoes," Lucas murmurs through his fingers.

"I heard."

"If they've dusted for prints, well, yeah, they'll find my fingerprints and shoe prints all over Claudia's house and yard. But, Jesus... I didn't kill her! I never touched her."

"I know you didn't," I say, flinching when he says "touched." He more than touched her; he made love to her, his hands all over her. His lips on her golden skin, on her mouth, on her eyes. But I don't point this out. This is not the moment. I'm a freaking saint. Here I am offering Lucas my full moral support. Yet he, less than an hour ago, accused me of murder. Nice.

He jerks up, eyes round, face freezing in horror. He has just remembered something.

I glance over at the cop. She is glued to her phone. I cup my hands around his ear and whisper, "Don't worry. I grabbed your flip phone out of the shoe when I heard them at the door and put it somewhere safe. They won't find it."

His face relaxes. He closes his eyes with relief and fumbles for my hand with his sweaty palm. "Thanks," he whispers back. "I had forgotten all about that thing."

*"That thing" broke my heart into a million pieces.* I put my mouth to his ear again. "Are you sure you got rid of the matchbook?"

He nods.

"Where did you burn it?"

He nods toward the kitchen, and whispers, "In the sink." He clears his throat and says to the officer, "Can I get some water?"

She looks up from her phone. Surveys the room around her. There is nobody to contradict her. They are still upstairs, shifting stuff around. "I guess so. Sure."

"Maybe I can make us some coffee," I suggest.

"We can all go," she agrees.

Lucas pulls me up by the hand and leads me to the kitchen. He nods toward the sink. I run the faucet for a long time, using the spray nozzle to make sure if any ashes are left, they disappear down the drain. I fill the electric kettle and flip the switch to on and spoon some fresh coffee into the French press. We wait for the water to boil while noises carry on above us. Shuffles, scraping. The wait feels torturous. Our house is old and the walls and ceilings not well insulated, so their rummaging around grates in our ears. Pretty much all our shoes are in the bedroom closets save a couple of pairs of sneakers by the front and back doors, which I am sure they will inspect. They are taking their sweet (or not so sweet) time. Are they working from a print they've found at some crime scene? Or was there a full-length photo taken at Chez Suzette showing the shoes Lucas was wearing? Some new evidence must have aroused their suspicions.

I pour the boiling water into the pot, steam rising, and let the coffee brew. The officer is standing by the doorway, on a call, only briefly acknowledging us, but still in a bodyguard stance.

"If you have something to tell me, honey, now's the time." My voice is almost inaudible.

He throws up his hands. "Like what?"

I turn my back to the cop in case she can lip-read, and whisper, "You asked me to come clean, so I'm asking you back."

He doesn't answer. Simply yanks open the icebox, grabs some orange juice and stalks out of the room. I trail behind him to the living room with the coffee and a couple of mugs, and the officer follows us. He switches on the TV with the remote. He always watches TV when he doesn't want a confrontation. Uses it like a barrier between us. The two detectives are still upstairs. Our officer seems content with the fact we are not going to pull out a gun or try anything smart.

"Coffee?" I say.

She shakes her head. "No thanks."

One of the news channels lights up the screen. We catch the tail end of the main story.

"Police have discovered Claudia Spector's abandoned Mercedes near a remote canyon in Malibu County, California." Lucas powers down the sound but it is still audible.

I glance over my shoulder at the officer. She is standing behind the couch so can't see our astonished faces. Her features show no emotion. And Lucas, strangely, doesn't switch off the television. Both of us are riveted, despite ourselves.

The news anchor continues, "A mixture of dried blood and bleach have been found in the trunk of the vehicle. DNA tests reveal the blood does in fact belong to the thirty-five-year-old movie star. No arrests have been made at this time. The investigation is ongoing. Stay tuned, we will be back with updates when we know more."

"Oh, my God," I say, goggling at the screen.

"This can't be real." Lucas zaps the TV off, glugs down his juice, staring at the blank screen in shock. He doesn't look me in the eye when he mouths, "Look, I swear... I swear to God, I had nothing to do with it! It wasn't me!"

"It was someone," I whisper.

He shakes his head, still in disbelief.

"I wonder if they'll ever find the body," I say.

"This can't be real. This is... it can't be really happening.

That photo of us together... shit... everyone will be blaming me!"

"Ssh, keep your voice down."

Boots clunking down the stairs. Voices, even a chuckle of laughter. How disrespectful, I think. For them to be laughing when someone's life as they know it is being played with and could end. These officers are in our home. Our *nest*. For them it's just another day of work, like when contractors come into your house and leave a trail of dust everywhere. They don't care. It's a job, nothing more. For us it is a total invasion of privacy. It feels like burglars are in our home yet paradoxically we have "invited" them in. They have that powerful and legal warrant in their hands; there is nothing we can say or do. One of them stumbles out with a couple of boxes of evidence.

"Thank you so much for your time," Detective Hawkins says. Her politeness sounds almost sarcastic. "I think we have everything we need. Appreciate your cooperation."

We are both too freaked out to respond. Neither of us says a word.

The door closes.

One by one, they are gone.

For now.

# THIRTY-ONE

Forensics must have put a rush on the job because the next morning Lucas is arrested on suspicion of murder.

When he is arrested, I am out. I had gone to pick up the dogs early, then I took them for a hike in the hills of Topanga Canyon. I am not at home when they come for him and read him the Miranda Rights. I am not at home to see the terror in his eyes and the realization that he wished he had never set eyes on Claudia Spector to begin with.

I picture him in handcuffs, being led away from our beautiful beachside home, the icy metal pressing against the warm bones of his wrist, clinking with the onyx cufflinks I gave him for our second wedding anniversary. The cool of his crisp white shirt, the cuff of his tailored suit—the attire of a top lawyer, not defending a client but defending himself. Professing his innocence, assuring them, perhaps, how he loved her. How he could never hurt her. That he is not a killer.

They will not believe him.

Despite it all—the lies, the gaslighting, the affair—I convince myself of his innocence.

She, too, is in my mind's eye. The cascade of honey-blond

hair. Her parted lips that kissed my husband maybe a thousand times. Her bright gray eyes, her open legs, the curve of her back as she cried out his name.

Blood, and bleach, they told us on the news. Her blood. Her DNA. A perfect match.

Tears stream down my face as I scramble back to my car, the dogs barreling ahead of me, obliviously excited to be going home after their walk in the hills.

Poor Lucas.

I am no legal expert but I suspect that Lucas will be charged with first-degree murder. At best, second-degree. You cannot cite manslaughter when you put a body in the trunk of a car and try to cover it up with bleach. The same bleach that winds up on the soles of your shoes. His will be considered a heinous crime because it involved planning, deliberation, and premeditation. At least, I'm pretty sure that's how they will see it. However, they still do not have an actual body. So how can they accuse him of murder? They have no proof, only circumstantial evidence. Will he be able to arrange bail?

Despite the evidence against him and the stark truth of what he's done, I can't help myself. I still love him, deep down. He's still my husband.

But then that's the kind of guy Lucas is. Charming, lovable, charismatic. A man who has women falling all over him.

The kind of man who gets away with murder.

# PART 2

## BEFORE

# THIRTY-TWO

## CLAUDIA

Claudia's heart is in her ears. The blood is pounding so hard in her brain she thinks she's going to have a cardiac arrest right here and now. The trunk of the car is dark and smells of bleach, and dust. But the smell of her own fear is stronger.

*So this is what it's like to die?*

This is not a scene from a movie, but reality. There are no assistants to unlock the trunk, to pull her to safety, to wrap a robe around her and give her a calming beverage and tell her what a great acting job she's done.

Why, why, why? Why did she get herself into this mess?

If only she had never met Lucas. The jealousy, the payback... none of this would have led to where she is now. Trapped in the trunk of her own frickin car!

She hears herself scream. *Let me out!* Her bent knees ache but she kicks and rolls and shoves as best she can.

*So this is what it's like to be murdered?*

She closes her eyes in the pitch dark to try and calm herself down. She doesn't have her cell phone with her to light her way, to call for help.

She has nothing.

Nothing but her fear. Her panic.

She is a body in the trunk of a car. By the time they find her DNA all over it, fibers from her clothing and hair… and no doubt her blood…

It will be too late.

*

# FIVE MONTHS EARLIER

# THIRTY-THREE

## CLAUDIA

Claudia is in a state of flux. Her wedding plans—and her entire world, in fact—have been crushed overnight like someone treading on a helpless bug on its back waving its legs. Crystal has broken off their engagement. Worse, she announced it on *The Isabella Mox Show*, chatting to Isabella about the breakup as if it had already happened. Claudia stares at the TV in disbelief. It's a miracle the news didn't leak. How did they kept it under wraps with a live audience? Did they all have to sign an NDA?

As Claudia watches the show on repeat, still incredulous, tears leak down her cheeks. Crystal, dressed in a silky black pantsuit, does a teetering little dance on her entrance to the theme music, in impossibly high heels. Sits on the couch, back straight, legs crossed, regal and starry and stunningly beautiful. "It was mutual," Crystal lies on the talk show, her head lowered, her Liza Minnelli eyes peeking up from the curtains of her thick, dark lashes. Her beauty—those famous cheekbones, the enormous eyes—is now a source of pain for Claudia.

"We both decided it simply wasn't going to work out," Crystal coos in her breathy cigarette voice, even though she doesn't smoke. "Filming's so demanding, you know? You have to spend so much time apart. It breaks my heart, Isabella, it really does, but sometimes you have to put on your big girl panties and face up to reality."

*Big girl panties?* Claudia loathes that expression at the best of times. She has been dumped via a talk show? Crystal didn't have the decency to tell her face to face?

Crystal is about to start filming in Canada. When they last spoke, she told Claudia they had no internet and bad reception. Clearly a lie. Claudia has been so blind. She wondered why Crystal packed up all her things before she left on location. Why had Claudia not seen *that* red flag? Crystal waved it right in her face! It's amazing how dumb you can be when you're in love. They'd planned to buy a new house together. Bigger, by the beach. They had talked about adopting a child, of starting a family. Of having a menagerie of dogs and cats, promising each other that after their marriage they would never accept a job at the same time, that one of them would stay home. Crystal had promised her the world yet was now ditching her in public for that very same world to see, and all Claudia can do to save face is go along with it to spare herself humiliation.

This is the result of filming, she thinks. Of working in movies. It's so easy to fall in love with your co-star. And just as easy, just as fast—for one of them, at least—to fall *out* of love. Making a movie is a giant buzz for all involved, even the crew. Momentum building and building, working in a closed, intimate environment divorced from the outside world, and then, bam! The movie finishes and you're left depleted. For a while you ride on that fabulous wave of creation, believing it's real. That's why so many relationships are doomed in this business, Claudia muses. Because their very foundation is make-believe.

"That's it," she tells herself as she swipes globs of runny mascara from her eyes and switches off the TV. "That is it!

Never ever again will I get romantically involved with another actor on set. Or off set, for that matter."

Actors suck. They're fascinating, yeah, but all *me me me*.

She can't deny that she too is guilty of the same thing. Two actors together—apart from Paul Newman and Joanne Woodward and a few other rare examples—is an egotistical match made in misery.

Never again.

In fact, no more romantic relationships, period.

It is Friday when she promises herself this. On Sunday, her insecurity reaching new heights—or new lows—and after weighing herself while simultaneously bingeing on Twinkies, Claudia, clad in sneakers, cap, shades, jogging gear, and earbuds, heads to Runyon Canyon. She wants to pound off the pounds she has gained while being in what she had *thought* was a loving relationship. Normally she'd go running with her trainer, or bodyguard—whom she hires from time to time when things get rough—but her trainer is busy today, her bodyguard unavailable, and her driver, who often accompanies her on runs, has hurt his toe and can't partake in any sport. If she keeps her head down and runs fast, she's pretty sure she'll get away without being spotted.

But, fifteen minutes into the run... bam! Music turned up loud, head down, and distracted by thoughts of Crystal's betrayal, she collides into another body.

"What the hell!" a voice yells at her.

"What the hell, you too!" she shouts back but immediately regrets it. Even with her shades and baseball cap, she isn't safe. Has she been recognized anyway? This asshole has probably slammed into her on purpose to get a reaction and will shove an iPhone in her face any second now. And then it'll be all over social media—viral—within about two minutes flat, followed by the news tomorrow. It's amazing how quickly nonsense news travels these days. If this guy Tweets, she won't even make it to her car without being mobbed first.

Now on her butt, and realizing she may have sprained her knee, she thinks it wise to apologize. Celebrities are not allowed to lose their cool or snap or grimace or scowl. Celebrities need to be gracious and friendly at all times, whatever the situation. Even when that crazy stalker had held a knife up to her throat, she had smiled. Told him they needed to talk.

"I'm sorry. I wasn't looking where I was going," she says to the runner.

"No problem. I'm fine, was just surprised. I wasn't really looking where I was going either. Are you okay?"

She looks briefly up at a man standing before her. Also in jogging gear, a golden retriever panting by his side. He holds out an arm to help her up. She keeps her head tilted downwards, hoping the cap will render her incognito.

"I'm fine," she says, not moving. She doesn't want to take a stranger's arm, but there's a wincing pain in her knee.

"Here, let me help you up."

"Honestly, I'm fine. You go on now, don't worry about me." Another dog, seemingly from nowhere, bounds up to her and licks her on the face. She wipes the slobber from her cheek with her baggy T-shirt and smiles, remembering her late black lab, Milo. Never mind, she'll take a shower, she's sweaty anyway. It makes her miss Milo like crazy. He died a couple of years back and she was so brokenhearted she hasn't dared even think about getting another dog. She can't go through that pain again.

The man pulls the dog away but doesn't apologize, just acts like it is completely normal. This dog, like the other, is also a golden retriever. Twins. Two panty dogs encircling her, tails in her face, the man's arm still held out. No *phone* in her face though. So far, anyhow. That's something. She cradles her knee. It hurts like hell.

The man speaks again. "Look, I'm not going anywhere till I

know you're okay. Let me at least walk you to your car. I assume you came by car?"

It's a normal assumption. Most people don't live in walking distance of Runyon Canyon and the hill makes it hard to bicycle. Roger, her driver, is waiting for her in the limo outside the park, but she's certainly not going to share that information with this guy, or anyone for that matter.

Claudia tries to get up on her own but topples back down again. "Shit."

"I'm an attorney. Sue me if you like, I have insurance." He says this without smiling.

Claudia laughs. That's the last thing she expected anyone to come up with. "It was my fault," she admits.

"Maybe, but this is America. Come on, let me at least help you to your feet. See if you can stand okay. If not, I'll call for help."

Her heart hammers at the idea of a scene. Even something as uninteresting as this could end up being all over social media, in people's news feeds, or even on the front page of some trashy paper. They do things like zoom in on your flesh, drawing a circle around a spot of cellulite, with an arrow in case the reader misses it. This is the real bummer side of being famous. People feel they own a part of you. Every zit, every expression, every high or low. It's theirs to claim. Movies are bad enough, but TV—hanging out in people's living rooms—has shot Claudia into a new realm of stardom, and of public entitlement. She no longer belongs to herself. Sometimes, she is pawed and grabbed. Sometimes people hurl insults at Bobbie—her TV character—telling her she's done another character on the show wrong and needs to apologize. Once, an elderly lady slapped Claudia/Bobbie on the face and called her a tramp.

Coming on this run alone has been a mistake, clearly.

"No! I mean, I'm fine. Sure, you can help me up, but please don't call anyone." Claudia offers him her hand and the man pulls her to a standing position. Finally, she looks him in the eye. Reluctantly. "Thanks."

"You're welcome."

She's waiting for him to click, to realize who she is, but he doesn't seem to register. His forearm is solid. Muscular. He's lean, though. A tennis body, not a boxer's body. Why she's inspecting him like this, she isn't sure. Perhaps because she has learned to be extra wary ever since the stalker episode. You never recover from something like that.

"Take a few steps," the man urges.

Claudia obliges. Her knee will be fine. Nothing her massage therapist can't sort out. "Thank you so much. Just a little bruise. I think I'm going to be fine. Your dogs are cute."

"Ariadne and Sappho. You've made quite an impression on them. They like you."

"Oh, you're into Greek mythology?"

"I am. Which entrance did you come in on?"

"Mulholland," Claudia says. "You?"

"Fuller."

"Honestly, I'm fine, I'll just walk back."

He frowns. "You know what? That makes me uneasy. My car's so much closer than yours if you're parked way up there. Let me drive you to your car."

She shakes her head. "Thanks, but no thanks." There's no way in a million years Claudia is getting into some stranger's car. Just because the guy has two friendly dogs does not make it okay. He could be an axe murderer. Unlikely, with two golden retrievers and a wedding band on his finger but...

"That's very gallant of you but, seriously, I'm fine." She looks into his eyes. Blue... a piercing blue. The guy is decidedly handsome. Blond. Around her age... mid-thirties, she guesses. He still doesn't show any sign whatsoever of recognition. It's refreshing. So rare these days.

She smiles. "Besides, your wife's probably waiting for you at home with pancakes or something." This was her and Crystal. A run, then homemade pancakes and freshly squeezed orange juice on Sundays. If neither was working, they'd make spicy Bloody Marys laced with horseradish to give the drinks an extra kick. They'd hang out by the pool reading magazines or the *New York Times*. Later, they'd watch a movie. Usually a classic with Barbara Stanwyck or Joan Crawford. Claudia loved Sundays. But today she is all alone.

He makes a face. "Sadly, no, no breakfast with my wife. Those beautiful days are over."

"Divorced?" Claudia inquires. Why she is getting personal she has no idea. Maybe because it's nice to have a casual conversation with a person who's in the same boat as she is. Alone on a Sunday. Their other half gone. She is all cried out over Crystal and to have a simple chat in the park with a stranger who doesn't know who she is feels pretty good. Something spontaneous like this hasn't happened in years.

The man fiddles with his wedding band. "My wife passed away," he says, shifting his gaze to the ground. "But I still wear my ring." The ring glints in the sunlight.

"I'm so sorry," Claudia replies. When the man looks up his eyes are brimming with tears; he seems pretty cut up about his loss. She feels sorry for him, poor man, losing his wife so young. She adds, "So sorry for your loss."

He nods. "Well, listen. If you promise me you're okay and you refuse to let me take you to your car, this is where I leave you."

"Sure," Claudia says. "Thank you for being such a gentleman."

"Any time." He pulls out a card from his shorts. His legs are strong, lean, and tan. "You may be wondering why I carry business cards with me on a run... well, it's just habit, I guess. Call me if you need anything. Or"—he grins, flashing a perfect Hollywood smile—"if you decide to sue me for bodily injury."

She laughs. "You shouldn't put ideas in my head."

"If you need anything, anything at all, just call."

"Okay."

They part ways, the dogs barking and leaping, blond tails wagging excitedly behind their owner as he sets off in the opposite direction. The retrievers then dash ahead of him almost tripping him up. Smiling, Claudia observes the man as he sprints. He's pretty fast. Agile, with a great physique. She runs her fingers over the card. It's engraved in navy-blue letters. Good quality. *Lucas Fox, attorney at law*. Not an actor, for once. Or a producer or a director. Just a regular person. Nice name. She pops the card into her pocket.

She wonders if she'll call him. She doubts it.

But then again, you never know.

# THIRTY-FOUR

## CLAUDIA

"Everybody wants to be me. Men want to own me and women want my life. At least, they think they do."

Claudia gets up from the chaise longue and steps toward her mosaic-tiled pool that glitters blue and gold in the afternoon sunshine. Shrugging off an antique kimono, which shimmies and floats to the ground in a scarlet puddle of silken glory, she thinks about the lawyer guy she bumped into in the park last weekend, wondering if the statement she just made now is true. He was so laissez-faire and unimpressed by her; perhaps a man like that would not want to own her. It would be nice to date someone who wasn't an actor for a change.

She steps into the water, topless. Topless, so she doesn't get a tan line. She has a whole closet of these beautiful robes. She collects treasures. Clothing, furniture, first edition books, art, and... people. Above all, people. Especially those less fortunate than herself. Her young entourage is lapping up every word she says. Hanging out with Claudia Spector in her Hollywood Hills mansion with an open bar, staff running to and fro with snacks and drinks, and getting to consider yourself an actual *friend* and confidante of the star herself, is anyone's dream come true.

Claudia knows this. She was a nobody once. She remembers when she first met her idol, Janette Waters. She felt like she had died and got a special seat in Hollywood heaven. And now it's her turn to be mother bird. She loves taking people under her wing.

She slips into the cool water, tilting her head back so the sunrays hit her face, bathing her in light and warmth. It's a warm day in May. Not too hot, just perfect. She doesn't wear a hat or even shades. She has become a true California girl since leaving her hometown in Nevada, fifteen years ago. A full-bodied tan, a worked-out physique. She isn't interested in being one of those pale, ghostlike actresses who shun the sun. Her golden tan and golden tresses are her trademark. She is the beautiful girl next door. But clearly not *really* the girl next door. Not anymore. She's a superstar. And that's what her fans love her for. She thinks again about the attorney and wonders how it was he had no idea who she was and what would have happened if she had taken up his offer and accepted a ride in his car. Today she is hanging out with mostly a bunch of strangers. How did that happen?

She lies horizontal in the water, buoyant on her back, and continues, aware, even with her eyes closed, that her small audience today is captivated with every wise word she utters. They have left their phones in a basket by the front door. A special rule of Claudia's. What happens in her private home stays in her private home. They need to live in the moment. She doesn't want anything—even the most innocuous snapshot—winding up on social media.

"They'd trade places in an instant if they had a magic wand. They think it's so easy, like I have the dream life, and I do... on the surface. Truly? They have no idea." The "they" she speaks of includes these people circled around her now, but because they are the chosen ones, they don't see through themselves. They're her *friends*. They are here, behind the high gates of her impossible-to-access home, whose garden smells of Pepita pink jasmine, hibiscus, wisteria, and lilac, and all things sweet and heady, and where hummingbirds dip and swoop, and sip nectar with their long beaks, their energetic wings whirring so fast you can't see them move.

It's a Saturday, and these hopeful actors are actually getting to have a *conversation* with one of the most famous women in the world. Despite the fact that Claudia is doing most of the talking. Holding court to her enraptured guests, they lap up every syllable she utters, believing in this moment they are her very best friends. She has that effect on people. When she speaks to you, when she singles you out, you are unique. Special.

Literally, one in a million.

"I know, I know," she goes on, talking to the deep blue sky, but with closed eyes. "I've got no right to complain because this is everything I wanted. Public figures don't get to gripe about a camera stuck in their face, cruel things said about them in the media, the lies and stories that get spun."

"Be careful what you wish for," a girl in a polka-dot bikini offers, and laughs.

Claudia doesn't reply because this particular truth cuts a little too close to the bone. Now she wishes, not for success with her career, but success with a romantic relationship.

She chats on in her lazy drawl, "They have no idea about the sacrifices I've made, the wear and tear on my soul. I worked my ass off to get here. Fought my way to the top. Did stuff no woman should have to do. Would I change a thing? Probably not. Still, I wish people would understand it's not all a bed of roses being famous. I mean, it is, but the roses have a shitload of thorns digging in your side when you sleep."

"So true," Amelia says. Amelia is Claudia's niece. Her sister's daughter, whom Claudia is only just getting to know. Her dad is military, always moving to some different part of the country, or abroad. She's a bumptious twenty-one-year-old who has left home and decided she wants to act. Claudia is coaching her, getting her ready to audition. She doesn't believe Amelia is ready yet, but she will be soon. She has sent her to her hairdresser, Sam, who has given Amelia a retro pixie cut not unlike Mia Farrow in her prime. She knows that Amelia needs an edge, because getting a job, sadly, is not just about talent. The haircut makes her stand out and really suits her. Claudia is keeping a reticent but steely eye on her niece. She doesn't want Amelia to be ruined. So many nasty, gross men in this business. The man's-world landscape has not changed as much as outsiders believe. They are everywhere, these predators. For now, they are slithering under the woodwork, biding their time, inventing new ways of getting their way without being caught. And there are those just as guilty—sometimes... gasp!... women, believe it or not—aiding and abetting these slimeballs. You have to watch out in this town. She feels protective of Amelia and any young woman forging her way as an actress.

Today, no men are here hanging out at her home. It isn't that Claudia's not interested in helping men, but she certainly doesn't go out of her way. Men have had it easy for way too long in this industry. They aren't scrutinized or judged for their looks the way women are, don't have to dodge so many slings and arrows. The percentage of good parts for actors is so much higher than for actresses, too. How many female-centric stories are there? Not so many. And the pay? She doesn't even want to get started on that. Yet, she has noticed, men still whine about how tough things are.

*Try being a woman in this town, pussies.*

She does some laps, stretching her long slim limbs as she swims. Something Claudia loves about her life is her free time between the seasons of the show she's doing, *Go Ask Bobbie.* Each movie she has made she has dreaded might be her last, but with such a primetime, blockbuster series—and earning a cool two million per episode—she has that wonderful feeling for once, of knowing she has a secure job. She's the star of the show. She doesn't panic about getting fired.

Why is it that actors are so insecure? Even legends like Dustin Hoffman admit to being insecure. She doesn't know what kind of human chooses to be an actor, but lacking in confidence and low self-esteem seems to be a trait they all share. Mixed with a swashbuckling, exterior bravado that camouflages this niggling self-doubt makes them all paradoxes of their own creation. A group of misfits.

Actors choose their line of work so they can hide behind a character, she thinks. Step outside of themselves into another's shoes. Shoes that feel so much more comfortable than their own. Most actors don't know who they even are. She's still finding out who she is, for sure.

She's definitely a work in progress and is the first to admit it.

She's aware that she has been apologizing half her life. If she can be seen as fabulous, she can eliminate the shame that lives inside her. Or so she always hopes. But, sadly, it doesn't work that way. However fabulous others think her, she can't shake the notion that her good luck could be snatched away from her at any moment because they'll find out her fabulousness is fraudulent. Not even therapy has made any difference. She isn't able to pinpoint the source of this shame, this unprecedented impostor syndrome, but it's so deep-rooted and such an integral part of her, she supposes she has to accept it. Own it, too.

She swims to the edge of the pool. She'll do a real workout later, in her gym. It is equipped with the latest Pilates Reformer, cardio equipment, a ballet barre, and a mirror taking up one side of the wall. Her trainer is coming at nine. Today's a Pilates day. She likes training at night. It helps her sleep.

"You guys feel free to stay and party," she tells Amelia's group of friends. "No phones. I'm going inside, I need to work.

Please don't disturb me. Help yourselves to food and stuff. Remember, no hard drugs. Weed's okay. No tobacco. If I catch anyone with a cigarette or rolling a joint with tobacco, you're out. Be ready for the screening at six."

Her home is equipped with a state-of-the-art movie theater. Sumptuous velvet seats that recline, and plush velvet paneling on the walls. A twenty-foot-wide screen. A popcorn machine. They're going to watch *Midnight Cowboy*. She likes to discuss performances, the script, the shots, even the costumes. She has a mini drama college going on, right in her screening room, and she's the unofficial teacher. She loves to share her knowledge about all things film. If they want to be actors, they need to start getting serious about their craft, right now. You can learn a lot by watching the greats.

God, she adores this medium. She could eat, breathe, and shit movies all day long. Theater, too. Though doing Broadway is off-limits these days. She's too famous to expose herself on stage every night. Too many nutjobs around. After the armed stalker who had managed to sneak into her trailer on location, two years ago, holding a knife to her neck, telling her how much he loved her—and who is thankfully now in jail—she has to be careful.

Claudia emerges from the pool, droplets of water shining like jewels off her back, and pads barefoot into the house. Her French tutor is coming in twenty minutes. An hour and a half of grueling French verbs and grammar. The dreaded French dictation. Her tutor will read out the text, sentence by sentence, and Claudia has to listen, her ears sharp as a bat's, and write down exactly what she hears. He's a French native from Lyon—strict and no-nonsense—and has assured her there's no point beginning conversation classes until she has the other stuff mastered.

Claudia's a workaholic, throws herself into all her roles. Once, she waited tables, incognito, to prepare for a role. She's driven a bus, swept the streets, and even cleaned toilets. That was at the beginning, before she was a household name. And now she's on a mission to educate herself, give herself a gift of something that doesn't rotate around her looks, her body. Reconstruct herself from the inside out. She covets the idea of being a cultured, learned woman. Surmount that piece-of-shit feeling that she isn't good enough, and conquer her insecurities.

Perhaps it would have been possible if a certain someone had not collided into her life. Someone who is about to change everything.

# THIRTY-FIVE

## CLAUDIA

Busy with a bunch of scripts she has promised her agent she'll read, Claudia feels another punch of loneliness. Her posse of young friends left late last night. Apart from birdsong outside, silence rings in her ears. It's Sunday. Will that guy go running in the park again? Her housekeeper, Juana, shoved her jogging gear into the washing machine, and his number is now illegible. She considers going to the park. Would she bump into him a second time? She shakes her head. She's still raw from the breakup with Crystal. She's better off single.

She has been entertaining and playing hostess to her young entourage—Amelia's acting class friends—too often lately. Since losing Crystal she has needed to fill a void. She isn't doing them any favors, though, as they'll get a rose-tinted idea of how life works in Hollywood. She knows how fortunate she has been. Being honest with herself she has let them spend time with her, not so much because she craves their company, but for the feeling of a full, ambient house. Noise. Bustle. Chatter. But these youngsters need to make their own way, follow their own path. "Follow your bliss" is a term she picked up somewhere along the way, from some guru or meditation class, and has bandied the cliché about probably too much. She knows only too well that there's nothing blissful about trying to climb the career ladder in Hollywood. Most of them won't even make it to the first rung, no matter how hard she tries to help them. Even talent doesn't secure you a chance. Even nepotism. They have to do it for themselves. Fate's a curious thing, but of late she has begun to believe in it.

What *is* her fate?

She pours herself a glass of merlot and lets it roll down her throat, quarter-way through reading a crappy, clichéd romcom that she'll definitely turn down. Why has her agent sent her this drivel? She has told Helena she's ready for a serious role. A serial killer, or a judge. Something intense. Nothing romantic or quixotic. She wants to play an ugly, raw character with flaws.

When Claudia arrived in this town, with eighty-nine dollars to her name, nobody helped her, nobody picked up the tab. She knocked on doors until she found a job, first in retail selling jeans, lumberjack shirts, and workers' clothing, and when she had saved a little money, she set up a market stall on Melrose, on Sundays, selling vintage clothing that she had picked up in Goodwill and various second-hand stores. She had a good eye. Nearly all the money she made she poured into her career. The headshots, the dreaded résumé full of carefully crafted "embellishments" (because she had to start somewhere), the demo reel and acting classes. All so pricey. Ironically, it wasn't her reel or headshot that gave her the first foot in the door, or an agent, but a young student filmmaker who bought a 1930s velvet jacket from her at the market, who happened to be looking for a teenager to play the part of a runaway in a short movie she had written. Claudia, twenty-one at the time, appeared younger than her years.

That day at the market, after a very late start, Claudia

looked pretty disheveled. Her hair was a stringy, greasy mess, she wasn't wearing a stitch of makeup, and her old Ugg boots had holes in the toes. It was pure luck she happened to match the vision of the young director that particular day. As they say, she was *in the right place at the right time*. "You're my Sadie!" the director cried out. Claudia didn't earn a cent on that short film. She was only paid expenses and had to provide her own props and costumes, but it was her launchpad. An agent saw the film at Sundance. It got nominated for an award. The agent—Helena Ronstein, whom she is still with—signed her straight away, and the rest... well, it wasn't history exactly, but it was the beginning of two years of grueling auditions and at least getting a chance for Claudia to participate, to audition, to call herself a real actor. She had broken the agent barrier. Got past the gatekeeper. Most hopefuls never even reach that far.

It took her three years of auditioning to land a decent job. It was a TV pilot for a horror series. It went nowhere, but it was a start. Commercials paid most of the rent, and then finally, just as Claudia was thinking about setting herself up full-time with her vintage clothing business, she got a part in a romantic comedy. Not the lead, but the best friend. And her quirky deadpan character and perfect comic timing caught the eye of the legendary director Don Weyler.

Claudia often reminisces about her past, totaling up her lucky breaks. She always feels grateful. Feeling grateful, she suspects, is, if not the key to happiness, the key to sanity. She knows other actors, some from acting classes she took way back when, who had talent coming out of their ears and who have gotten absolutely nowhere. This is a business where luck plays a huge part. She is truly grateful for everything.

She pulls another script from the pile. A movie that will be shot on location in Poland. Nope, she isn't up for filming that far away from home right now. She'll turn that one down.

She brings her wineglass to her lips but nearly drops it, hands shaky, her body suddenly tense with fear. Are those footsteps she hears? Roger, her driver, has gone home. Juana isn't due in today. Her assistant, Mary, is away. As far as Claudia knows, she's alone in her house. "Hello?" she calls out. "Is someone there?" She stands up and slowly moves to the fireplace. On the mantle is a large wooden box where she keeps a handgun. It isn't loaded, but it's a good deterrent. Her logic tells her there's no way someone can have entered her property with her sophisticated security system in place, but the rush of adrenaline slamming through her body is a whole other beast. "Hello?"

A figure enters the room, barefoot. "I'm sorry, it's just me."

Claudia lets out a rush of air, struggling to right her thrashing heart. It is just Amelia's friend Minnie. The one who sat by the pool, hardly speaking, with a book in her hand. "Minnie, what are you still doing here? I thought Roger had taken you all home yesterday."

"I fell asleep and nobody woke me up. I guess they all forgot about me."

"And you've been here all night, all day, sleeping?"

The girl nods. "Sorry."

"You scared the shit out of me! I'm sorry, but I'm very busy, you can't stay."

The girl looks down at her toes. So pitiful, Claudia thinks, her pale legs skinny, her arms frail and lean. Hollywood will surely take a bite of this delicate thing and spit her right out again.

"Have you had anything to eat?" Claudia asks her.

The waif shakes her head.

"I'll fix you something, then call Roger. He can take you home."

Minnie shuffles her feet. Lifts her eyes. "I don't have a home."

"Well, you must have somewhere to go. A friend's?"

"Me and my boyfriend broke up. He went back to Minnesota, didn't like LA."

"You from Minnesota, too?"

"No. Buffalo."

"And you didn't want to go with him?"

Minnie shakes her head again. "He's going to live back at his parents."

"I see. Well, you can stay with Amelia." Claudia looks her guest up and down. She hardly said a word when they were hanging out yesterday, with her nose buried in a novel.

Minnie speaks up now. "Amelia told me she hasn't got enough room for me. I can't stay with her."

Claudia draws in a breath. This is rich, considering she's paying Amelia's rent. She guesses Amelia must've moved a boyfriend in. She is meant to be getting serious about her career, not taking a free ride. When Claudia was a teenager she had two jobs, bought all her own clothing, and if she couldn't afford something, she saved up for it. What is it with Amelia's generation? They expect things to be easy. Expect their parents to fund their lives. Fancy phones, a dozen pairs of designer sneakers, tickets for concerts, travel. She has seen how some of these kids live, courtesy of their permissive, clueless parents, who somehow have amnesia when it comes to their own pasts, who tell themselves how much harder things are now for their children these days than it was for them. No, things are not harder. Scarier, yes, with climate change on their heels and the pressures of social media. But the younger generation has become more spoiled, more accustomed to daily luxuries and instant gratification. What is she supposed to do with Minnie? She doesn't want her staying but she can't leave her on the street.

"You're an actress?" she asks Minnie.

"No way!"

"No way? What's that supposed to mean?"

"I mean, not in a million years can I act. I get nervous when someone even takes a photo of me."

"So why did you come to LA?"

"To work?" Minnie says this like it was a question.

"What kind of work are you looking for?"

"I want to be an assistant?"

Her upward inflection has Claudia raise a brow. "You don't sound so sure."

"I *am* sure," Minnie says. "I want to be a PA. I can type. I'm pretty nerdy with AI and stuff."

"You have experience?"

"Some." And then she adds, "Yeah, I do. I have a ton of experience. I worked in a dentist's office and was a receptionist at a veterinarian's last summer. You'd be amazed how complicated the system is. I knew all the dogs and their owners."

Claudia tilts her head, considering the awkward situation of finding a young helpless stranger in her home. Minnie has left her hometown and is showing a certain amount of chutzpah and independence, just by being here. Surely that can only be a good thing?

Claudia says, "I don't have a job for you, if that's what you're hoping. I already have an assistant. Mary. She's been with me for years. She happens to be on vacation right now, but... look, Minnie, if you came here for a job, I'm sorry but I can't help you. Is that why you fell asleep? You were hoping you'd get to—"

"No! I promise!"

She regards her guest/gatecrasher for a moment, trying to figure out what her agenda is. Perhaps she's genuine. An image rises in her mind of when she first came to LA. The amount of doors that were slammed—sometimes literally—in her face. How people in lofty positions of being able to help a young person out didn't give her the time of day. It pains her to see a young woman with nowhere to go. She must be the only person

Claudia has met recently, under the age of twenty-five, who doesn't want to be an actor.

"Come on then, Minnie. Let's go to the kitchen and I'll fix us something to eat." Somehow Claudia knows it isn't just a meal she'll be fixing, but this girl's life.

# THIRTY-SIX

## CLAUDIA

Two weeks on and not a lot has changed in Claudia's bubble. Now late May, the evenings are warm and balmy. Since splitting with Crystal, Claudia has declined every single invitation. To parties, to opening nights, to weddings, to anything with an envelope. She has stayed at home behind her grand iron gates, more alone than Greta Garbo. She hasn't invited her niece's young friends back to her home either but has set Minnie up in an apartment in West Hollywood, paying her rent until Minnie finds a job. She is forever waving her godmother wand it seems, but, hey, that's what money's for. Claudia is a sucker, and she knows it. This charity-begins-at-home agony-aunt thing is one of her weaknesses. She has given Minnie two months to find a job, after that she'll have to go back to Buffalo where she comes from.

There is one invitation, though, that Claudia feels she can't pass up. It's from her old friend Jordan, a football player whom she has known since high school, who has made it big. How often does that happen in life? Two people from a little town in Nevada whose dreams of fame and fortune and doing what they love best have come true?

She can't let him down.

It isn't just because she needs to be there for an old friend, but Claudia has heard, from Jordan himself, that Crystal is coming. She knows there'll be photographers everywhere, and a zillion famous people she isn't in the mood to mingle with right now, but she needs to be strong, override that feeling of being annihilated by another human being. See Crystal, face to face. Show Crystal she doesn't care. Give the best performance of her life. Although Claudia initially planned to turn Jordan's invitation down, she's livid that someone can have such control over her emotions. No, Crystal is not going to take her dignity and social life away from her. Claudia will prove to the world, and to herself, that she's not fazed one bit by Crystal's betrayal. She'll flirt with other people, why not? Flirt right in front of her ex. Dressed to the nines while she's at it.

Childish, tit-for-tat behavior, yeah, but dammit, it's one way of getting through this tunnel of turmoil.

She will be *fabulous*.

She chooses a scarlet, silk crepe Marilyn dress from her wardrobe of tricks. It didn't actually belong to Marilyn, but it could have. Ruched around the bust, in at the waist. Flowy and elegant but also sexy. She'll call her stylist to organize some jewels to wear to Jordan's shindig. Real jewels that she'll borrow, from De Beers or Harry Winston. They'll send along a bodyguard to accompany her, no doubt, but that's fine. Pairing the red dress with some high stilettoes in nude—to elongate her legs even more—Claudia runs her eyes up and down the mirror in her bedroom, gazing at her reflection. No, it's over the top... makes her look like she's trying too hard. She looks desperate.

This party isn't the Oscars, not even red carpet. It's a Hollywood pool party, for heaven's sake. What is she thinking? She doesn't even care. She'll go to the damn party in shorts and flip-flops. Let them take photos of her that way: simple, back to basics. She has nothing to prove. This is who she is. Like it or lump it. And, no, she won't flirt. She'll show her face, say hello to Jordan, have one drink and leave.

She arrives at the party early. This way, she can leave early. Beautiful people are mingling and fawning over each other. Greeting one another with air kisses and "Long time no see!" "Is that really you?" and "Oh my God, I can't believe you're here!" or the snotty putdown line she hates so much, "What are *you* doing here?" In living rooms, in halls, in the kitchen, and in and around the backyard, where a kidney-shaped pool takes center stage, these wannabes and stars are rubbing shoulders, while cocktail waitresses bring canapés and drinks on silver trays. Sports personalities, agents, managers, actors, producers, directors, and more... they're all here. Claudia spots a fair share of drug taking amidst the hubbub. Not for her. She's been there, done that. She brushes past an amorous couple, ducking her head under a string of fairy lights weaved between trees, catching tidbits of conversation.

"So, yeah, that scene was pretty intense, but I have to admit that was my double, not me."

"Not your ass in that iconic shot?"

"Nope. My contract strictly forbidded nudity. Forbade nudity? Excuse my grammar, I have no idea." The girl lets out a wheezy laugh and takes another drag of a big fat spliff.

Claudia walks past other conversations like, "Well, you know why *he* got the part? It wasn't talent, that's for sure. You know who he's fucking, don't you?" and, "Seriously, she's like the best dermatologist in the city. Those barcode lines above the lip? She can fix those, no problem."

Claudia is looking for Jordan. So far, no joy. She heads off toward the tennis court, where there's another bar set up. Her gaze scanning the grounds, the next thing she knows she has bumped into a Rolexed, cufflinked wrist, drink spilling all over her. Lucky she isn't in that red dress, heels, and decked in jewels. Still, she'll now stink of mojito or whatever pungent, wet aroma she smells on her body, staining her clothing, sticky on her flesh.

"Excuse me."

Was it her fault? Probably. The truth is, she's clumsy. Not many people know this about her; she has practiced grace and movie-star poise for long enough. But hard as she tries not to be, she's a klutz by nature.

The owner of the arm with the drink attached laughs. "*You* again?"

It's a little dark, just small round solar bulbs lighting up a pathway. Claudia squints her eyes at the figure in front of her. "Lucas, right?" She recognizes the man whom she collided into in Runyon Canyon. The attorney. He's alone. No date by his side. She can't believe he's here. Is this fate?

"How's the knee?" he asks.

"Absolutely fine. But now I'm going to have to get into the swimming pool to wash away the stench of alcohol you spilled all over me. Do you make a habit of colliding into distracted women?" She is aware she's flirting.

Lucas laughs again. "Only when they're beautiful and have two left feet. Which, I've found, is quite a unique combination."

Claudia rolls her eyes at his lame but admittingly original pickup line. "Have you seen Jordan? I was trying to find him."

"He's by the tennis court. Come on, I need to replenish these drinks anyway, thanks to you. How d'you know Jordan?"

"We were friends in high school."

Lucas stops walking, turns and rakes his eyes slowly over Claudia. "That's right. I know exactly who you are now. Jordan has told me all about you."

"Oh, yeah? What did he say?"

"Just how you're old school friends, and come from the same town."

It's a relief to Claudia that Lucas isn't fawning all over her.

The common denominator is a friend they share. A friend who isn't even in the industry. *Lucas must know who I am,* she thinks, *but seemingly doesn't care one way or the other. I like that.*

"You're here alone?" Lucas asks.

"Yeah, I am."

"Me too. You like going places alone?"

Claudia considers this before she answers. She loves hanging out with friends, but since Crystal... well, she has come to the conclusion that Crystal had alienated her from her friends. Always declined invitations. Discouraged Claudia from having people over. She was jealous, too. Hated it when Claudia had made new acquaintances or spent too much time with old work colleagues. All this possessiveness, only to be unceremoniously dumped? Crystal has a lot to answer for.

Claudia replies, "I don't always like being alone. But I'm not afraid of my own company." And then to veer the subject away from herself, she asks, "How do you know Jordan?"

"He's a client of mine."

"Is that why you're at this party early then? To be supportive? Schmooze a bit?"

He chuckles. "No, not schmooze. I don't need to do that anymore. My schmoozing days are behind me."

She gives him a slow smile, remembering the early days of her career. How she would have given anything to be invited to a party like this, and now she couldn't care less. "Me too. Usually I don't party much. At least, not lately. I had planned to arrive early here, say hi, and leave."

"Me too."

They are standing under an oak tree, almost in the dark. Taking a step back to avoid a couple of drunk and swaying partygoers heading for the bar, the tip of Claudia's flip-flop catches on a rock. Stumbling, Lucas reaches out to steady her. She grabs his arm. His other hand remains on the small of her back. Something about the physical contact is so sensual for her. An electric current shoots right through her. Nobody has touched her since Crystal. Nobody but her massage therapist. She and Lucas stand unmoving, gazes locked in a sort of inquisitive stare. *He feels it too, doesn't he?* Her body pulses. She can sense it. In this moment, she does not want to head toward the tennis court and chat to Jordan, or anyone else. She wants to kiss Lucas.

And get kissed back.

"You want to split?" he asks, still with his hand, not on her back, but on the curve of her ass.

"Yeah, let's get out of here." But then she says as an afterthought, "How do I know you're not an axe murderer?"

He shoots her a wry smile. "You don't. But you can look me up online, if you like. Or better, I'll do it right now. Here," he says, showing her his phone. He has googled his business, Fox & Co. He presses on "images" and up he comes in a photo. There's another man, identical to him but older and with gray hair, the two of them in suits, standing side by side, the logo of the office in the background.

"Your dad?" Claudia inquires.

He nods.

Claudia laughs. "You didn't have to do that. Prove you were legit. I was only kidding."

"What you see is what you get," he says. "No surprises with me."

What she sees is a sexy, fun, spontaneous guy who is really into her and doesn't seem to care about her fame. She hasn't done this kind of thing in years: go off with someone she has met at a party. Excitement buzzes through her, around her, inside her. She likes this guy. She calls it out for what it is. She's on the rebound. She needs some attention. Some *physical* attention. She wants his hands on her, all over her. She wants to get laid.

*Forget about Crystal.* The great thing is that because this person's a man, she can't compare the two of them. Won't feel let down or disappointed. She'll take him for what he is at face value: a very cute, single, and horny guy who wants to have sex with her. He isn't an actor, or director, or producer. There'll be no scandal, no Hollywood intrigue, no exploitation. Just a normal man, with a normal job who'll give her what she needs, no strings attached.

Just perfect.

# THIRTY-SEVEN

## CLAUDIA

The sex is incredible. Claudia thinks of scenes from movies from the eighties when people tore each other's clothing off within five minutes of meeting each other. She loves watching these old films. Like the limo scene with Kevin Costner and Sean Young in *No Way Out*. When they were both gorgeous and in their prime and when Claudia was just a baby.

In her own limo, with Roger at the wheel, it is as if she and Lucas are reenacting that scene and the wild, risky passion that only comes after two strangers meet. She feels reckless taking a chance on Lucas, an unknown entity, a total stranger. But that's also part of the excitement.

*Body Heat, Basic Instinct, Fatal Attraction.*

A time before mobile phones or internet, a time before Google, when people had to judge each other at face value, when if you made a date with someone you had to show up and not rely on sending a text letting them know you'd be late. When people who were crazy for each other stayed by the house phone, waiting for it to ring, not going out in case they missed a call. How strange that must have been—she was too young to know about those things then. But she's seen enough of it in old movies to hanker after the romance it invoked. The sense of intrigue.

She is not going to ask Lucas for his Instagram, Twitter, or Facebook handles because she doesn't ever go on social media. She *loathes* social media. Claudia doesn't need that time-suck in her life. Sure, she has social media accounts with millions of followers, but she doesn't run them; she doesn't have the time or inclination to get swept into the vortex of scrolling and posting. Her PR company does that. She wants to be recognized for her work, not for being a person who is famous for being famous. She is so over all that self-promotion; there are enough Kardashians in this world. She's too private for that. Social media does not do anyone's mental health any favors either. The forum and website she started for young girls that she had been so excited about in its infancy, GenerationWhy.com, has turned into a bully, shaming fest, the opposite of what it set out to be. She is done with the online world. The reason she chose to act in the first place was so she could hide behind her characters. Be someone else entirely. The last thing she wants is to expose her true self. She regrets doing that *Vanity Fair* article. It was Crystal who pressured her into accepting. Crystal craves attention, nurtures her celebrity status, and now Claudia thinks about it, she suspects that she had been using her all along. The media attention they garnered was quite something. Crystal never intended to marry Claudia, did she? It was all one big publicity stunt. All Claudia has ever wanted career-wise is to do her job: act. The celebrity thing actually gets in the way. Is that such an anomaly these days? She guesses it is.

It's refreshing to meet someone outside showbusiness who is just a normal guy.

Claudia is not quite daring enough to invite Lucas back to her home, though, so they take a bungalow in a hotel in West Hollywood, where she knows the staff will be discreet and where she comes from time to time to seek solace or have a meeting behind its Disneyesque, faux Gothic walls. Hardly have they closed the blinds, when she and Lucas begin to rip off the other's clothing, tumbling to the bed. As Lucas thrusts inside her, tongue locked with hers, sweat on sweat, it makes Claudia remember that sex with a man can be out of this world. Raw. Visceral. Primal. Almost painful. She has no regrets whatsoever.

There is nothing like sex for the sake of sex.

This is exactly what the doctor ordered.

They meet up a few times a week after that and do little more than fuck. There is no time for conversation, and anyhow, neither cares particularly what makes the other tick. If they do vent their problems, the other is, in truth, probably not even listening. They're available for each other's pleasure, nothing more.

Soon Lucas begins coming over to Claudia's house. Sometimes in his lunch hour, sometimes after work. They order takeout, not for culinary delectation or as a focal point for interesting conversation to get to know each other better, but as fuel to keep on going. Stamina food. Two, three, four times in a row, they can't get enough of each other.

"I need you, babe," Lucas whispers in her ear as he pounds into her, a fistful of her hair in his hand. This is their fourteenth date, if you could call it a date.

"I know," she moans. Another climax is building. "Shut up and keep moving." She slams into him and feels her body on the point of explosion.

"You are soooo sexy," he breathes. "You smell amazing."

Her body rises to meet his, her hips grinding into his groin. She cups her hands around his tight ass and claims her pleasure. "Oh, God," she cries out. This is the right way to expel Crystal. Replacement therapy. It is working like a charm.

He takes his pleasure too, the pair of them coming in unison. She knows how rare this is, how special.

"I can't stay the night though," he murmurs five minutes later, their legs entangled, sweat glistening on Claudia's brow, his breath warm against her mouth.

Claudia doesn't really care. In fact, she prefers him gone by morning. Yet lately, she wonders—just out of curiosity—why he never wants to stay.

Hardly has Lucas left her house when Claudia feels a primal need for him again. Little by little, she becomes more dependent on Lucas's presence in her life. Her sexual desire is transforming into something softer, needier. Her craving bordering on the insatiable, yes, but with a twist. She wants more of *him*, more than just a physical relationship.

*Hormones are unfair.* She's aware that sex gives women a higher level of oxytocin than men: the bonding hormone that can't distinguish between lust and love. Claudia knows logically that she is not falling in love with Lucas—no way, she hardly knows the guy—but some invisible force is causing her to feel a desperate need to connect with him on some deeper level than merely sex. Guys get a dose of dopamine—the pleasure hormone—and women are saddled with the bonding "love" hormone.

How is that fair?

She wants to get to know Lucas better.

# THIRTY-EIGHT

## CLAUDIA

One day in June Claudia finds Crystal waiting for her after filming. They are wrapping up the final season of *Go Ask Bobbie*. This is the penultimate episode. Somehow, Crystal has wangled her way to the entrance of Claudia's trailer. Is she working on the same lot? Claudia makes a mental note to find out who is responsible. After what happened two years ago with the stalker, she is furious. Luckily, she has her bodyguard Pete with her. He comes with the job, paid for by the studio. Not even curious to know what Crystal is after, Claudia wants nothing to do with her. How can you profess your love, plan a wedding and then dump that same very person via a TV talk show? Claudia is aware she has been spared, knows a marriage with Crystal would have been a disaster, but she'll never forget what this woman has done to her.

Never.

Crystal stands by the trailer, arms out, proffering a grin and a massive bouquet of red roses cradled in her arms, while also clutching a magnum of Dom Pérignon. What the hell she thinks she's celebrating, Claudia has no idea. She hasn't seen Crystal since watching her on Isabella's show. Claudia herself was a guest only a week ago. And when Isabella asked Claudia about her relationship, she said, "Yep, it's true, Isabella, I'm in a new relationship."

"Oh," Isabella said. "I was actually referring to Crystal."

"Water under the bridge," Claudia replied.

"No chance of a reunion, a kiss and make-up? You two were such a cool couple."

"Like I said, water under the bridge, or rather, a drought under the bridge. I have a relationship with someone else now. But I can't say who it is... you know, to protect his privacy."

"*His* privacy?"

It had caused a stir. Claudia hadn't meant it to come out. Lucas didn't seem to notice, thank goodness. But for Crystal it was like a siren.

The champagne and roses signal one thing, clearly. She wants Claudia back. "I'm sorry, sweetie," Crystal starts, taking a step toward her. "I miss you, can we start again?"

Claudia turns her back on her ex and walks away. It gives her a shiver of pleasure when she asks her bodyguard to tell Crystal to leave her trailer and to "Please take your roses and champagne with you. Oh, and Ms. Spector has asked me to make sure you don't forget your big girl panties, too."

Lucas—it turns out—has cured Claudia of Crystal. How else is she able to be so strong, so resolved? The only problem now is that Lucas himself is on her mind. Way more than is healthy. She can't get enough of him.

She thinks of the family of owls in her backyard. The owlets are about to leave the nest in the pine tree at the end of her garden. Every winter Claudia is treated to what sounds like a woodwind concert in the treetops: the love song of the great horned owl attracting a mate. He usually begins his song in early January, and then a duet takes place between him and his ladylove during courtship. The love duet only lasts a few weeks in late winter, but the males continue to vocalize: the song changing up from romantic to territorial, once the pair has chosen each other and mated. The male owl both guards his mate and hunts for food for her while she incubates the eggs. Then he provides for the chicks. Later, both parents share the task of feeding their chicks, until, as fledglings, they will leave the nest during summer, which is what is taking place now at one end of her backyard.

This is the kind of bond Claudia realizes she longs for. It seems ridiculous to fantasize about an owl's life, but when she thinks of her life ahead, this is what she aspires to: a family life. Children. Her career has taken all her energy. She is ready for a change, ready to commit.

Lucas has told her she is his North Star, that he can't live without her.

Words like this hold weight. She allows herself to dream, to plan a future with him.

She has a premonition, almost, that Lucas is the person who will change her destiny.

# THIRTY-NINE

## CLAUDIA

Claudia is on a mission to find Minnie a job. Even something part-time. Claudia visits Minnie in her apartment every now and then, helping her cook up a résumé, and sometimes brings her a piece of furniture, or things from her house she no longer wants. A way of helping Minnie out and clearing away the old simultaneously. One time, a couple of chairs, another time, a trash bag of old clothing, although there is certainly nothing trashy about the contents, including a sleek Calvin Klein sheath dress she once wore to an awards party, and a collection of silk blouses. All in the hope she can smarten up Minnie's attire.

They do stuff together too. On one occasion, Claudia donned a wig, oversize hat, and long coat, and they went to see a show. She loves the retro movie palaces in Downtown LA from the 1920s, like the Theatre at Ace Hotel with its vaulted ceilings covered in mirrors and Spanish Gothic style. It has been fun hanging out with Minnie. Her niece, Amelia, is preoccupied with her new boyfriend and no longer interested in her acting classes, so Claudia finds her efforts shifting from Amelia to Minnie, especially since Minnie doesn't seem to have many friends, and Claudia feels bad for the girl being alone in a strange city. She remembers what it was like for her at the beginning. She needs to find Minnie a job so she'll make new friends and gain independence.

While Claudia and Lucas are digging into Juana's delicious chili—after a run in the park one Sunday—and enjoying a glass of red, and while Sappho and Ariadne roam her backyard, Lucas brings up his problems at work. Lately, he has been doing a lot of overtime, telling Claudia about some Japanese client he needs to win over in order to take over his father's law firm. Lucas complains he is overworked, stressed, and has too much on his plate. *Join the club*, Claudia thinks wryly. It's normal for actors to work long hours and into the night. Actors have to think about their jobs twenty-four-seven when they're filming, and when they aren't, they need to prepare for the next role. Grueling physical workouts are just one of the components of their job, to make sure they're doing a character service and to make sure—with the camera picking up every detail, every extra pound—they look good. Learning skills like fencing, horseback riding, boxing, ballet, the tango. If you want authenticity, you can't rely on a double. Not to mention learning lines down pat, or perfecting an accent or even another language. Good actors never stop perfecting their craft or preparing for a role. It amuses her that Lucas is such a lightweight. Still, she is pleased he is sharing his problems with her, that their relationship is developing into something more.

"I have a solution," Claudia tells him, pushing a forkful of Juana's chili into her mouth.

"I wish," Lucas grumbles, his lips turned down in a pout. "You have no idea what my dad's like. If I don't reel in this client, I'm done for. Seriously, my father's a ruthless son of a bitch. After all the shit I've done for him, he's capable of shutting me down, handing the firm over to the highest bidder. He doesn't give a damn about me."

Claudia takes a sip of wine, then says, "I know a girl named

Minnie you can employ. She needs a job, she'd be perfect. Reduce the stress a bit, help you out." She's pretty sure Minnie would probably not be much of a solution for Lucas, but working for Lucas would certainly be a solution for Minnie. Minnie isn't her responsibility, true, but Claudia can't help herself. She's a fixer by nature. None of her friends are looking for an assistant, but Lucas? Maybe he is the answer? Minnie's smart, and more than capable of doing girl Friday work at a law firm and help lessen Lucas's load. Once she gets some experience, she can move on to something she enjoys more.

Lucas groans. "Right now, I'm not in a financial position to hire anybody new."

"She won't be expensive. She's only twenty-two. She needs a break. It would be great for her résumé. Apparently, she's into AI and stuff. She might be good."

Lucas frowns. "I don't know. I'm not a charity. Anyhow, please let's not talk about work, it's tensing me up." He traces his fingers down Claudia's face, then, angling her chin toward him with one hand, and unzipping his fly with another, he says, "I need release, babe. Need to get work off my mind."

But Claudia isn't in the mood. She's done with the sex, sex, sex thing. It's time they engage in more meaningful conversations, get to know each other in a more profound way. Things have changed. At least, *she* has changed. She has deeper, more developed feelings. She shakes him off. "I can't right now, I need to learn my lines."

"Come on, babe! Since when have lines gotten in the way?"

Claudia is ready to move to the next level with this relationship. Ironic that she's the one who has championed a no-strings-attached kind of thing, and now she is sick of it. Sex with him is amazing, but she wants something more serious, more fulfilling. No, "fulfilling" is a bad choice of word. Intimacy is what Claudia craves. She doesn't want to fuck anymore. She wants to make love. And from the sweet things he tells her about not being able to carry on without her, she assumes he wants the same things she does.

Claudia takes his hands from inside her jeans and steps away. "Give me five minutes."

Lucas blows out a noisy breath of exasperation, his pants undone. His sex drive is something else. "Claudia, no, where are you going?"

"To the bathroom." She needs space. Time to think without Lucas clouding her judgment. A moment alone. As she sits on the lid of the toilet sipping her wine, Crystal comes to mind. When they were an item, Crystal had planted the idea in Claudia's head that the two of them would start a family. Adopt. Claudia had abandoned all notions of adoption and having kids once they split up. But now, with Lucas, maybe they could try? The adoption plan with Crystal was a practical one: neither had wanted to spend nine months pregnant. It would have gotten in the way of work. Thinking about this now, in retrospect, that notion was pretty uncompromising and emotionally sterile. That is no way to bring a child into the world, is it? To put convenience first... or rather, a career first. If you want to start a family, you have to go all in. Make a proper commitment.

Claudia's plans have always been based around her career. Now at the top, with everything she has always dreamed of—amazing roles, awards, an incredible home—she needs to do something for herself, not simply her career. Has she ever put *herself* first when she thinks about it? Ever? And here is Lucas. He's no longer her lover, but her boyfriend. The two of them could start a family. Why not? He has told her time and time again how crazy he is about her. Is she in love, too? Men get to experiment—or rather, dither about starting a family or having children—until they are sixty plus. Another unjust factor (like the oxytocin) which makes Claudia suspect that God might be a guy after all. Whatever. It is what it is, and she needs to start thinking seriously about having kids; she doesn't have forever.

She takes another long sip of Vega Sicilia, a delicious Ribera del Duero a friend recommended. A good red always sets her mind at peace. Thinking about Crystal, and how easily a relationship can blow up in your face, she is at war with herself about what do next. Her needs and wants versus practicality. There is more to life than just a great career. Yet she has to get it right this time. *Think, Claudia. What do you want? Where should you go from here?* She needs to take a breath, calm down, not try to push an outcome. Most importantly, she needs to find out where Lucas stands in all this.

Her relationship with Lucas has happened so fast she needs to take it in steps, to make sure she isn't jumping the gun. Meet his parents, visit him at his workplace. They haven't done any of that so far. They have been in a little bubble, always at her house, behind her big iron gates. Alone. Private. Apart from members of her staff, nobody has even met him. A good test would be to go away for a weekend together. On neutral ground. He always comes to her place; they never go to his beach house because it is being remodeled, dust and workmen everywhere. He has shown her photos of the mess.

A weekend away together would be a great start, a good test to see how they get on, away from it all, just the two of them.

"Babe? Are you done? What are you doing in there?" Lucas is pounding on the bathroom door.

"Just a minute." Claudia runs the faucet and washes her hands. She dries them on a hand towel embroidered with her initials—something she picked up at a vintage store. She opens the door to find Lucas standing there, still waiting, lips turned down in a frown.

"Honey, what took you so long? I've been lonely."

Claudia hooks him around his neck and pulls her forlorn puppy-dog boyfriend in for a deep, lusty kiss. When she's finished, she speaks into his mouth. "Why don't we take a vacation?"

He pulls away slightly. "Like where?"

"Lake Tahoe? We could go for the weekend. Take a cabin in the woods?"

He cocks his head to one side like a dog trying to understand a new word. Or maybe he is calculating something in his mind, weighing up the pros and cons of going on a minibreak.

"Okay," he finally agrees, pulling down his slacks and setting his hard-on free. "Whatever you want, babe, just... give me another one of those sexy kisses again."

# FORTY

## CLAUDIA

The weekend in Lake Tahoe is sublime. The azure waters and epic hikes amid the pine trees and the fresh air make for the perfect getaway. They stay in the less touristic West Shore, where from some overlooks they can see more than fifty feet deep, down into the shimmering crystal waters. They take out some paddleboards, careful not to tumble into the ice-cold water. Even in late June, the alpine lake, fed by snowmelt, is not known for its swimming.

On the second day, they head out in kayaks. The peace and quiet is blissful. The sound of each other's laughter, the plopping of the paddle in the water making ripples as they glide along. Lucas is different from everybody she has ever known. There is a lightness of being about him. A buoyancy. Like a cork that never sinks. He doesn't take anything too seriously. She loves this about him. He takes the heaviness out of her and throws it to the breeze. If she talks about how hard her upbringing was, being raised by a single mom, how her father abandoned them, he says things like, "You are who you are because of that and that's a beautiful thing." Or "Embrace the moment, babe. We're here together, and that's incredible. We are *alive*!" There's something addictive about Lucas, in the sweetest possible way. He takes her pain away, because when she is with him, she forgets herself. She imagines how this could be her future. Simple. Uncomplicated. Lucas would make a great dad, because he has a childlike quality about him. He sees the today. There are no lurid tomorrows for him. No angst about the future.

It's as if Claudia has discovered her own personal universe with him, far away from work, from the city, from everyday demands. It's just the two of them, alone and together. The cabin, set amidst the woods above the lake, is rustic, and although it's summer, they light a fire in the evenings. They roast marshmallows and drink heady red wine. A huge wool-pile rug on the hearth makes it movie-worthy: the clichéd scene where the couple make love in front of a roaring fireplace?—that is them.

Orgasms can make you lose your mind. Literally. Claudia knows this because she played a human biologist in a movie one time. The lateral orbitofrontal cortex—the part of the brain that is responsible for reason—becomes less active during sex. In fact, it can make you temporarily lose your memory, suffering (well... not "suffering" exactly) from transient global amnesia. Still, even knowing these facts, this does not deter Claudia from making certain impaired judgments, which she only sees as impaired later, when it is impossible to turn back the clock.

People always assume decisions are actively made, but they can just as easily be *not* made, for example moments in time where the brain relaxes and decides no action is necessary. Claudia is not the first and certainly won't be the last to let herself be the victim of rash decision-making when it comes to a partner.

If Claudia has been floating on clouds during the weekend

in Lake Tahoe, the following week has her plummeting to earth, aware that the clouds are nothing more than vapor. She is free-falling, with nobody to catch her.

Lucas becomes more unavailable. Busier with work. The more she calls, the more elusive he is. She wonders if that silver ring she bought him, a skull with turquoise eyes, was a bad omen.

This is not what she expected.

Minnie is due to start working for Fox & Co. Claudia did not initially appreciate how it was to her own personal advantage that Minnie was working for Lucas. All she had considered was Minnie herself. But now she sees it might be useful. Minnie can let Claudia know what his movements are.

"Is Minnie your real name?" Claudia asks her after her first day at work.

"No. But it's what my family has always called me. Like Minnie Mouse. My brother couldn't pronounce Jasmine, and Minnie stuck. When people call me Jasmine, I forget they're talking to me."

"Jasmine's your real name then?"

Minnie nods.

"It's a beautiful name. You need to get serious, Minnie. Call yourself Jasmine and dress more formally. You're working in a lawyer's office. You can't wear miniskirts and flash off all those ear piercings. You need to wear a suit, or at least some black slacks and a blouse. Or an elegant skirt. What happened to the blouses I gave you?"

"They look weird on me. Really beautiful, and thanks, but not really my style."

"We'll go shopping next week and get some cool outfits, okay? Ones that are right for you. This job's your lucky break. It could lead to better things. Lucas knows people in the industry. If you work hard and follow his lead, things could really work out for you."

Telling Minnie to follow Lucas's lead is Claudia's first mistake.

# FORTY-ONE

## MINNIE

I am so freakin pumped! First day on the job and I feel like I own LA. Finally, I belong here. I can call my parents and let them know I HAVE A REAL JOB!

When I told Mom Claudia Spector was my friend she was like, yeah right. Nobody believes me. It's so weird. I mean, like they believe I've met her but cannot believe she's my actual friend and we hang together. But Claudia told me to play it down and promise not to talk about it to other people. Made me swear on the Holy Bible that I would never ever talk to the media and never ever post anything on TikTok. I respect her too much and no way would I risk my friendship with her. I am literally over the freakin moon. I live in LA and I have a real job!!!!!! And a megawattage movie star as my friend. It's insane!

But now Amelia's mad. I think she's jealous, but that's so not my problem because she basically ditched me to hang out with Mike. And Claudia kind of felt sorry for me (I think). And now Mike is kind of ghosting her and Amelia suddenly wants to do stuff with me. We'll see. I did feel a little used by her, but I am so not the type to hold a grudge. And I guess if it hadn't been for Amelia I wouldn't've gotten to meet Claudia and wouldn't've gotten the job at Fox so I'm super grateful. And now I can pay Claudia back for my rent, although it'll take me a while. Not that she has asked me, but Mom says it's the right thing to do, so I'm trying to save money. Make my rent and car payments. But it's so expensive in LA. Like gas and food. Thank God for Taco Bell. I'm living on bean burritos cos it's cheaper than cooking. Or maybe I'm just lazy?

# FORTY-TWO

## MINNIE

So.

Work. Hmm. I dunno where I fit in. Mr. Fox is super friendly and has told me to call him Lucas. Fine. But old Mr. Fox? His dad? Lucas has warned me to keep out of his way. Very weird. And now I'm kind of worried my job is even serious but then Lucas has given me cash to buy things like supplies and stuff and tells me to keep the change—which is sometimes thirty dollars or more—so I know he can afford to pay me. He made me sign a non-disclosure agreement. Like what I see and hear here in the office stays in the office. For clients' protection. No problem. My job so far is running around doing small chores, but doing nothing in particular. Like he's trying to invent something for me to do but he hasn't come up with a real job yet. Maybe that would be cool for some people, but I don't like it. It's boring. Today I answered the phone and took messages. Oh, and get this. There was a photo inside his desk that I found in a frame of him with a woman with his arm around her. His wife, right? Who is dead, he told me. But then? The phone rings and when I ask who it is, she tells me she's his wife. Ava.

When Lucas gets back from lunch (I think with Claudia) the conversation goes something like this:

"Hey, Mr. Fox... I mean, Lucas. How was lunch?"

"Great, Minnie. Thanks."

"Where did you go?"

"Spago."

"With Claudia?"

"No. A client."

"Your wife called."

He goes white. "My wife?"

"Ava. A woman who said she was your wife."

"Shit." He goes silent and looks pretty freaked out. Like I've caught him with his hand in the cookie jar. "Look. Minnie. It's not what you think."

"What do I think?"

He gives me a half smile. "Don't be smart."

"No. Seriously. I dunno what the deal is. What should I be thinking? Or saying?"

"You should not be *saying* anything to anyone." Then he comes over to my desk and takes me by the hand. "Minnie," he says. "Minnie. Oh, Minnie." He scrunches up his face like he's in pain.

"What?"

"My wife and I are... look we're not really together but..."

I can already see he's lying. "What should I tell Claudia?"

"What? Claudia? You do not tell her anything. Jesus. Minnie. You keep your mouth shut about Ava. Okay?"

I frown. Look at him like he's a jerk. Which he clearly is. Claudia's my friend. Claudia got me this job. I shake my head with a no. "I can't do that. It feels wrong."

"Shit," he says again. "Remember, Minnie, you signed an NDA."

"Yeah, but that was about clients and stuff. This is personal."

"Still. You signed."

"So. What are you gonna do? Sue me?"

"Christ. What was I thinking?" He starts mumbling to himself. Like he's only just twigged that me and Claudia are friends and she got me the job and of course I'd find out about his wife within minutes of working here. How dumb can someone be? He *is* kind of dumb. A cliché dumb blond. I mean maybe he's a good attorney? But I kind of doubt it. The guy hasn't got any common sense.

"Minnie. Oh shit. Look. My wife is ill. Like mentally ill. Really ill. If you tell Claudia then Claudia might confront her and she... look... anything could happen. Ava's been in psychiatric care before. In a hospital. Like a mental breakdown. You get it? She cannot know about Claudia and so Claudia cannot —*cannot*—know about her."

"So why did you start dating Claudia?"

"Minnie." He looks at me with his big blue eyes like I'm not getting it. "She... she... came on to me and I caved. Who wouldn't? Please. I beg of you. Please keep this between us."

I don't reply.

"It will hurt both of them. Please. Minnie. Have a heart."

*A heart?* "Excuse me?"

"Look. Minnie." His voice goes into a whisper. "I'll pay you a bonus."

"Like a bribe to keep me quiet?"

"It's not like that. It's—"

"I feel badly for both of them."

"Me too! You think I like the situation? My wife mentally ill? On the edge? Claudia would go insane with jealousy. My wife might..." He starts pacing around the room. "Please, Minnie."

"You need to choose between them. I guess a wife should get priority over a girlfriend, right? Even if Claudia's my friend."

He shakes his head in denial. "Anyhow, it's over between Claudia and me."

"Err, I don't think she knows that, Lucas."

"She will. Soon. Is five thousand dollars enough?"

"You'll give me five thousand dollars if I keep my mouth shut?"

"Yes."

I let out a great big sigh. "Then I'll feel even guiltier."

"It's a way of saying thank you so nobody gets hurt."

"I dunno."

"Seven thousand dollars."

"Seriously?"

"Seriously."

"When will you pay up?"

He narrows his eyes. "How can I trust you?"

I raise a brow. "Excuse me? I think I should be asking the same question."

"Do you always speak to your bosses this way? I should fire your cocky ass."

"Fire away. Doesn't look like I have a legitimate job anyways. Why did you even hire me in the first place?"

"Good question. I wasn't thinking. Shit. Damn it!"

I consider my options. Seven thousand bucks on the line. If I get fired, I'll have nothing. Claudia may end up hating me because... what's that expression about shooting the messenger? "I'll think about it," I tell him.

"No. No thinking about it, Minnie. You need to let me know now if you're on my side."

"On your side like I agree with what you're doing? Two-timing? Or on your side about the seven thousand?"

"Boy, you have a smart mouth."

"Just asking."

"Are you willing to keep quiet if I give you compensation?"

"All right," I say with an eye-roll.

"Promise?"

"I promise. You promise, too? To give me the money?"

"Sure. If you keep quiet, sure."

"Okay."

"We have a deal?"

"We have a deal."

We shake hands.

I think I have just made a deal with a devil.

# FORTY-THREE

## MINNIE

Claudia calls me a few weeks later. Not to see how I am or to hang out, but to get info on Lucas. I am in such a crappy position. And now I'm getting the impression she suggested me for the job just so I could spy on Lucas. Which is so not cool. Both of them are behaving like assholes.

Amelia is back with Mike. I'm in LA with a job I hate. Being bribed. Used. And now I think I want to go back home. One day of rain in this place is all it takes to make you realize LA is not the paradise you think it is. Everybody uses everybody. I paid Claudia back my two months' rent, paid off a chunk of my credit card and now I'm up five hundred dollars in guilt money, but still have my car payments, so cannot leave this job. I'm no better than them.

Claudia wants to know where Lucas is going and who he's seeing. I so want to say, *He's married, duh! His dead wife is alive!* But I don't. I feel depressed. Down. Shitty. I've sold my soul and I want to go home. And OH! Big news. Ava popped by the office. Guess what? She's not a crazy suicidal nutjob. She is normal. She's a script supervisor. Has a normal job. She's pretty too. In my opinion she's more beautiful than Claudia. Dark wavy hair. Big brown eyes. Not skinny and neurotic like Claudia. I told Ava my name was Jasmine because I wanted to look professional because I knew she was looking at me like what the hell is this person's job and what's she doing here, and I agree. What the hell is my job and what am I doing here? Here meaning the office and here meaning LA.

Claudia isn't inviting me to do stuff anymore. Like I was her plaything and now she's bored with me. It's like she planned the whole thing. Got me into this office to spy. Am I being paranoid? Or maybe she senses something's off? Maybe she knows I know something and that's why she's being offhand with me. Whatever. The result's the same. I'm alone. No friends. No family. I miss my mom. I miss my ex-boyfriend. I want to go back east where I belong.

I'm so confused. So lonely. At home in my apartment I eat ramen noodles alone watching Netflix alone or crap on TikTok alone which makes me depressed seeing how everyone else has such freaking great lives and I'm such a failure. When Claudia wanted to hang out I was on top of the world and now she doesn't give a shit about me. Ditto Amelia. Because now Amelia and Claudia are doing stuff together and not inviting me along. Lucas is the only one who's being friendly. Too friendly. Lechy in fact. He's been coming on to me lately. Touchy feely. But it's nothing I can't handle. And I can use it to my advantage, seeing as he's so light-fingered—with bribes too. Actually he makes me laugh. The only thing that makes me laugh these days. I might even consider him if he was single. But he has two relationships. So he can shove his wandering fingers right up his ass.

"Minnie babe." Lucas leans over my desk. I finally have something serious to do. I'm sorting out his Excel spreadsheets to get them in alphabetic order. Arranging his files so they make sense so he can find them more easily. I'm really into AI and it's amazing what it can do. Lucas is impressed with my work and says clichéd stuff like, "You're not just a pretty face." He's actually been real kind to me. Asks me how I'm doing every day. Even took me surfing one time. And okay I do see what the fuss is about. When he puts the attention on you it's like you're the only woman in the world. But no. He's my boss. No way will I be sucker number three. Plus he's too old for me. And maybe there are even more women in addition to Claudia and his wife. I wouldn't put it past him if he's bagging others too outside his marriage and his affair with Claudia.

"You're doing great, babe," he says with a grin.

"I'm not your babe."

He winks at me. "You are to me. You look cute today. Love that little tartan skirt."

"Everybody tells me to change the way I dress."

"Don't change a thing, Minnie Mouse. Your legs are total eye candy." He licks his lips. Looks me up and down. So subtle. *Not*. The bulge in his suit pants says it all. "It's so great to come to the office every morning, Min. And see those gorgeous legs. It lifts my spirits, you know?"

I remind him that what he is doing is sexual harassment and I could sue his ass. He looks sheepish for a second then goes on to tell me about the saga with his dad and the Japanese client, da dee da de da. Yawn yawn. I'm only half listening. Lucas loves to complain and I'm supposed to sympathize and nod and be a great listener. I play along. Six more months of this and I'm gone. I'm going back to Buffalo. I'm done with this place. I don't even like the sun anymore. I pray for rain. It's roasting here in summer. But like I said, when rain does come you see Los Angeles for what it is. A pit of snakes and ugly boxy buildings with no soul in a mass of traffic jams. There is no heart to LA. Not even Downtown has a heart. Just one big mass of urban rot spread over hundreds of miles dotted here and there with millionaire/billionaire enclaves like Bel-Air and Hancock Park or the best part of Laurel Canyon where Claudia lives. Ritzy places where I will never get to live. Walking in LA is not the same as walking in a real city. Everyone drives everywhere because this place is so big. There is no intimacy. The other day a policeman threatened to arrest me for jaywalking. Seriously. You can't even cross the road freely. Lucas lets me drive his Lexus to do errands so I can't complain. Still. I swear I feel like killing someone. I have this rage inside me that I can't explain and now I get why angry people end up being shooters. I feel like getting a gun and going on a rampage. I won't. Of course I won't. But that's how I feel inside.

I want to scream the world down.

I am *angry*.

I am so fucking angry and I don't know why.

# FORTY-FOUR

## MINNIE

I did a dumb thing. Ava's been away. Working or something. Sounds like Lucas is scared of his wife. Claudia has stopped calling me so maybe their relationship is on again. Who knows. I don't even ask. Best not to know. Anyhow, Lucas instructed me to go pick up the dogs from their kennels in Topanga and bring them back to his house ready for Ava when she gets home, so she doesn't have to schlep up there in the traffic at rush hour since he doesn't have time but he promised her he would go himself.

Fine. Mission accomplished. Dogs back home and happy.

So. I'm in their bedroom checking out Ava's wardrobe and okay I tried on a cashmere sweater for fun and the doggies are excited to be home and I'm fooling around with them and they're jumping on the bed barking and I hear someone coming so I rip the sweater off over my head but it's tight and I'm stuck in this article of clothing and I feel an earring catch. I shake out the sweater and the earring isn't there and there isn't time to hunt around and I stuff the sweater in the closet and race out of the room, nearly crashing into someone, thinking it's Ava but it isn't.

It's the cleaning lady.

I try to make excuses so I can hang around longer and find the earring but she's not buying it. She has the vacuum cleaner in one hand and the nozzle in another and she's like "I need to clean this room please go downstairs and take the dogs with you." She is a scary older lady with steely eyes and a foreign accent and makes me feel like I have to obey her.

So I do.

Now there's a stray earring of mine lurking around somewhere in the thick pile carpet in Lucas and his wife's bedroom. With any luck the cleaning lady will vacuum it up and that'll be the end of it. It isn't valuable just a zirconia hoop I bought at Claire's for ten bucks.

It's still ten bucks though.

Oh and I have Lucas's mother spying on me on top of everything else. Seems like she knows about Claudia and is not happy. She came to the office the other day and cross-questioned me about her. Called her a tramp and said Mr. Fox is very unhappy about her too. They know where Claudia lives! How do they know that? I swear to God I think Mrs. Fox has been trailing Claudia because she even knows what kind of car she drives. She told me that Lucas has denied dating Claudia. Pretends he hardly knows her. Told his mom she was imagining it, so she wanted to hear the truth from me. I said I had no idea. Another person who told me to dress better. I am so over grownups bossing me around when I'm a grownup myself.

Fast-forward to a day later and all hell has broken loose about the freaking earring. Which I had warned Lucas about. Which apparently Ava found like an hour after she arrived home. Which the cleaning lady had not vacuumed up which must mean she isn't very good at her job. Or she's *too* good at her job. Maybe she found it herself and thought it was real diamond and is super honest. Lucas could've told his wife the truth but no. My boss is not capable of telling the truth. He's a pathological liar. About small things. About everything.

He can. Not. Tell. The. Simple. Truth. It's like he lives and breathes for lying. He feeds off lies.

"You know how to do Photoshop, right?" Lucas asks me back in the office.

"Sure."

He dings me a photo of Ava in a red dress and it arrives in my messages. "Get rid of the earrings she's wearing in this picture and replace them with your earrings. The earring that ended up in my house."

"*What?*"

"You heard me."

"I can't just—"

"Do it, Minnie. You got me into this mess, now get me out of it. And make it look realistic."

He has no clue. "You think this is easy?" I say. "I need to find a picture of me wearing my earrings, get the proportions and the angle right and get rid of the shadows on her neck of the old earrings she's wearing and... listen, Lucas, it's not as easy as you think."

"Just do it. Send me the doctored pic when you're done. It had better look authentic."

Five minutes later, Claudia calls, trying to scoop me for info about where Lucas is and what he's up to. Clearly he has not called her lately. She asks me for his home address. I tell her I don't know. I feel like blabbing the whole story. That his wife isn't dead, but very much alive. That Lucas has been lying to them both about everything. That his psycho mother knows where she lives and she should watch her back. I should save Claudia the heartache of her being so into a guy who behaves like a spoiled child and is deceiving everyone.

He is a serial liar.

A sex addict.

She should know. So should Ava. Claudia would freak out big time. I know her. She's super proud. I can't even imagine how salty she'd get if she discovered the man who's been living rent-free inside her head all this time is such a jerk. Worse, I cannot believe I'm helping him be such a jerk. But I still have debts and need the money and he's my boss so what can I do?

When the photo is done Lucas gets me to go to the printers and get it printed up. Find a silver frame. Frame it. Display it on his desk as if it's a permanent feature. Next thing I know his wife is at the office. I manage to avoid her. Slip out before she notices me. Talk about feel guilty as hell. First his mother now the wife. I am tangled in his web of lies and family intrigue.

A few weeks later Lucas makes me do a whole bunch of photoshopping again. This time not just one photo but a whole series. Changing backgrounds and locations. Using old photos of Ava—some in a bikini some in a dress—transplanting her from Malibu to the Caribbean. Beaches, a five-star hotel. This time I do it on my phone with a photo editing app using location presets and a background eraser tool. Swapping one background over for another, I superimpose the Caribbean backdrop. Adjust the exposure and saturation. Probably very obvious and a little artificial if you look closely but at this point I don't even care. Why is Lucas pretending they were on vacation when they weren't? I have no clue. If I ever question him he tells me I'm being sassy so I have given up asking what the hell is going on. Like I said he is such a *Liar Liar Pants on Fire*. He must get a kick out of spinning tales.

I have never felt like such a bad person and so ashamed of my actions. If I'd had any idea being a personal assistant was going to be this sketchy there's no way I would've gotten into this situation in the first place. I feel like a villain. I'm really beginning to hate the guy. Totally using me to trick and lie to his wife. And he's screwed up my relationship with Claudia because I can't look her in the face and lie so I don't even call her anymore. I did tell him as much. Said I refused to do more photos, but he bribed me again with a bonus. I guess that makes me just as guilty as him.

Like I said. I have sold my soul to the devil. A blond womanizing devil with blue eyes who hides behind a cute smile and a big wallet.

When my car's paid off then I'm getting out of this dump of a town.

I'll keep my mouth closed about what Lucas has done. About what I've done.

For now.

When I leave the office for the day I drive down to the beach and yell my lungs out.

I can't take this shit anymore.

# FORTY-FIVE

## CLAUDIA

*Keep your enemies close.*

Claudia is watching *All About Eve* for the twentieth time. The Bette Davis film about a young starlet, Eve Harrington, who Bette Davis's character, Margo, takes under her wing, yet Eve then betrays her, usurping Margo's theatrical career, snatching her best life away from her in the "sweetest" most ingenious way, right from under Margo's nose. One of those people nobody suspects until it is too late. A clever conniver. An operator who works at the expense of others. Others who have stuck their necks out for her.

After all Claudia has done for Minnie. Minnie, it is clear, is having an affair with Lucas. The way she's so cagy and secretive about him. The way, coincidentally—after Minnie started working for Lucas—he started becoming inconsistent with his calls to Claudia. Hot and cold. Not answering her calls and texts. Giving her sporadic, intermittent attention. Sometimes being loving, and then... nothing. Her niece, Amelia, has confirmed it too. Has told Claudia that she's ninety-nine percent sure Minnie is sleeping with Lucas because of the way

Minnie's behaving, and the way she goes beetroot in the face whenever his name is mentioned.

What a fool Claudia has been! Minnie isn't a sweet innocent girl, but a user, an opportunist and, unlike Claudia, probably opening her legs for Lucas whenever he clicks his fingers. Minnie is an easy target. She won't be thinking about starting a family with him or caring about meaningful conversations. She'll be using him to get ahead, just the way he's probably using her. For sex. Wow, Minnie fits into the stereotypical Hollywood mold perfectly. She has no doubt lied about not wanting to be an actress too. Next thing, she'll probably see Minnie on primetime TV in a starring role.

She doesn't blame Minnie, per se. Minnie is young, impressionable. But, boy, does her betrayal sting. Claudia had felt like her older sister, her mentor. All that time she invested in the girl. Taking her under her wing. The movies they'd watched together. The long drives and visits to museums, Minnie helping Claudia pick out a wig and disguise. She felt so much closer to Minnie than to her niece, her own flesh and blood. She wants to find Minnie and shake her. Knock some sense into her. *Lucas is a user!* The betrayal burrows its way into her psyche. Yet another failed relationship.

*Oh, Minnie, honey, what have you gone and done?*

It's been a long day trailing Minnie's movements. Claudia waits for her outside Lucas's office. Minnie is wearing her signature short skirt and combat boots, and a long, flowing coat embroidered with flowers. Claudia needs to see with her own eyes. She needs proof because she still can't believe Minnie would hurt her this way.

It isn't easy following someone in your car. You need to stay close enough not to lose them, and far enough away so it isn't obvious. They make it look so simple in the movies. She has even shot scenes like this, but in real life, with traffic and drivers who cut you up on the roads, and traffic lights everywhere, it is nerve-rackingly tricky. First, the trip took her all the way to Topanga, where Minnie picked up Sappho and Ariadne from doggie daycare. Then the trip continued through Topanga Canyon all the way down to the PCH to Lucas's beach house. Claudia cannot believe what an idiot she's been. Lucas had shown her all these photos of his house in the throes of being remodeled. Told her how the contractors had at least three more months to go before they were done. Lies! There are no workmen around, no signs of building work. The house is perfect! No debris like in the photos. In fact, the photos he showed her were not even of the same house!

As for Minnie, not only is Minnie strutting around in a miniskirt and driving his Lexus like she owns it, but she also has the keys to his house. The miniskirt thing really bugs Claudia. After all those pretty outfits she gave her. Thousands of dollars' worth! The friendship she thought they shared. Lucas is screwing Minnie with her long, twenty-two-year-old legs... of course he is. Being a movie star does not give Claudia precedence over pretty young things. Youth always triumphs in Hollywood, doesn't it? Lucas has moved on. Minnie is fresh, tender meat. To think that Claudia has wasted so much energy fantasizing about starting a family with him when he is clearly getting his rocks off elsewhere! No wonder he kept putting her off about meeting his parents.

*What the hell!*

But now Claudia remembers how Lucas has told her about problems at work lately, that he's distracted, stressed. Maybe there's some mistake, some puzzle piece she isn't seeing? Is it possible she's jumping to conclusions? Minnie wouldn't do this to her. Or would she? Perhaps this house belongs to someone else? A friend of Lucas's who is babysitting the dogs? Crystal treated Claudia so badly, maybe she's being paranoid, expecting the worst?

No! No! No! Claudia is looking at Lucas's beach house

before her, it has to be. Why would Minnie pick up the dogs from daycare only to dump them at a neighbor's? Plus, why would she have a neighbor's key to their house? This is definitely not the house in the photos, true, but Claudia knows, just knows that house was a ruse. Did he get them from stock photos online?

The *effort* it takes to spin all these lies! Isn't telling the truth a whole lot easier? If he has lied about this, he could be lying about anything, right? For whatever reason, he did not want Claudia to come to his house. And certainly, a beach house in Malibu is nothing to be ashamed of. What is he hiding?

There's only one way to find out what is going on. Ask Minnie herself. Claudia will be able to tell if she's lying by looking into her eyes. She hasn't seen Minnie for a while, partly because Claudia's been busy with work, partly because Amelia was jealous ("I'm your niece, why are you hanging out with my friend instead of me?"), and partly because Minnie sounded so shifty and evasive about Lucas every time they had spoken on the phone.

Now is not the moment to confront her. She'll invite Minnie over to dinner. Talk this through in a calm, reasonable manner.

Later, she calls but Minnie doesn't answer, and when she sends Roger around to her apartment to pick her up in the limo, Minnie isn't at home.

# FORTY-SIX

## CLAUDIA

It is now September. Two months have flitted by and Minnie is still avoiding Claudia's calls, answering her texts in monosyllables. Claudia feels like a car with a punctured tire. A sports car Minnie was riding around in for fun—a joy ride—which she abandoned when it no longer served her needs. To help her process the betrayal, Claudia has shifted all her energy into work. She has been on location in New York these past two months, in the sweltering heat, filming *Cat's Cradle*. Work, as usual, has been her balm, her medicine.

Finishing up on the movie, and hardly back home in LA for a day, Claudia gets a call from Lucas, who has been silent for six weeks or so. As if he can smell her presence, sniff out her still unhealed wound.

"Hey, babe," Lucas chirps in a midnight phone call. "Sorry I've been so unavailable lately."

"That's an understatement," Claudia snipes, wishing she could be more laissez-faire about the whole thing. While she was away in New York, she had hoped she'd be able to wipe Lucas out of her head. It had vaguely worked.

Vaguely.

But not completely. He is now a part of her life whether she likes it or not.

Claudia has tried her best to block them both out. Lucas and Minnie. And now Lucas is calling her again as if nothing has happened? Like they are still on! So much has changed in that time. She has been itching to call him, but how can she consider a relationship with a man who has been, a) ghosting her and b) in all likelihood cheating on her?

*Screw him.*

Claudia still hasn't gone to bed. She was engrossed in a script her agent sent over when the phone rang. The part, of an eighteenth-century prostitute—or, as she prefers to say, sex worker—is interesting. A role she could really get her teeth into. Even though she's awake, she does not appreciate it when people call late, on principle, unless it's an emergency. After nine at night and before nine in the morning is impolite, especially when it's probably a booty call.

Lucas's voice sounds irritatingly upbeat. "So sorry I haven't called, babe. I miss you. I need to see you."

Despite herself, Claudia feels her insides churn. She has missed this lying son of a bitch too. When she lets people into her heart—which isn't very often—she cares too much. Lucas has gotten to her in more ways than one.

She is about to rail at him. Better, though, to see him in the flesh, in situ, while he lies to her face. Ask him about Minnie. Look into his eyes. See for herself. She is ninety-eight percent sure he is sleeping with her. Hence his silence lately. Hence Minnie's silence. A double betrayal of trust. But what if he isn't? That two percent doubt niggles at her. She so wishes there might be an explanation and supposes she needs to give him an opportunity to explain himself, just on the off chance. There is nothing worse than being accused of lying when you aren't. She owes him that much. She can't decide what to do.

"How's it working out with Minnie?" she asks him now,

wishing the words hadn't left her lips. *Better to see his reaction in person.*

"Babe, why are you asking me about work in the middle of the night?"

*Work?* His response takes her aback. She retorts, "Lucas, you can't just call out of the blue after, what... six weeks, especially at this hour, and expect me to be at your beck and call!"

"Honey." He doesn't say more. The "honey" sounds sweet to her ears, damn him.

"I think you owe me an explanation about your beach house," she throws out.

"My *house*?"

"You never invited me because you told me it was being remodeled, that there were workmen all over the place, that there were piles of cement and sand everywhere. And the photos you showed me didn't even look like your real house anyhow."

A beat of silence.

Then Lucas answers, without taking her question on board. "Claudia, you want to see me or not?"

She isn't going to let him off the hook so persists with her question. "Tell me about your house, why don't you?"

"*What*? What the hell is this?"

She reels off his address. Why is it that this conversation is running away with her, dragging her dignity along with it? Not what she wants at all.

"Have you been *following* me or something?"

She doesn't answer.

"Jesus." Lucas groans. "That is so uncool. Claudia, seriously? This is not like you at all."

Her mouth has no filter tonight. She blabs out, "You're sleeping with Minnie, aren't you?"

A roar of laughter. But the laughter sounds forced. "I can't believe you'd think that. You know what? I don't need this shit,

Claudia. All I wanted was to see you. Have a good time. And you're, like, going all psycho on me. I can't deal with this. I don't need this."

"Fine. I'll call Minnie and ask her right now." Claudia ends the call. *Going all psycho on him?* How dare he? Throwing her phone on the couch where it lands with a soft bounce amid the pillows, she can practically feel her blood about to boil over. Nobody treats her this way! Seriously, *nobody*... no one has dissed her like this for... she can't even remember how long. How *dare* he treat her like... like some random woman he was screwing in an on/off relationship! Like some fuck buddy or something. She is *Claudia Spector*! Studio heads, powerful directors, and producers treat her like... like the star she is. And Lucas is some dumb, two-bit attorney walking all over her! Or trying to, at any rate. She will *not* be his doormat!

She sits on her couch, fuming, her breath coming hot and hard. She is about to dial Minnie. But it's nearly one o'clock in the morning. And Minnie won't answer anyway. She gets thinking about Lucas's house. Why is he harboring secrets concerning his house? What's the big deal? Something doesn't sit right with her. At all. It flashes into her mind then straight out again. His wedding band. No. That doesn't make sense.

Or does it?

Fishing her sneakers out from under the couch, she jams her feet into them, frantically doing up the laces, breaking a nail in the process. "Fuck! Fuck, fuuuuuuuuck!" Her yells ring through her empty house. Her heart is palpitating... with anger, with indignation. For a second, ever the professional actress, she clocks her behavior. Useful for future scenes. She could tap into this feeling of frustrated wrath. Her stomach in knots, her eyes burning with rage, her hands visibly shaking.

*Stay home, stay home, don't be an idiot. Let sleeping lawyers lie.*

*Lie* being the operative word.

But Claudia continues getting herself ready. Rampaging, stomping, disregarding her sensible inner voice that echoes through her head, trying its best to calm her ire. She grabs her purse from the kitchen, and a cardigan from the back of a chair. A bag of Doritos and her Thermos of water. Whatever warnings the voice inside her head counsels about driving to Lucas's house at this hour and humiliating herself, her physical being does not take heed.

She'll sit in her car all night if she has to.

She *has* to find out what Lucas's secret is.

# FORTY-SEVEN

## CLAUDIA

The family-size bag of Doritos is now empty. Corn-chip crumbs spill down her front, into the folds of her sweatpants and nestle in cracks all over her car seat, smushed into the carpeted floor by her feet. Tomorrow she'll probably break out in zits and ulcers. She's been an idiot not to eat a proper dinner, take care of herself. Considering all the delicious meals Juana prepares with such love and care, and all Claudia has to do is stick them in the microwave.

Claudia takes another slug of water, craving a Diet Coke instead and wishing she'd stopped at a gas station to load up on snacks and drinks. The Dorito binge has done nothing to placate her wrath. She longs for Hershey's, Starburst, sickly-sweet candy of her youth. She wants to stuff her face.

She continues her watch on the window. A woman who isn't Minnie lives in Lucas's house. It makes the Dorito binge rise in her throat, the dumb surprise of it—how has she been so clueless?—making her temples throb. By her comportment, the ease of the young woman's movements, the way she ambles around the room, it's obvious to Claudia that this person belongs here. She is not a girlfriend, nor a visitor. This woman moves in a way... hard to define, which is synonymous with the status of marriage. Lucas comes into shot, so to speak. He says something to her and she smiles and moves away from the window. Out goes the light. He has probably said, "Come back to bed."

The woman has to be Lucas's wife.

The wedding band. It was on his finger, plain as day, the morning Claudia and Lucas had met in the park in May. He told her his wife had passed away. When their gazes met there were tears in his eyes. She had taken Lucas at face value, believing he was who he said he was, the way people used to do before the internet took over the world, and before fake news, and before everyone became so cynical and suspicious of one another. She hadn't done a deep dive on him online because, unless she is doing research for work, she makes a point of not going down the social media rabbit hole.

Lucas is fake news all right.

Claudia, dumbstruck, her gaze glued to the window—no longer backlit but dark since the light is off—considers what she should do next.

Her jaw clamped tight, her fists unconsciously balled, she thinks with a sickening heart, *This could be me.* If she had succumbed to his request to hook up tonight: Lucas's warm lips on hers, lingering and hungry, hair mussed from making love. Them in the shower together, water sluicing down their backs, their hands all over each other, exploring every curve and crevice of the other's body. He knows she has a little scar on her left hip from a bicycle accident when she was a child. She has seen the white slash of scar across his butt from a wipeout with his surfboard. Intimate moments, intimate, shared secrets. Or when his gaze roamed the planes of her face, her eyes, her nose, while he told her how beautiful she was, how she had "stolen" his heart.

Stolen. The word has so much more meaning now, it's not just a cliché.

This man is playing with emotions like he's picking up a guitar one day only to change it for a flute the next, perhaps loving the instruments with equal measure. Are there others too? *Why didn't Minnie warn me he was married? Surely she must have known?* A tiny sob snatches a breath from her, followed by a whoosh of anger surging through her chest. Anger is good. She will not, *cannot* allow herself to feel wistful about this faux relationship based on nothing but lies and betrayal. She should simply drive home. If she has any sense of pride or self-preservation at all, this is absolutely what she should do. But that ball of fire in her heart cries out to be sated before it gets quenched. She hankers after some kind of closure. A finale.

*Lucas needs to be taught a lesson.*

The light goes on again. Why, she wonders, do people get undressed by lighted windows at night? Do they *want* to attract voyeurs? Have they not seen Martin Scorsese in his cameo role in *Taxi Driver*? Sitting in the back of the taxi, watching his wife, thinking and expressing horrible, violent thoughts? In the movie, the woman in the window is a silhouette, but Claudia sees so much more than a shadow now. For four whole minutes she observes a very attractive woman, around her age, possibly slightly younger. A woman whose silhouette shows she is wearing a baby-doll nighty. The kind women wear when pregnant.

She'll go to the door. Ring the bell. Confront Lucas. Tell the wife who she is: Lucas's lover. Or rather, ex-lover. It is over between them, that's for sure. It won't be a tit-for-tat tattletale revenge. No. This woman deserves to know the truth. Deserves to know her husband is a cheating, lying, deceiving... what's the right noun? Claudia is so incensed she can't think of the perfect word for him. Whatever it is, it deserves to be spray-painted on his Lexus. No, that isn't clever enough... the payback needs to be something he can't trace back to her.

She is so laser-focused on the window of the house, half waiting for Lucas or his wife to burst out of their home and ask her what the hell she's doing in their driveway, that when someone taps on her car window, her heart feels like it might explode. Terror grips her by the throat, she can hardly breathe, let alone scream. A face, pressed up and distorted against the glass, leers in at her. What is this, *Friday the 13th*? It is several seconds before she realizes who it is.

Crystal.

She, Claudia the stalker, is being stalked.

She cracks the window an inch. "What the hell, Crystal?" she hisses in a whisper.

Crystal might blow everything. In this moment it hits Claudia that, no, she will not confront Lucas in his own home. It's up to the wife to discover for herself what kind of person her husband is. The wife is not Claudia's friend; she does not owe this woman the truth. It's not Claudia's problem. She'll find another way to get even with the bastard.

"Open up." Crystal tries the door handle.

"No! Go away! What are you doing here?"

"What are *you* doing here?"

"It's a free fucking country."

Crystal jimmies the handle again. "Come on, Claudia, open up, let me in the car, I just wanna talk."

With an exasperated groan, Claudia releases the lock and starts the engine. Lucky for her, her car is electric and relatively silent. She does not want to make a scene after all. She has found out enough, seen the truth with her own eyes and now she needs to get the hell away and never look back. Crystal opens the door, slips sideways into the car, placing her small butt on the seat, her legs swiveling themselves into place as she clicks the door shut and snaps on her seat belt. "Drive," she says. "Before they see us here."

"They?" Claudia is aware there is a "they." She has seen it tonight up close and voyeuristically personal. But what does Crystal know that she doesn't? And why has her ex followed her here?

"That's why I kept *trying* to call you," Crystal emphasizes. "To *warn* you about Lucas. But you've evidently blocked me. The guy you've been dating is married."

"Yeah, I kind of got an inkling of that," Claudia responds sarcastically. "Where's your car?"

Crystal stretches out her legs. "I got an Uber here."

"You *followed* me?"

"Yep. I told the driver, 'follow that car' like they do in the movies." She lets out her silky laugh. "Funny how movies come to life sometimes. You ever notice that? How things play out in real life like on screen? *Minority Report* isn't far off. You watch."

"What do you want, Crystal?" Claudia pulls out of the driveway and heads off toward home. She doesn't trust Crystal, and to have her as a passenger in her car is the last thing she imagined would go down.

"I want for us to... well, at least be friends."

Claudia shakes her head vehemently. "We'll never be friends. Not after that stunt you pulled on Isabella's show."

"I don't know what got into me, sweetie. Please accept my apology." She sighs.

"A little late for that, don't you think? I can't believe you're even in my car. I can't believe I'm even speaking to you." It's late. Nothing Claudia has done this evening makes any sense. She's hungry. Tired. Her life feels out of control. Two disastrous romantic relationships resulting from her own personal picks, her own crap choices which have led her to where she is in this moment. Stalked by her ex while she was stalking a married man. It's a joke. The kind of story that romantic comedies are made of. Except this story's romance is all dried up. Worse, it was never there in the first place; the romance was in her head, a fabrication of her own imaginings, of her own desires. Neither Lucas nor Crystal love her for her. She has been used. Is *being* used still. By both of them. She is doomed to be alone forever. She can rely on herself financially, but emotionally? It's tough to be a one-woman show. But she guesses that is what lies ahead. She'll manage. She always has and always will.

"Where are we going?" Crystal asks.

"I don't know. I'm starving. I could really use a hot meal. Canter's, I guess. Or there's a new place open late in Thousand Oaks that's closer."

"Okay, I'm up for that."

Claudia snickers. Crystal has some nerve. "I'm not exactly inviting you."

Crystal lays a hand on her knee. "We need to talk."

Claudia shoots her ex a sneer. "No, we don't need to talk. There's nothing to discuss."

"Please."

Claudia disengages Crystal's hand. "Tell me about Lucas, since you seem to know so much."

"He's an attorney."

"Duh, even I know that."

"He's married to a woman named Ava. She's a script supervisor. A big fan of yours, funnily enough."

Claudia laughs. "That *is* funny. Quite the ironic twist. She wouldn't be a fan if she knew I've screwed her husband. And you know all this, how?"

"Through my friend Sunny, who's also a script supervisor and pretty tight with her. Apparently Ava has always wanted to meet you. She even gushed about you a few months back in one of those women's magazines. *Marie Claire* or *Red* or something..."

"She's famous?"

"No. One of those 'day in the life of' kind of things. She's just a regular person. Pretty, though. I mean, *very* attractive. I delved into Lucas online when I found out you were seeing him. Then came across her on, like, page six of Google and then tracked down their Instagram page. Then, you know, found more stuff out from there. Seriously, I shoulda been a private detective instead of an actress. My latest movie's going to flop. I smell failure coming my way. Swing a left up ahead if you want to go to Thousand Oaks."

Claudia frowned. "Are you sure?"

"Yeah, there're roadblocks otherwise. Yesterday I was in a jam for hours. Trust me, hang a left."

Claudia can't even remember the route she took to get down here earlier; she was in an auto-pilot frenzy of fury. Taking a left doesn't make sense, but she does as she's told, too frazzled to disagree with Crystal, and she doesn't mind driving the extra miles anyhow. There's something therapeutic about driving at night. Usually Roger takes her everywhere. Being in the driver's seat makes a nice change. She buzzes her window down to let in a gust of fresh canyon air, which she needs to keep her awake and maneuver the switchback turns in the dark road. Despite herself, she's enjoying Crystal's company. How crazy is that? No, she is not about to let her ex back into her life again, but seeing her here in the flesh beside her, chatting away as if nothing in particular has happened, is actually okay. The genie is out of the bottle. Crystal does not look as beautiful to her anymore, does not make her insides jitter with butterflies. She is not as glorious and sexy as she remembered, not as special. To be honest, she seems a little burned out. Mascara smudged, her hair a straggled disarray, rings under her eyes. The two of them walking into a restaurant might stir up a lot of gossip. She is in a pretty sorry state herself. No makeup. Saggy old jogging pants and a ripped T-shirt. *What the cat dragged in*, both of them a mess. Somebody is bound to take a photo on their phone. Her stylist will freak out seeing all her hard work over the years undone in one fell swoop. Maybe Claudia doesn't even care anymore.

She thinks of Lucas, how he deserves payback for what he's done and how surprised he'll be to see the gossip, not that he probably gives a shit. She muses on all those lies so effortlessly spoken from his pretty-boy lips. But mostly, on how humiliated she feels for being such a dunce. *Humiliation really eats at you, gnaws at your soul*. It's the kind of emotion that takes up prime-time in your head. More than jealousy even. More than anger. She wishes she could let it go.

"What else do you know about Lucas's wife?" she asks Crystal.

"That she's pregnant. That she's very good at her job but wants to be a stay-at-home mom."

A wave of… not envy, but some gut-empty feeling equally as powerful washes over Claudia. Now she can add shame to her roster of emotions. Lucas's poor wife, expecting a baby while he is peacocking around behind her back and lying to everyone in the process. The hairs on her arms and neck bristle just thinking about it. She feels angry on her own behalf too. "And you know all this for sure?"

"Yeah, Sunny saw her recently."

"Does she know Lucas was cheating on her?"

"I don't know. If so, she never mentioned it. Does your car have a low tire?"

"Not that I know of."

"Well, next place that's safe to stop, better stop. Just in case and we can take a look. It feels bumpy to me. Plus, would you mind if I drive instead? You're making me super nervous on these bends."

They get out and trade places.

They never get to the restaurant with Crystal at the wheel.

# PART 3

## BEFORE

(One month before Claudia's disappearance)

# FORTY-EIGHT

## AVA

A purple September sky hovers low and heavy. The calm before the storm. I can sense it in the air. Something other than my pregnancy is brewing, but I can't say what. Lucas's affair with Claudia is never far from my mind, even though he promises it's over and has offered to destroy the prenup to show how dedicated he is to me, how strong our marriage is, and how he trusts me. He wants my pregnancy to go without a hitch this time around. Being a family man is all he talks about these days. He has begged my forgiveness, over and over. I *had* been considering it, weighing up the pros and cons... but last night, I saw a car pull out of our driveway and it made me question everything again.

Someone may be watching me. Or Lucas. Or both of us. And I'm pretty sure I know who that someone is.

When I get a call from "caller unknown," my suspicions are... if not confirmed, definitely piqued. Call me crazy, but I feel Claudia's presence. Somehow, I know she is still in the picture. Still a third wheel in our marriage.

Then Sunny calls. "All right, love, how's it going?" she asks in her usual chit-chatty way, her London accent always bringing a smile to my face.

We chat about work for a while and she regales me with stories about her extended family from India coming for a visit and how exhausted she is after the summer, but also how glad she is to no longer be living in London, how all her relatives are full of doom and gloom about the UK. *The grass is always greener*, I think. Then she tells me something that blows my mind.

"I think your wish may have come true," she announces, a grin in her voice.

I immediately think of Lucas. How I want our marriage to work. How I love him and would do anything for a stable home-life. This is what I have been wishing for. I wish for the good parts of Lucas without the bad. The Lucas I fell in love with who makes me laugh, feel nurtured and complete. This, I have been praying for and willing with all my heart.

"My wish?" I say.

"I was going to surprise you, but I thought I'd better give you the heads-up."

"What's this all about, Sunny?"

"You're a Claudia Spector fan, right? You're always banging on about how you want to meet her one day, how great you think she is."

It's as if Sunny is playing some prank on me. Like she's just punched me in the gut. A Claudia Spector fan? Not anymore, that's for sure. But it's true, I always had hoped I'd meet her one day. Sunny and I work in showbusiness. There has always been a faint possibility of meeting Claudia Spector on set. After all, I've met a ton of other movie stars over the years. I almost want to laugh at the irony of it all. I have not told a soul about Lucas and Claudia. "I think she's a great actor, yeah," I hedge. I have never mentioned Lucas's affair to Sunny. At this point, I have not mentioned it to one single soul, not even my neighbor Jill, who is also a *Go Ask Bobbie* fan.

"How would you like to meet her?" Sunny bursts out.

My body goes through a bunch of sensations that no words can properly describe. A free-falling of the heart? Butterflies swooping in and out of my stomach? My morning coffee coming up my esophagus? I can't even say. It's like my body is being assaulted in a medley of ways at the mention of Claudia Spector's name.

"You're kidding, right?" I check. "You met her on set?"

"No, nothing like that. I'm talking about meeting her for *real*, not just a hi, how do you do in passing."

I am racking my brains. Has Sunny got wind of Lucas and Claudia and this is her way of telling me? How could she possibly know? This cannot be a coincidence. People don't just call you up one day asking if you'd like to meet a world-famous movie star out of the blue. Has Lucas been going around boasting about his affair? He may be a jerk in many ways, but boasting isn't his style.

Sunny lets out a snort which is somewhere between a laugh and a giggle. "Not kidding. Crystal's a new friend of mine."

"We *are* talking about the same person, right? Crystal Cormac? Claudia Spector's girlfriend?"

"Claudia's ex, yeah. But they broke up."

"I had no idea you knew her."

"Yeah, we're friends. I mean, not bosom buddies, exactly, but I got to know her recently. Then I thought of you, how keen you've always been to meet Claudia."

"I read all about their breakup. I mean... I saw it. On TV. Crystal ditched her on Isabella Mox's show." My palms break out in a sweat. I set my mug of coffee down for fear it'll slip from my hands and go crashing to the floor. I put my phone on speaker.

"Well, they're friends again. I mean, they must be because Crystal asked me if we'd like to go over to Claudia's for dinner."

"Wait. Slow down. *Us*? For dinner?"

"Yeah. You and me."

"But why would she want to have total strangers over to her house for dinner?"

My heart is now racing, scampering. As if it's trying to run away like a rat on a sinking ship. A chaotic profusion of possibilities slams into my brain. What does Claudia Spector want? Does she know who I am? Does she want to win me over so she can get closer to Lucas? Or to get me out of the way, period? She certainly has the clout to do so. It flashes through my brain that she might want me dead. Or maybe she wants to pay me off so she gets to keep him for herself. Claudia Spector, inviting me —a relative nobody—to her house when she's screwing my husband? Something's wrong. Very, very wrong.

"Remember when you did that working woman piece?" Sunny asks.

"The one that wound up in *Woman's Style*?"

"Yeah, well, Crystal had read it and evidently told Claudia, and somehow they—"

"Sunny, let me stop you right there. As much as I'd love to feel flattered and excited to meet Claudia Spector and feel that it's *me* she wants to meet because I'm such a fascinatingly cool person, you need to know something very relevant." I pause to make sure she's actually listening.

"Which is?"

"Claudia Spector's fucking my husband."

"Lucas?"

"The very same husband, yes."

"No *way*!" She lets out a chortle of laughter.

"Yes way."

Sunny giggles, clearly thinking I'm kidding around. "You're taking the piss."

"I'm not. I found evidence and he admitted it to me."

Sunny gasps. "She's still seeing him?"

"He swears not. But... well, between you and me, Lucas... Lucas lies. I can't trust him."

"I'm so sorry, hon. I'm *so* sorry, I've always thought you two had a perfect marriage."

"It's okay. I mean, no, it's not okay, but we've sorted it out. He swears it's over between them."

"You think he's telling the truth?"

"I so want to believe he is." *And even if I don't, I'm stuck here anyway...*

"Yeah, well, this does make things a bit complicated. And weird."

"Telling me." I sigh into my phone. "So, yeah, I'd love to meet Claudia Spector. I mean, I think she's great, as you know. Or did. But now... I don't know if it's such a good idea."

"You're curious as hell, I bet?"

I let out a short, nervous laugh. "Curious, yeah, of course. But scared. What does she want from me? I'm a nobody. Why does she want to meet me? Keep your enemies close and all that?"

"To apologize to you?" Sunny's tone is tentative.

"You think? I don't know. Something's up, Sunny. But if we don't go meet her, we'll never know, I guess. Unless you can ask Crystal? Get a feel for what Claudia wants? Find out what her motive is?"

"Um... Thing is, I kinda already said yes. I assumed you'd jump at the chance. Crystal's coming to pick us up."

"When?"

"Six thirty this evening. We can meet at my house and we'll go with her together to Claudia's."

"Why can't we go in our own cars? Why do we have to get picked up?"

"Security, I suppose."

"Ha! Claudia's security, not ours. We get picked up, then we can't leave her house any time we want, can we? We'll be trapped there behind those iron gates without our cars."

"It's meant to be gorgeous."

"Yeah, Sunny, but it's not your husband she's been having an affair with. What if she wants to... I don't know... hurt me or something?"

"I doubt that. She's meant to be a really great person. Really friendly."

"It's all a bit weird."

"It is. You're right. But I still fancy going. Come on, it'll be a laugh. I'm dying to meet her!"

"Let me think about it."

# FORTY-NINE

## AVA

Women don't dress for men as much as people assume. But women do dress for other women. Especially ones we admire.

Or fear.

I burrow through my closet trying to find the perfect outfit. A dress and heels? No. What if I have to run for my life? But where to? I've read that *Vanity Fair* article a zillion times. There's a high iron gate at Claudia Spector's property. Which makes me assume there must be high walls to go with the gate or there would be no point. What happens if I need to escape? Am I being totally paranoid? Overthinking this? Sunny thinks so and has no qualms whatsoever about going for dinner. Me? I am visibly shaking as I get ready. I want to say no to this invitation. I feel like the girl going down into the basement in a horror movie. The irresistible draw into the unknown while everyone is yelling at the screen, *Don't be an idiot!* Or *Look behind you!*

I can't tell Lucas where I'm going. Obviously not. He would forbid it. Completely flip out if he knew. I can't risk letting him know, however tempted I am to throw it in his face. So, I simply told him that Sunny and I are going out to dinner. "A girls' night out to catch up," and when he asked where, I said I didn't know, that we'd decide on the fly. He's downstairs watching a movie, and I'm trying on, then ripping off, then hurling half my wardrobe onto my bed, outfit after outfit, feeling like I have "nothing to wear" while dresses and skirts and tops of every color and style are piling into a mini mountain. It's hot outside. I end up choosing white sneakers, shorts, and a pretty pink and green stretchy corset top, then swap the sneakers at the last minute for ballet flats. I can still run but at least I've added a touch of elegance to my otherwise oddball outfit. The corset top looks sexy. Ish. It shows off my tiny baby bump and my fuller than usual pregnant breasts. I want to give Claudia a clear message: You may be a movie star but I am just as hot as you are. Oh, and FYI, I happen to be pregnant with *my* husband's baby.

I'm so desperate to get my look just right I end up raiding Lucas's closet, grabbing a blazer of his that's kind of cutely oversized on me but somehow works. And to be honest, I suddenly feel ridiculous squeezed into this top, so hiding it with a huge blazer helps. I'm late and getting out of it is not an option right now unless I want to reach even higher levels of stress.

At the end of it all, looking at myself in the mirror, I don't know what to make of myself. Do I look ridiculous? Or super on trend? I have no idea, but I can't leave Sunny waiting any longer.

Crystal is sitting in her car outside Sunny's apartment, ready to take us to Claudia's house. She introduces herself, gliding her gaze over me briefly as if checking out the merchandise, and of course I suspect I must be either overdressed or underdressed. It's absurd that I feel more self-conscious meeting Claudia Spector than I ever have been with any boyfriend to date, even Lucas. This is not only about being starstruck, but nervous. Terrified, actually. What am I playing at? I keep asking myself why I am meeting a woman who was, and maybe still is, having an affair with my husband. Crystal has said nothing. Does she know about Claudia and Lucas's affair? Or is she being used as some kind of pawn? The whole thing feels bizarre. I want to ask her outright, but I don't.

The car moves off. I stare out the window in a daze. Suddenly, I want to go home. What I'm doing is off-the-charts reckless. I hate Claudia Spector for what she has done: barged her way into the middle of my marriage, stirred it up with a giant golden spoon with no thought to anyone but herself. She is a *movie* star, let's remember. She's used to people worshipping her. She probably always gets what she wants. Has she forgotten what it's like to be small? To be a normal person fighting for your family in this unjust world? Has fame made her so arrogant she can snap her fingers and summon the wife of a man she's been having an affair with to her side?

Well, yeah, clearly, she can. Because here I am.

I bet she wants to pay me off. As if love is a commodity that has a price. *Sorry, Claudia, I can't be bought.*

I am chiding myself for, as usual, not thinking things through. I want to break up this "happy" party. Beg them to turn the car around. They're laughing and gossiping while I sit alone and scared and angry with myself in the back of the car.

Sunny is in the front with Crystal, hooting with giggles. They're talking about people they know in common, all in showbusiness, nattering away to each other with no thought of me and my nerves. My mouth is dry, my brain overloading with ideas and possibilities about where this meeting will lead. Worse, where it might end. I cannot deny I have a temper when pushed. What if I lose it with Claudia? Who would blame me? I hate the word bitch, especially being a dog lover, but it's the word that comes to mind every time I picture Claudia Spector in the arms of my husband.

We approach the imposing gates of Claudia's home. Grabbing a pen from inside my purse and fishing around for something to write on—which turns out to be a matchbook from Chez Suzette—I scrawl out her address. I'm not quite sure why I do this. A memento to remember this evening by? A clue for police if they wind up discovering my body in a dumpster somewhere? A spit in the face to brandish to Lucas how I called his bluff and met the infamous Claudia Spector in her *home*! Or simply a way of remembering where she lives if I ever need to come back and stick a knife in her throat?

Sunny looks over her shoulder. "All right there, Ava?"

I nod. *But, no, I'm not all right.* "This is it? Her house?" I shove the matchbook in my jacket pocket, embarrassed in case I look like too much of a fangirl or a would-be stalker.

Crystal punches in a code on an intercom keypad hidden by a bush. "Yep. This is it." The way she says "this is it" makes my stomach fold over. It sounds so final. A double entendre. *This is it.*

*This is the end.*

The gates open and then speedily close behind us once the car is inside. Crystal heads up the driveway toward the house, which is white, broken up with dark timbering, sitting atop a hill. The style is French Tudor. We approach a huge stone fountain; the driveway curves around it. Crystal parks the car so its nose is facing away from the house and we get out. There is an instant feeling of serenity and peace behind these gates. Birdsong, the sound of the water in the fountain, the whisper of a warm breeze in the trees. Tall palms and Italian cypresses, two avocados, mango, and peach. The driveway is not asphalt but paved in real stone, with grass growing neatly in the cracks, thick and green, making it look like a natural chequerboard. I'm glad I didn't wear heels.

Now she is standing, I observe Crystal properly for the first time. She's not nearly as tall as I had imagined. Without her usual thick black eyeliner and mascara—her signature look—she's quite ordinary, quite unremarkable, not the siren you see on the screen. Her breasts are not larger than life either, but a regular size. She even has cankles. She is not an actor in the same caliber as Claudia, more of a "celebrity" so she is always on TV, often doing talk shows and commercials. She pretty much plays the same part over and over in movies: the bitch who turns out to have a heart of gold. In front of me now, all I see is a regular person who could be anybody. In fact, I probably wouldn't have even recognized her in a different context.

"Follow me," she tells us. "Claudia'll probably be in the pool."

We climb stone steps, either side of us a network of herbaceous borders packed with flowers and shrubs. Butterflies seem to be everywhere. The mansion must be set in at least an acre of land. At the top of the steps there is a beautiful pool shimmering in the sunshine. It is tiled in blue and gold mosaic, the effect stunning. Around the pool are white chaises longues. It could be a boutique hotel, but all this, in the middle of LA, belongs to just one person. It makes our wonderful house by the ocean look humble. I stare in awe around me. Trees everywhere and an immense feeling of privacy. You can't see the neighbors. At least not from here.

"This place," Sunny says, grabbing my hand. "Have you ever seen anything like it?"

"It's gorgeous," I agree. I move in slow motion as in a dream. Or nightmare. I'm yet to find out.

Still no sign of Claudia. It occurs to me for a second that Crystal has usurped Claudia's life. That Claudia is doing a movie somewhere and Crystal is "borrowing" her house. Their split was talked about for months, and now we're to believe they're friends?

But then Claudia emerges from the open French doors and walks toward us.

My heart thrums with trepidation and an ominous foreboding I can't put into words.

# FIFTY

## AVA

"Hello!" she cries out. "Welcome!" Her smile is wide, her face filled with friendliness. Like Crystal, she is smaller than I imagined. Slighter. More petite. She is in a teal-blue bikini, a white sarong wrapped around her middle. Her feet are bare. She does not have cankles like Crystal. Her ankles look tiny and almost snappable. "Did you bring your swimsuits with you?"

"Crap," Sunny says, rolling her eyes. "I totally forgot. And forgot to tell you, Ava."

"Ava, how lovely to meet you, especially since we have *so* much in common. I'm Claudia." She takes both my hands in hers. Not a handshake. Nor a greeting with an air kiss. This seems appropriate. Not too much or too little. Her smile is surprisingly genuine, her remark flippant but not catty. Her warmth takes me by surprise, but then again, acting is her trade.

I have no idea how I should reply. *Yes, we do have so much in common. We do, but lay off my husband, he's mine, bitch.* Or even, *Hell, you know what, come to think of it? You can have the bastard. For free!*

I don't have a clever answer so offer her a smile back. And, yes, I am bowled over by her, I cannot deny it. All the things I had rehearsed to say on my way over here do not come out. I should ask her right this minute why she invited me here, but so many emotions roiling inside my gut stop me. What is happening is so surreal, I still can't quite accept it's true. The affair. The invitation. *Accepting* her invitation. I take a deep breath. Claudia Spector is in front of me, holding my hands.

She drops them and says, "Thought a barbecue would be nice. All vegan, hope you don't mind. I'm not sure how long I can keep it up for, this no meat thing... at least for a while, I hope. I'm trying to do my bit for the planet, you know?"

"That's fine," I answer politely, still tongue-tied. "I'm sure it'll be delicious."

"I've got a million swimsuits, feel free to borrow one. If you'd like to cool off first?"

*Cool off?* I must look flustered. "No, that's okay," I quickly answer, suddenly mortified about the prospect of showing myself half-naked in front of her. She might size up my body. Check out the competition. I'm not like her. I don't have the time or financial means to be massaged and pampered all day long with fancy oils, and with a private trainer on call twenty-four-seven to help sculpt my body into an oh-so-perfect shape. I want to yell at her, *Why have you invited me? What do you want?* But I don't. I feel shy. Confused. Angry. Excited, despite myself. By my own actions as much as hers.

*I'll let the evening unfold and see what happens.*

Claudia looks like she does in the movies, yet more delicate. Her famous blond hair is glossy but messier. Her skin glows with health and is faintly tan, a couple of light freckles sprinkle the bridge of her nose. Her eyes are a clear gray blue and when she looks at you there is a focus there that makes you feel you are truly being seen. She is very natural. Very comfortable in her own skin. I am half in awe, half in shock. This woman was having an affair with my husband!

Is she *still* having an affair with my husband? My guess is yes. And that's why I've been summoned.

"What would you both like to drink? Got cocktails, champagne." Her gaze slips down to my stomach. "Oh, that's right, Ava, you're pregnant. I've got some delicious freshly made lemonade."

The lemonade sounds perfect and exactly what I'm in the mood for, but I say, "I'd love a non-alcoholic beer if you have one? Or a soda?" I choose things that are hopefully in a bottle or can. An insane fantasy lurks in my brain that I may get drugged... my drink spiked or something, and then murdered by Claudia. Or not by Claudia herself but by her fixer, her henchman. Don't movie stars have these types of people who do stuff for them and pick up their mess? Maybe the "henchman" is Crystal.

"I have a great idea. You know for the theater they make fake bottles of champagne? I have a whole bunch of them. It's sparkling apple juice in reality but, you know... in a champagne bottle so you can pop the cork on stage. And for movies, too, obviously. I have a whole lot of real Cristal that I got for my wedding that never happened, and also apple-juice Cristal made by them especially. Isn't that fun?" I understand in this moment Claudia is the type of person who likes to take control. I asked for beer or a soda but now a five-hundred-dollar-plus bottle of champagne is being offered instead and its theatrical counterpart, so who the hell am I to say no to that?

"We have so much of it in the cellar, you know. Of real Cristal. A play on names. Crystal, Cristal, you see?"

*Cellar?*

My blood runs cold. Hands in pockets, I wrap my blazer tight around me as if protecting myself. This place has a cellar? Sweat gathers behind my knees.

And then Claudia yells into the void, "Juana, would you bring out an ice-cold bottle of real Cristal and the apple-juice

Cristal, please? And four champagne glasses?" Again, she takes my hand and leads me to one side of the pool where there's a big, round, mosaic table—that matches the pool—under a tamarind tree. An emerald-green hummingbird is batting its wings by a feeder. There's a pond with round lilies and croaking frogs. This place is a true paradise.

I am about to ask her about Lucas, but instead come up with, "I bet you find it hard to ever leave."

She looks at me quizzically like I've said something with a double meaning. Does she think I'm alluding to Lucas? Then she answers, "I do. I've been here over five years and I'll never sell. It's a real Garden of Eden. I planted pretty much everything you see. Can you believe it? There're so many rare species of plants and trees in my backyard. I have a gardener who helps me, of course."

*Of course.*

"It's beautiful," I agree. "You don't have a dog to enjoy it though?" The famous Annie Leibovitz photo of her and her dog kissing comes to mind.

A cloud of sadness passes over her face. "I did. But I was so broken hearted when he died I don't know if I can go through that again. Sometimes I borrow dogs. Ariadne and Sappho loved coming here."

My heart feels like it has stopped and she has punched me in the gut with iron fists hidden in velvet gloves. Her words are cruel to my ears. This is how she breaks the affair to me? *My* dogs, *my* girls whom *I* rescued from the puppy mill have been innocently enjoying a stranger's "hospitality" that came wrapped up in an infidelity package with a woman screwing *my* husband? Imagining her hands all over Lucas is bad enough, but that she also cast her net and hauled in my dogs and now *me* feels like the ultimate insult. She is admitting to my face, right here and now, by telling me she has met my dogs, that she is "close" to my husband. Does she take me for a fool? No, I guess she assumes I know about the two of them and I'm okay with it, because, hey... she's *Claudia Spector*, after all, the world-famous movie star, and I should be graced by her presence! A rush of adrenaline surges through my veins, anger streaming along with it. How dare she!

"Excuse me?" I fire at her, incredulous. Crystal and Sunny are still by the pool, out of earshot.

Claudia tosses a whoosh of hair behind her ear with a flick of her hand. "I'm sorry, Ava, I didn't mean to upset you. You know that's why I invited you here, right? To discuss Lucas? Did Crystal mention that to you, by any chance? The reason why I thought we should meet? I wanted to let you know what happened between Lucas and me, and, well... sorry, it came out all wrong. I apologize."

I stare at her, unable to respond, my tongue knotted up with my warring emotions. Finally I blurt out, "Look, I've known all about you and my husband for quite a while. And he swore to me it was over between the two of you."

She bites her lip. "It *is* over. Look, Ava, I *would* apologize if I'd done something wrong. I mean... I *have* inadvertently done something wrong, obviously, but I was totally unaware. I had no idea Lucas was married. I'm sorry, I really am. I drove to your house the other day. I saw you. In the window."

I open my mouth to say something, but no words come out. So my instincts were right. Claudia was, and still is, very much around. She has never left. Lucas, as usual, has lied to me.

"Did Crystal not explain?"

"I... I... no. I mean, I guessed. I mean, sure, otherwise why would you even want to meet me?"

"To make sure you knew what was going on. I hated the idea that you were in the dark. And I wanted to meet you face to face." Her gaze meets mine. There is dejection in her eyes. She looks me up and down. "You're so pretty. So nice, Ava. Why would he cheat on you? I don't get it."

My voice has still not found itself. I want to say a million things, and I want to say nothing. I want to smack her in the face. I want to burst out crying. I spout out, "I feel pretty cut up about what you said about Ariadne and Sappho, you know. My dogs coming here? Lucas taking a piece of me and giving it to you. My dogs are like my kids. Wasn't it enough he was unfaithful to me? Wasn't that enough that he was having an affair? But he had to go and rub salt in my wound." I feel a sob about to break in my throat but I hold myself together for my pride's sake. "It hurts. A lot. I suspected but... well, I didn't think Lucas would betray me so badly. He had no right to do that."

She nods and gives me a look of sympathy. Or is it empathy? "I bet. I can't even imagine how you must feel." Her fingers reach out to mine.

I pull my hand away instinctively. Cut to the chase. "You're in love with my husband, aren't you? Are you still seeing each other?"

Her eyes widen in alarm. "No. No! We are *not* still seeing each other. I only found out about you yesterday. I swear, I had no idea he was married. He told me his wife had passed away, and like a fool I believed him."

A second whammy. This hurts even more than her remark about Ariadne and Sappho. "He told you I was *dead*?"

"Yeah. I'm sorry. And he told me he still wore his wedding band in memory of his late wife. He had tears in his eyes when he mentioned her... *you*. I guess that makes me pretty dumb, huh? But I swear if I'd known he was a married man there's no way I would've started a relationship with him. Or even flirted. You have to believe that. I am *not* a home wrecker. No way in a million years would I have done anything that might've hurt someone else on purpose. My dad was... look, Ava, I am *so* sorry, but apart from being an idiot, I didn't do anything wrong. I guess I wanted to ask you to meet me partly to absolve myself?"

Tears spring to my eyes. Relief. Hurt. A feeling of betrayal that hurts like crazy. In this moment, I hate Lucas. I so want to not believe Claudia. But I do believe her because I know how deep Lucas's lies can go. I can see him now, with his poor-widower act. Somehow, I know she's telling the truth.

Tears are rolling down my face. I wipe them away with the tips of my jittery fingers. I take off my blazer and hang it on the back of the garden chair, stifled by a rush of heat to my body. "How did you meet my husband?" I still cannot believe I am here talking to Claudia Spector about her affair with my husband. I literally pinch my arm to make sure this isn't some sort of trippy, surreal dream.

She tells me about the day they met in Runyon Canyon, the party at Jordan's. Their weekend in Lake Tahoe. How he stopped all contact, then suddenly, a couple of nights ago, called late, wanting to see her. How she became suspicious about his house, followed Minnie from his office, saw me in the window and how Crystal showed up. How Crystal enlightened her because of the Sunny connection and gave her a potted history of who I was.

Who I *am*.

Notably, that I am pregnant with Lucas's baby.

"And you don't want to see him anymore?" I double-check.

She snorts out a huffy breath. "Sweetie, I'm not that much of a masochist."

Nibbling along the already-ragged flesh, I rip my teeth into a hangnail on my thumb and it starts to bleed, but I can't let it go. "I can't tell you how angry I am."

She sighs, her voice a touch irritable. "I told you I was sorry."

"Not you. *Him*."

She nods. Her housekeeper, Juana, bustles over with a silver tray of two champagne bottles, impossible to tell which is real and which is the dummy. Also, white linen napkins, coupe glasses, olives, and chips. Claudia takes one of the bottles and eases out the cork. She is gracious and kind with Juana, telling her how she wouldn't be able to function without her. Claudia is a regular person who does not flaunt her movie-star-ness around in her everyday life. So different from the arrogant person I was raging about earlier, the character I had cooked her up to be. She's at ease, friendly, sincere, and has a genuine kindness about her. How can I hate her for what she did when she genuinely had no clue she was doing anything wrong?

Yet...

I *do* still hate her. I hate her because my husband fell in love with her. He held her body when he should have been holding mine. Kissed her lips instead of mine. I am being unfair, I know, but I still feel mad with her for stealing something that belonged to me, and doing it with such ease. I have had to fight for my marriage, fight for Lucas's love. And she breezes in and snatches it away. And now she has brought me here like some queen snapping her fingers. What are her intentions?

"I swear I had no idea," she assures me. "I was naïve, yeah, an idiot, but I didn't hurt anyone on purpose."

She tells me everything. All his embellished lies about why she wasn't invited to his beach house, how he would mention his late wife every so often, reminiscing about "their" life together with genuine sadness. How she (I) died tragically of cancer. I nod, the hurt scooping out my insides. It's easy to say that Claudia should have been smarter. But I know Lucas. He's a master liar. I can see how she was tricked. A gamut of emotions flit through my mind. Mostly fury and humiliation. It was one thing for him to fall for Claudia. To cheat on me. That I can wrap my head around, because like it or not, shit happens. But the lies. The endless, complicated maze of lies. The betrayal. The sneaking around behind my back. The plotting and scheming. This is what hurts the most. All this is what makes me the maddest of all.

A rage is building inside me. He left me for dead and didn't call 911 and then, when he met Claudia in the park, he told her I actually *was* dead! Was that what he secretly wanted? Me... dead? How fucking dare he play with my life like that?

I let Claudia know about his behavior. The gaslighting, how he accused me of having an affair when it was him all along. She is open-mouthed and angry on my behalf as well as her own. I feel a bond forming, not of a fan and a movie star, but a real live connection between two wronged women. Whatever happens, Lucas's duplicity will link us forever.

"We're victims of Lucas's lies," she tells me in a grave tone, her blue-gray gaze fixed on mine tenderly.

"We are," I agree. "But I don't want to be a victim. A victim has never been who I am. I'm a fighter, Claudia."

Claudia pushes a lock of hair from her face. "Me too. But I've been down on my luck with relationships lately."

I look at her square in the eyes. "How would you like to turn that around? How would you feel about playing the player?" I pour the fake apple-juice champagne into two glasses, pushing one of them along the table toward her, and lift the other in a toast. I don't consider the fact that Lucas is the father of my future child. I don't consider that, deep down inside, I still love my husband and am capable of forgiveness. I don't consider that I have so much more to lose than she does.

I am swept away in the moment. It is in this instant I sow the seeds of fatality.

# FIFTY-ONE

## AVA

I make a shameful confession right here by the pool. Claudia is the first and only person I tell this to. Of all people I think she will understand.

Sometimes we want to punish a loved one we have been hurt by, don't we? Sometimes, in an inoffensive, white-lie way. Other times, our payback can go a little deeper. And, on some occasions, a "what if" can morph into something huge.

I guess that's what happened with me and Lucas.

What if...

*Sometimes you have to lie to get to the truth.*

"It was after I found that earring in our bedroom," I tell her.

"Which, like I already told you, wasn't mine," Claudia assures me.

"Anyway," I say, feeling the sting of what she has said, knowing there must've been others, that the earring still remains a mystery. "I decided to test Lucas's loyalty, prove to myself how much he loved me—or didn't—evaluating his love for me in the worst possible way." We are still sitting at the mosaic table, the light fading, the twitter of birds and the rustling leaves in an evening breeze, witness, too, to my revelation. Claudia is all ears. Sunny and Crystal have gone inside.

She takes a sip of her drink. "Why? What did you do?"

"It started off as a kind of joke. I had an extra can of Campbell's Cream of Chicken Soup after using it for a vomit scene in a film I was shooting. Lucas hates ready-made meals and rebukes me if I stock canned foods in the pantry."

Claudia fills the evening air with a burst of laughter. "Oh, my Lordy Lord, I am so loving the idea of cream of chicken soup for vomit, that is *genius*. I'm going to steal that for future films. But, Ava, I thought you were a script supervisor, are things like that part of your job?"

"Nope. But... I like to help out now and then. And people doing vomit scenes badly is a pet peeve of mine. Anyhow," I go on with a smile, secretly congratulating myself on my professionalism, "I was about to throw the soup away—something which goes against every fiber of my being when there are hungry people who would do anything for food—but then I had a crazy idea." I pause, remembering my lightbulb moment. "To begin with, it was a kind of 'play dead,' fun, silly spoof, you know, to get a reaction out of him? To see what he'd do? It would last just a few minutes, and then I'd say, 'Fooled you!'"

"This is beginning to sound intriguing," Claudia says.

"But then I got thinking... I was so hurt and angry. The earring I'd found. The nights he worked 'late' at his office, and once, it sounds like a cliché but it's true, I discovered—not lipstick on his collar—but an *actual* lipstick in one of his jacket pockets. A shade and brand that wasn't mine."

"Well, I don't wear lipstick, unless for work or red carpet events, so it wasn't me. Jesus, how many women were there?"

"I'm asking myself the same thing."

"Carry on with your story."

"I thought... what if. What if I died? Would he even care? It's the kind of thing that crosses most people's minds at some point, right? *If I die, so-and-so will be sorry for what they've done*? I remember first thinking this when I can't've been more than six years old. How my mom would miss me if I were dead, how guilty she'd feel for screaming at me about what a 'bloodsucker' I was."

"She called you a *bloodsucker*?"

"That's a story for another time, but yeah. I plotted to run away from home or planned my own death in my head quite a lot when I was little, but I was too chicken to go through with it."

Claudia, her elbows on the table, leans in closer. "Thank God."

"But with Lucas that day, something propelled me to go through with my charade. Like, I really needed to know how he felt about me, if he cared. The chunky creamy soup was just one of my props. I found some liquor in the cabinet, an old vial of pills I'd been prescribed after my D & C that only had one pill remaining."

"You had a miscarriage? Ava, I'm so sorry."

I sigh. "Anyway, I showcased that pill on the divan of my bed, for extra effect. Creamy chicken soup smeared over the bed linen. I mean, I work with set dressers and set decorators all the time so I know how small details can make all the difference to making a scene authentic."

"Sure. Of course."

"I showered, put on a little makeup... I mean, I wanted to at least look good, you know, so hopefully Lucas would wallow in his mistake all the more, thinking about what he'd lost. I'd forgotten about the camera above the bed, actually. The fake smoke detector I'd set up after the earring incident to find out if he was bringing women home."

"Wait... you set up a fake smoke detector?"

"I did. A spy camera. After the earring episode, to catch him out."

Claudia bursts into laughter. "I knew the moment I met you, Ava, we'd be friends. Carry on. This story is fan-freakin-tastic."

"Did I tell you I did acting classes one time? I wanted to be an actor."

"Like everyone who comes to Hollywood."

"Exactly. Anyway, there's something, as you well know, about acting out a part that's very addictive. They don't call it the acting 'bug' for nothing, I guess. It gets under your skin, doesn't it? And all those classes I'd taken with my acting coach, well... I was looking forward to testing my skills."

Claudia claps her hands together in excitement and anticipation. "Keep going, this could be a great scene in a movie."

"I got swept away by my own creation. Playing dead was more fun than I'd imagined it would be. I might've been tempted to laugh..."

"To 'corpse' as we say in the business."

"Right. But all I had to do was think of the earring, the tube of lipstick, to get me into character with deadpan concentration. I didn't think about how wrong it was till later."

"Why was it wrong?"

"Oh, I don't know. It's a little disrespectful to people who really do try and end their own lives, isn't it?"

"Ava. Love has no boundaries."

"Right," I say, wondering if her words reflect her own actions. For a second I feel a sting of realization. I add, "We all do things we're ashamed of, don't we? Sometimes it's hard to backpedal."

She looks at me for a beat. Does she feel guilty for what she did? The way I did after I played out that fake suicide attempt?

But she says, "Don't stop your story! What happened next?"

"I waited. Waited to see how he'd react, one eye three-quarter mast to see what he was doing out of my peripheral vision. He was pacing around, cussing to himself and then... he called his daddy."

"You're joking?"

"Not joking. You can imagine the letdown! Well, it was more of a wakeup call. Except, by this point I couldn't—or didn't want to—snap out of it and let him know I was faking it. I let him roll me over onto my stomach and I pretended to retch so he'd know at least I was still alive. In fact, I was guilty of letting out a spluttery cough—which, like I said, happens to be a pet peeve of mine with actors in vomit scenes."

"Oh, my God, that is so *true*! I've seen it a million times. When actors cough instead of puke. So, what happened when he called 911?"

"He never did call 911."

"Did he at least call a doctor?"

"No. Just his dad, who told him not to bother."

"And he listened to that sage advice?"

"Yep."

"Did he know somehow you were faking it?"

"No. If he did, he would've said." I go on to tell her about the earring photoshopping, the gaslighting. Claudia is open-mouthed.

"Anyhow," I go on. "I didn't think things could get worse between me and Lucas. My husband had shown me, in no uncertain terms, he did not give a damn about me. But then you came along. Or at least, I found out about you. At that point you were already on the scene, actually, because I found your messages in his burner phone."

Claudia goes quiet. "I am *so* sorry. Please don't hate me, Ava. I swear I had no idea Lucas was married."

I gaze at her, surrounded by the scent of jasmine and honeysuckle in her stunning Garden of Eden and think to myself, *There will always be a tiny part of me that will hate you, Claudia, however innocent you are.*

# FIFTY-TWO

## AVA

Sunny and Crystal join us and pop the real bottle of Cristal. Because they are here, our conversation is no longer focused on Lucas. The tone lightens, and we laugh, joke, and horse around.

Somehow, I mistake one glass for another and wind up drinking half a glass of the real thing. Remembering my grandmother telling me that she drank all the way through her pregnancy because that's what they did in those days, I release myself from my flare of panic and guilt. More and more of both bottles are produced... an endless stream, but I am careful and stick to the dummy version. I can't even remember eating, but I guess we do. Vegan hotdogs and burgers, roasted tomatoes on the barbecue. I end up splashing about in the heated pool. It is luxurious like some Moroccan hammam, or inspired by some other exotic country. All four of us frolicking around, Crystal and Sunny inebriated and wild, Claudia opening up to us about so many personal things, including her lonely childhood, her jealous siblings, a six-month spate in the hospital with meningitis as a child. Then the conversation changes to Hollywood gossip and our favorite movies. Claudia and I both cite *Mary Poppins* as our number-one choice. We are lost and happy behind the big iron gates of Claudia Spector's home, enjoying her hospitality. A new-found friendship that makes me feel like we've won the lottery, despite the circumstances.

For now.

I am sitting on the edge of the pool with Claudia, legs dangling in the water, her arm wound around my shoulder. We are laughing about nothing in particular, and about everything. None of this seems real. And yet it is.

"You can bring the girls here," she suggests.

I know what she is referring to. "Sappho and Ariadne?"

"Isn't that cool? That we don't need him anymore? We can get along without him just fine." She lets out a peal of laughter. I'm not sure if she's tipsy or simply happy. "He needs to be punished," she whispers in my ear. "Let's keep this a secret, though. Between the two of us. We don't want to share this with them, especially not Sunny. At least, not yet." She nods in the direction of Crystal and Sunny, who are so wrapped up in Hollywood gossip they're not paying attention to us.

"He does," I agree. "Taught a lesson for life." I think of my faux suicide again. Even that didn't knock the wind out of him. Even that flowed off his surfer's back like water off a mallard duck.

"We've run out of champagne," Claudia is now telling me.

"Impossible! I thought you had an endless supply."

"Well, we haven't exactly 'run out' but we need to stick more in the fridge."

"Maybe Sunny's had enough. We need to start thinking about getting home." I conjure up an image of myself arriving home, Lucas wondering why I'm so late. I would probably start throwing plates around the kitchen, or toss his clothes out the window, or chop up his suits with a pair of scissors, or throw him a bunch of punches.

Claudia jumps into the pool. The light below the water makes it glitter gold and ultramarine. It's dark now. There are stars in the sky. Do I hear an owl in the trees at one end of her backyard? I feel like I'm in another world here, far, far away from Los Angeles.

She skims her palm across the water. "You can stay the night. Hell, you could move in. I've got the space. You could move into the guest house by the tennis court."

I laugh. "Thanks for the offer, but I have a home." *A home I am dreading going back to.*

"Is it yours? Your house? You personally own it?"

I slip back into the water. It is luxuriously warm and takes the edge off her very personal, prying question, which takes me by surprise. "Not exactly, but—"

"It belongs to Lucas?"

"Technically." I dip my shoulders down so they're covered. Why does she want to know the ins and outs of my finances? It occurs to me she wants to pay me off, after all. Bribe me out of my marriage. At this point I feel like telling her she can have Lucas for free if she wants him. *Good riddance*, I think. I have been trying to stoke the embers for long enough. Our fire has burned out.

She goes on, "Well, I guess if you divorce him, under California law, it's fifty-fifty down the line so you'll be set, right?" She swims a breaststroke in a circle around me.

I think of the prenup Lucas has offered to destroy, in exchange for his proposed new marriage deal: for me to stay in our marriage for at least three more years. Living with him in the marital home, spending nights in our marital bed, all utilities and other household expenses paid by him, no need to work or find a job.

But that was before I found out that he still desires Claudia and called her only last night wanting to see her. To fuck her, clearly. To carry on two-timing me. And her. Because she had been convinced by him he was single. And that I was dead. This... after he had *sworn* to me it was over? After he promised I was the only woman in his life? Assuming Claudia is telling the truth, he has betrayed me all over again.

"What happens if he dies, out of interest?" she's inquiring now, her slim arms stirring the water in lazy circles, the gold and navy-blue mosaics making dreamy ripples in the evening light.

I quote her Lucas's newly proposed marriage deal. "If Lucas gets hit by a bus, our child-to-be will inherit everything in trust, with me as guardian till the child is twenty-one. If I—God forbid—have a miscarriage or something, and there's no child, I'll inherit half of his assets, and his parents the other half."

She narrows her eyes. "And if you do give birth successfully and raise this child, you won't get a dime if he gets hit by a bus?"

"Well, I'll be looking after my child, so—"

She slaps the palm of her hand on the surface of the water. "He's an attorney, watch out. This deal doesn't seem so sweet if you ask me, Ava."

"It's better than the prenup we have in place right now, with me getting nothing at all if we divorce, so, you know, I guess I'm happy to sign." Then I remember all the conditions imposed on me and feel confused and bamboozled all over again. "Besides, if I leave, he's warned me he'll fight for full custody of our baby and, being an attorney along with his dad, I'm pretty sure he'll win. So I might as well take the better deal at least."

She computes in her head what I've just told her, and raises a skeptical brow. "Don't let him bully you. Hold out for better," she advises, now swimming over to the steps. "If he gets hit by a bus, you should get it all, don't you think? After the shit you've been through, especially. Don't let that two-timing wise-ass sweet-talk you into a deal you'll regret. Learn to be tough. You think I got to where I am now through talent alone?"

I feel emboldened by her honesty, her bravado. She does seem to be looking out for me. "Maybe you're right," I ponder, weighing up my options that seem to lean less to my advantage and more to his, now that Claudia has pointed out the obvious.

She slicks her wet hair behind her ears and glides over to the steps. "You'd be surprised how trusts can wrap stuff up so the recipient ends up with next to nothing. Imagine you need a new car, or a vacation, or even a new furnace or something, and every single time you have to beg the trustees for money? Who are these trustees, anyway? You can bet your bottom dollar they'll be on his side, not yours. And what happens after the kid turns twenty-one? Time passes quickly. You'll be older then and may not be able to work. And then what? The kid's twenty-one and maybe hates your guts, or is a greedy spendthrift, or gets involved in some shit-ass relationship with a person you hate who takes over, or your kid winds up with a drug or gambling problem and you're left without a dime?"

"I guess you've got a point," I admit. I try to picture my poor unborn baby in one of the aforementioned doomsday scenarios but can't. Claudia sure has an active imagination. But she is savvy and has, by the sounds of it, swum with the biggest sharks in LA.

"Hold out for everything, Ava. Don't compromise. Be a winner."

Her words resonate with me. So much so, I begin to hatch a plan.

# FIFTY-THREE

## MINNIE

Out of the blue, Claudia calls.

"Hey, Minnie, what's up?"

"Long time no hear," I answer.

Her tone is cool. "I was away filming in New York."

"Oh, yeah? And before that?"

"I did call but every time you... like... seemed a little off." She clears her throat.

I scoff. "*I* seemed off? You and Amelia didn't invite me to hang out!"

"Well, she's on again with Mike so isn't really returning my calls. I'm disappointed, actually. Just like my sister. Said she wanted to be an actor but she obviously doesn't have what it takes. Like discipline for starters. Minnie. We need to talk."

I go silent. I'm not sure if Claudia wants to see me or she wants info about Lucas.

"You want to come over? I can send Roger to come get you. I got two full trash-bags of clothing you can have." *Clearly trying to tempt me.*

"Um, no offense, Claudia, but your clothes? They don't look so good on me." I wait for her to mention Lucas. She doesn't.

But then she says. "Did you know Lucas was married? I guess you must've, huh?"

I don't know how to answer. I can see how bad this looks. I can't admit to Claudia how Lucas bought my silence.

Then she says, "How well d'you know Ava?"

"Lucas's Ava?"

"Yeah. Lucas's wife, Ava."

"I don't know her. Not really."

"But you've met? The two of you?"

"Sure. Like once."

"You like her?"

"She seems nice."

"She's at my house right now."

I nearly choke on my soda. "What?"

"Yeah. She's here with her friend Sunny."

"You invited her over?"

"Sure. Why not?"

"Because you're... you're—"

"Not anymore."

I want to ask her what the deal is. But it's none of my business. And because I never told Claudia about Ava, I look like a terrible person. But I don't want to get involved. Things are already bad enough. Lucas gave me those bonuses. A deal's a deal. He's my boss. If they've hit the off button then I should steer clear.

"Can Ava be trusted?" Claudia asks.

"How should I know? Ask her."

She breaks up with laughter. "Minnie?"

"Yeah?"

"You want to make it up to me? The fact that you basically hid something so important from me and got me into such a bad predicament?"

"I'm sorry, Claudia, I didn't—"

"If I paid you a lot of money... I mean a lot... would you do something for me?"

I think about this for a second. "Depends what it is."

"Could I trust you, though." This doesn't come out as a question.

Thinking of the money and how much I need it and how she's right to be upset, I say, "If I make a deal, I make a deal."

"Can we be friends, Minnie? You and I?"

I let that question sit and stew for a while. Then I tell her, "I thought we *were* friends. But then you kind of ghosted me."

"You ghosted *me*! And chose to hide something super important from me."

"I'm sorry."

"Minnie."

"What."

"D'you forgive me?"

"For what?"

"For... ghosting you. Somewhat."

"I guess."

"I forgive you for not telling me about Ava so you can forgive me, right?"

"Sure."

"So you'll come over? And help me with Ava?"

"What d'you want me to do?"

"I'll tell you when you get here."

I sigh into my phone. "I don't want to do anything mean."

"Of *course* not."

"She's there now? While you're talking on the phone with me?"

"She's hanging out with Crystal and Sunny by the pool. Or maybe they're watching a movie. They're around somewhere."

"Crystal your ex?"

"Uh-huh."

"Hmm. Okay. Interesting."

"Minnie."

"What?"

"Can I count on you?" She whispers this like it's a conspiracy.

"Like I said. It depends."

"On the money?"

"Maybe. If it's not worth my while…"

"Oh. It will be. I can pay you reeeally well."

"It also depends what you want me to do."

"D'you trust me, Minnie?"

"No. Not particularly."

She laughs again. "I'll send Roger over in half an hour. You at home?"

"Yeah." I think of that expression my grandma loves so much. *In for a penny, in for a pound.*

The point is, I won't let Claudia push me into doing something I don't wanna do. But at the same time… the money. Well. Maybe I'm the kind of person who can be bought after all. My track record proves it. Which kind of sucks. But the sooner I pay off my car, the sooner I'm out of LA. We all do shit we don't want to do for money. Right? Anyone who says they don't is lying.

"Okay. See you soon." Claudia ends the call.

I have no idea what she wants. Guess I'll find out soon enough.

# FIFTY-FOUR

## AVA

It is now around ten at night. Earlier, Claudia showed me to a spare bedroom overlooking her backyard, where I showered, and she told me to pick out anything from her closet to wear. Alone, I wander around the room in a soft, pink chenille bathrobe, fingering her things. A ceramic bowl on a table that has a stamp below from San Gimignano in Italy. A big old one-eyed teddy bear on the bed, that looks like it's from her childhood, worn and loved. A *Playbill* of Jessica Chastain in *A Doll's House* on Broadway.

The spare closet is dazzling. My gaze rakes through outfit after outfit, some I recognize from magazine covers or red-carpet galas. The glittery gold one she wore at the Oscars two years ago. The jacket with Frida Kahlo painted on the back when she was snapped walking along the streets of New York. The cream cashmere cape with rhinestones she wore in the church at the wedding of Prince Harry and Meghan at Windsor Castle. And I had thought at the time, *Only Claudia can get away with wearing almost the same color as the bride*. The black flared silk pants she wore with the pink top when she did that spread in Spanish *Hola!* There are shoes, too. I try on a high-heeled, red

Jimmy Choo. Two sizes too small. She is Cinderella, and I—oh, how I wish—her sister.

In the end, I pull out a T-shirt with Mickey Mouse on it. I attempt, in vain, to squeeze into a pair of her jeans. Too small. I can't get them past my thighs. She is such a fragile thing. I guess what they say is true. The camera puts on several pounds, so being slim is part of her job. What a drag to have to worry about your weight all the time. Being an actress must be harder than people imagine. Sounds like it isn't all glamour at all. I'm glad now I didn't go down that road.

I hear raucous laughter from downstairs. Crystal is hammered on champagne. Sunny, too. Claudia is scarily sober. That, or she holds her liquor well.

There is a soft knock at the door and Claudia walks into the room. She's wearing black cargo pants, flip-flops, and a pale blue tee.

"Come down to the cellar with me to get more champagne?"

I feel my eyes bulge in terror at the mention of that freaky cellar again. I thought she had dropped that idea. "There's no more?"

"There's a lot more but it's in the cellar. I hate going down there alone. Juana's gone home."

"Maybe they've had quite enough to drink," I hedge. "Maybe they should be drinking water instead." The last thing I feel like doing is going down to her strange cellar like some idiot in a horror movie, but I don't want to sound rude. Claudia and I have been having a blast, like we have really bonded. I like her. Perhaps too much. But do I trust her?

I stand there in her Mickey Mouse T-shirt, hoping she will let me keep it, not knowing how to get out of her request without sounding like a suspicious bitch. Then I sit on the edge of the bed next to the teddy and say something unexpected, probably so she forgets the cellar mission. "What drew you to my husband?" I twist a lock of hair around my finger. A habit of mine I have seen mirrored in Claudia. Strange how alike we are in so many ways. "Just curious to know," I add.

She inclines her head and thinks about it for a minute. I'm wondering if she's going to come up with the obvious: a part of his anatomy that never fails him, even when he's been drinking. After all, Claudia doesn't shy away from being brutally honest, even if it hurts. But she answers in a gentle voice, "His eyes?"

I nod. Those Bradley Cooper eyes did it for me too. "That's it?"

She shrugs. "His easy, casual manner, his spontaneity. Like there's no baggage with Lucas. There's a lightness about him that's intoxicating. Like when you're with him he takes your pain away."

My eyes fill with moisture. She has him in a nutshell. And that's why we both feel so betrayed by him, isn't it? He makes us feel good. Happy. In love. But it's not real. Or it's only real on his terms. Which is: *Accept my lies and philandering or lose me. Because you can't have it both ways... babe.*

"Don't cry, Ava." She walks over, sits next to me and takes me by the hand, pulls me toward her, swings an arm around my shoulder and gives me a loving hug. "It's over between us, I promise. Look, he's all yours, Ava. I swear I won't come between you. You're his wife. I was an unsuspecting mistress and had no idea. He's all yours."

I think how Lucas is like water. Whatever I do, whatever happens, he will go back to his primal state. He simply can't help himself. The floodgates of my emotions burst open. "But I don't want him anymore," I sob. "I can't be with a person I don't trust not even a little. If it isn't you, it'll be someone else. On and on. Forever. I'll always be wondering who, what, where, and feeling I'm not good enough. That's not a marriage. I can't live like that."

"True."

Her response stings. *True.*

It's cathartic to have someone I can share my aching heart with. Someone who gets it. Claudia and I are in this together. She doesn't want Lucas anymore. So what would that make me if I put up with his shit myself? A raggedy dishcloth. Soiled and used. I need to rise to her level. Call it quits with him and fight if I have to. When you shut a door, a new one opens, doesn't it? It takes guts. It takes faith. But if you don't believe in yourself, you will never grow.

"Come on, let's go downstairs and get those lushes some more champagne." Claudia pulls me by the hand. I am in a kind of daze, still working out how I feel about all this. I stumble after her. We wander through her multimillion-dollar home. It is so white and fresh-looking. Creamy, sumptuous couches everywhere, set against either polished, dark parquet floors, or antique terracotta tiling. The art on the walls is mostly modern. Then there are the giant photos of her and her black Labrador kissing. The Annie Leibovitz, but different shots from the one printed in *Vogue.* Instead of the profile, these are of Claudia laughing, mouth wide open, abandoned joy sparkling in her eyes. I feel warm inside, and remember that she is a good person. A person who kisses dogs. A person who has a big, generous heart.

I let her lead me on. To the kitchen, where she opens a door. Down some steps.

Down to the cellar.

A cellar with no windows, where nobody could hear me scream for help.

A voice inside my head says, *What the hell are you doing, dummy?*

I allow her to pull me behind her, her soft fingers entwined in mine. *This is Claudia Spector!* I tell myself. *She would never hurt anyone.*

Later, I will find out my assumption is wrong.

# FIFTY-FIVE

## CLAUDIA

Claudia is enjoying having Sunny and Ava over. It's turning out to be somewhat of a party, but most of all, meeting Ava feels to her like a cathartic, life-changing moment. Something is shifting inside her. Not in a negative way, but in a gear-changing way. Ava has—maybe unwittingly—precipitated this change.

The night before, after Crystal had stalked Claudia to Lucas's house—where Claudia discovered the existence of Ava, a very non-dead wife—Claudia had worked herself up into such a state of indignation about Lucas, they never made it to the restaurant in Thousand Oaks.

"Take me home," she had asked Crystal. "I've got a bunch of frozen meals in the fridge that Juana prepared for me. Soups and casseroles and stuff. I want to go home. Just so you know though, this doesn't mean you can stay over." She had forgiven Crystal but in no way wanted a close relationship again.

They drove along in silence while Claudia thought more about how lonely it was being famous, how trust became so much more of an issue when the stakes were high. She pictured Lucas's wife in her mind's eye. She should know, shouldn't she? Shouldn't she get the heads-up about what her husband was doing? She would want to be told if her partner was cheating on her, even by a stranger. She'd be doing her a favor.

"I want to meet Ava," she burst out suddenly. "I think she deserves to know the truth."

Crystal checked the mirror and gently slalomed around a fallen branch in the road. "Like I told you, my friend Sunny knows her. I could set up a meeting, if you like."

So, the following morning, Crystal called Sunny and Sunny then called Ava.

And the next thing Claudia knew, Ava was standing right before her: a guest in her home.

And here they are now, about to enter the cellar.

Crystal and Sunny have asked for more champagne, so she obliges. She doesn't ask them to go to the cellar and get it themselves in case one of them falls down the steps. Ava is stone-cold sober, so Claudia asks her to come with her. She sees the fear in Ava's eyes and laughs.

One thing Claudia is aware of is how powerful women can be pooling their resources and their trust in one another into a tight-knit knot. If only women truly believed in their power and trusted each other, they could rule the world. *It's about time they did, too. Men have had their chance and screwed things up for long enough.*

Yes, she is risking it, but without giving trust a chance, life is lonely. She has been a loner for long enough already. She will trust Ava, and she will give Minnie another chance and trust her too.

It is as if Claudia and Ava have met their "sister from another mister." There is an understanding between them, a bond. A synergy. A symbiosis. Their humble backgrounds, their deadbeat fathers, the way they have both had to fight for their lot in life, but most of all, Lucas—for better or worse—connecting them in such a powerful way. She loves Ava's mixture of vulnerability and strength. When Ava confessed everything to Claudia—her fake suicide when Lucas didn't dial 911 and by all intents and purposes left her to die—her heart opened up to her. She had pretended to Lucas she was dying as a practical joke to see his reaction, yet it had metastasized into something insidious and dark. It was funny but also heartbreaking. The doctored photos of her wearing earrings he had never given her. The barrage of lies during their marriage making Ava feel like she was, and still is, going crazy.

Amused by the fear in Ava's eyes, she promises, "I swear, Ava, I won't lock you in the cellar."

And when she leads Ava by the hand to grab a couple of bottles of champagne and Ava follows, it makes her realize something: Ava is trusting her, which means she can trust her back. It's no easy feat to make a new friend in this life. If loyal and trusting Ava can follow her down to a cold cellar, it says it all, really.

Unopened champagne bottles in hand, they end up sitting on an old oak wine barrel. Claudia had an idea to make them into flowerpots, but likes them so much as they are, she has kept them down here in the cellar.

"I'm thinking of going to Europe," she tells Ava.

"A vacation?"

"No, a job."

"What's the job?" Ava asks.

"A French film. I even get to speak French. The director's an old friend of mine. The money's a joke. It's like I'd be doing the job for... not even pocket money. Basically, a freebie."

Ava's eyes widen. "Wow, that's ambitious. To do a movie in a foreign language."

"I always push myself with my work."

Ava nods. The fear in her eyes has left her. She seems genuinely fascinated by Claudia's career choices. "You'd have to *learn* French?"

"Pretty much. At least, learn the script by heart. They'll

give me a language coach, you know, to get the accent right? But the part's an American woman, and apparently the French find our accents sexy. Who knew, right?" A hiatus of silence lingers between them. It is unsaid but clear. Claudia needs to get away from Lucas. From all of it. She adds, "I feel like disappearing from Hollywood. From life in general. Change things up a bit. A stint abroad would do me the world of good."

Ava shrugs. "Disappear, then."

Claudia chuckles. "I wish."

"No, I'm serious. Leave. Don't tell anyone where you're going. Turn your life on its axis."

"I'd have to let my agent know, at least." She says this, but instantly thinks, *why*? Her life is hers, not her agent's, not her publicist's. She smiles to herself, thinking of all the possibilities stretched out before her.

A catalog of scenarios flits through her imaginative brain. She's read enough crazily plotted movie scripts in her life, and true-crime stories that are sometimes even more far-fetched than fiction. A frenzied profusion of ideas gets her mind ticking away, cooking up all sorts of madcap schemes. Ava is right. Lucas deserves to learn a lesson. Claudia thinks of her father—that shmuck—and all the men who have cheated on their wives. Although what Lucas has done is so much worse than straightforward cheating. It's strange how she forgives women for their misdeeds so much more so than men. Crystal. Minnie. But men? She finds it so challenging to forgive and forget their shit-ass conduct. She imagines how she and Ava could pay Lucas back and then she could simply disappear. At least for a while.

"Have you ever read any Agatha Christie novels?" she asks Ava.

"I've seen a bunch of her movies. *Murder on the Orient Express* was my favorite. I guess I must've read a book or two of hers, but a long time ago."

"Did you know that Agatha Christie disappeared in 1926?"

"No, I didn't."

Claudia shuffles herself into a more comfortable position on the barrel. "After kissing her daughter goodnight, she drove off in her Morris Cowley roadster and was not seen for eleven days. It sparked a huge manhunt, even involving airplanes and more than a thousand policemen."

"Really?"

"The prime minister urged the police to find her. Even Sherlock Holmes's inventor, you know, Arthur Conan Doyle? Even he was recruited to find Agatha Christie. Apparently he was into occult stuff. He took one of her gloves to a medium to try and discover what had happened. Had her cheating husband murdered her? A lot of people thought so."

"Her cheating husband?" Ava's mouth quirks into a tiny smile.

"It's always the husband, boyfriend, or lover, isn't it?" Claudia says. She looks for Ava's reaction. Are they thinking the same thing?

"Go on," Ava urges. "Tell me what happened next."

"Well, finally, they located Agatha Christie's abandoned car near a spring named Silent Pool, which was said to be bottomless. But no Agatha Christie. The eeriness and intrigue loomed in everyone's minds."

"Oh, my God, I've never heard this story! And then what happened?"

Claudia continues in a quiet voice. "Eleven days later, Agatha Christie was discovered unharmed, safe and well, in a spa hotel in Yorkshire. She had taken a train there and used the name of her husband's mistress to check in. She had even joined in the dances and dinners at the then-hotspot hotel. It was a banjo player who recognized her from the newspaper headlines and called the police. She attributed her actions to total memory loss. Or at least, her husband, who came to collect her, said that's what it was. He was probably saving face."

"You're suggesting you could do an Agatha Christie?" Ava asks.

Claudia smiles, her teeth white in the cool dim light of the cellar. "Maybe I could take it a step further, with your help of course. I mean, you and I would need to work out the fine details."

"You disappearing. Lucas the jealous lover on the edge, acting on revenge? Or *you* the amorous lover and he wants you gone, out of the way of his marriage?"

"Exactly."

"Your car left abandoned somewhere? No trace of you. And Lucas looking as guilty as hell?"

Claudia grins. "It's a great plot, don't you think?"

"Maybe some clues for the police would be a nice touch. Like a little of your blood in the trunk of the car? Signs of a struggle?"

Claudia nods, still smiling. "That's exactly what I had in mind. How did you know?"

"Great minds think alike?"

Claudia laughs. "Let poetic justice take its course. Just for, maybe, eleven days? Enough time to give Lucas a shock to the system. Then I'll appear again. Plead memory loss if need be."

Ava can't contain her giggles. "Perfect."

"Oh, and I've recruited Minnie to help us."

"Minnie?"

"Lucas's assistant Minnie? She says you two know each other."

"Oh, right. Jasmine. You trust her?"

"I do."

# FIFTY-SIX

## CLAUDIA

A couple of days after Claudia and Ava have solidified their plan, Claudia calls Lucas, setting in motion their carefully masterminded plot.

He takes the bait immediately and is "pumped," he says, to meet her for dinner.

The restaurant is the kind of place where A-listers who want to be seen come, pretending they don't want to be seen. It's a game of charades. In the past, Claudia's publicist would make a call. Claudia would be dressed in some lavish outfit, on the arm of some gorgeous heartthrob, and the paparazzi would be there, waiting. She would feign ignorance and everybody would be happy. She, and whoever her date was, got the publicity, and the press would make money. They were all one big delighted family playing the Hollywood game.

Today it's different. She really does need to be careful. It has to look like a secret tryst between clandestine lovers. So she makes sure not to let her agent or publicist know what she's up to. The other day she mentioned something in an offhand way to someone whom she knew would alert someone in particular, who would be itching to take the photo of her and Lucas touching foreheads at Chez Suzette. The touching forehead thing is the cue to snap the picture.

"I didn't think you'd agree to see me," Lucas says at the beginning of the meal. They are in a half-moon booth upholstered in scarlet velvet. Snowy tablecloths. Waiters in white gloves. Wine that spirals into the thousands. Lavish, towering flower arrangements. It looks like old Hollywood, in the days when women wore perky little hats and styled their hair and never went out of the house without lipstick. The floor is a dreamy black and white marble in a diamond pattern. Not shiny, but antique. This place is all elegance and class. She'll let Lucas pick up the tab. He needs to pay the price for what he's done, literally and figuratively.

"I missed you," she says, fixing her gaze on his startling blue eyes. It's the truth. He looks sexy, as usual. She runs her eyes over him and thinks of his tight body, naked, the muscles in his surfer chest, the lean long thighs. The power tool between his legs. He's a great lay, there's no denying it. Tonight will be the last time they'll have sex though. She has cleared that with Ava. She needs him to come home with her. It is part of their plan.

"You can screw him, sure," Ava agreed at Claudia's house, when they were plotting the whole thing. "What do I care if you have sex with him one more time, he's already broken my heart. If he meets you for dinner and wants to spend the night with you after he swore to me it was over, then, hey... that's proof, right? It can't be clearer than that. I can't carry on being married to this man. I can't be used as sloppy seconds anymore."

"You'll need to carry on, though, like everything's normal," Claudia had instructed. "Even after I disappear."

Ava has agreed, reluctantly. Agreed to carry on being the perfect wife. Agreed to show solidarity and loyalty to her husband so nobody would ever suspect. Let a few choice people know about Claudia's affair with Lucas. Her neighbor Jill, for instance, so that when the photo is released to the media, gossip will spread like a Santa Ana wildfire.

Still, Claudia feels like she is betraying her new friend with this last romantic tryst. It doesn't seem right. It bugs her conscience that she is battling out these contrasting emotions. She is furious with Lucas, yet she still finds him attractive.

"You're sexy," she tells him, nudging her bare ankle against his thigh, tipping her toe into his suited, bulging crotch. What she really means, what she says to herself in her head is, *Your sum-total worth is your sexual prowess and good looks... nothing more.*

Maybe he catches a glimpse of her thoughts from the hesitation in her eyes. He says, "Sorry I didn't call for so long, babe. It wasn't personal."

"Why was that, by the way? That you didn't call?" She waits for the truth, knowing it won't come. If he fesses up now and admits to her that he's married, then she won't go through with the plan. She and Ava have agreed to this. *Give him one more chance*, Ava told her. They both know it's unlikely, but she'll try her best to extract some kind of confession out of him.

He tilts back a mouthful of red and swallows. "Work. It's been crazy."

Claudia gives him a knowing smile. She throws out casually, "I thought maybe you were leading a double life or something."

He looks her straight in the eyes. "I guess it *is* like two lives, in a way. My work life, which is insanely stressful, and then spending time with you, which is amazing."

*That is not an answer*, she thinks.

"You don't have a secret girlfriend hidden somewhere, or a wife?" Claudia knows she's being too obvious. Perhaps this time he'll come clean. It's evident, isn't it, that she's onto him? But Lucas just smiles. If he's nervous, he doesn't show it.

"How could I possibly want to go for hamburger when I can have steak?"

He's quoting Paul Newman, but badly. She is not the steak. He's gotten it wrong. The steak is at home. In effect, Ava is the steak and Claudia the hamburger. Whatever. The denial trips right off his tongue.

"I thought maybe you had someone else," Claudia clarifies. His last denial is not a lie. Not exactly. She needs him to *lie* to justify what she is going to do.

"No, babe. You're the only one for me. I can't even think of another woman when you're near me."

She needs to pin him down. "And when I'm not near you? Do you think of any other woman?"

He takes another swig of Margaux. He seems unfazed by her grilling. Almost like he's enjoying the challenge. "Claudia, hon, you're on my mind twenty-four-seven. Except when I'm working. I need to concentrate on my work, you get that, right? If I think of you when I'm in the middle of a meeting? A little embarrassing, you can imagine." He smirks.

She pushes on. "You haven't, you know, had a one-night stand with anyone else? An old flame maybe?"

"Nope. Just you, sweetie. Just you."

She has him nailed. Ava is expecting his child. Yet here he is. Lying to Claudia's face. Lying behind Ava's back. Meanwhile, Ava is forced to carry on living with him. Being loving with him—the model wife in fact. She has given him no reason whatsoever to stray.

Claudia scooches closer along the booth so their thighs meet, leans over and touches her forehead to his. She sees, in her peripheral vison, a camera flash go off somewhere. Good. The photo has been taken. "I need your body on top of mine," she breathes into him. She lets her fingers play against the hardness of his groin, trapped inside his suit pants, and a wave of sadness washes over her knowing that this is all an illusion. The romantic dinner, the delicious wine, the two of them together. It might have been so great if only it were real. If only he wasn't married to another woman. It really did seem, for a while, like the realest of passions. Even, she had fancied... love. This is the oldest tale in the book, isn't it? A woman believing that she is loved when it's only a figment of her desire, her will, nothing more? Her mother comes to mind. Her poor, long-suffering mom. Her dad had broken her heart. Into small spiky shards which could never be pieced back together again.

Lucas is just like her father. And Claudia... well, she's not much better, is she? Plotting and scheming like this? She wants to stop right now, but she has to end this. Has to put an end to his lies.

After dinner they drive to her house. They have wild sex on the sofa of her living room. She thinks of the art film she'll soon be shooting in France. She will be topless in certain love scenes. The director has promised she'll be half in shadow and how tasteful it will be. The French know how to do it right, and she's up for the challenge. America's darling star-spangled girl will shock the world. Before that happens, though, she will disappear. At least for a while. What she is doing, on so many levels, is wrong. But it feels imperative. Like a voice is guiding her, pushing her forward.

As she climaxes and hears Lucas cry out, "I love you, babe," she throws her arm out and a lamp smashes to the hard terracotta floor. She leaves it there. The next day she cracks her phone and chucks it on the couch, the spidery web of glass making it look so much worse than it is. The blood is easy enough. It is handy the amount of skillsets Claudia has mastered during her years of acting. Once, she played a nurse. It was at the beginning of her career, in a detective series. She took the role very seriously, as she always does when playing a part. Drawing blood is easier than it looks. The trick is to let it drip, drip, drip, out of the syringe in measured amounts, in a trail, and then smear some of it around as if there has been a struggle. She leads the trail to the kitchen telephone. Those blood-splatter experts are no fools, everyone knows this from watching *Dexter* and *CSI*.

The blood will be an authentic touch.

But the real clues will be left in the trunk of her abandoned Mercedes. Her DNA, fibers, and hairs. More of her blood haphazardly dripped around and then scrubbed afterward with bleach. She will do this in advance, to let it dry nicely. Apparently, forensics prefer to freeze-dry blood samples anyway; they never test fresh blood... she remembers that from a show she did. Lucas's dress shoes that Ava will hand over for preparation, her blood left to dry and then rubbed with bleach, and that Minnie will plant back in his closet when the couple are both out of the house (she has keys to their home, after all), will make Lucas the number-one suspect in Claudia's apparent murder case. Because, if Claudia plays it right, her "disappearance" will last for several weeks. Enough time to punish the cheating asshole, make him sorry for what he's done.

*A little jail time will teach him a life lesson.*

Then she'll plead ignorance. Say she hasn't watched the news or read the papers. *"I was in France. I had no idea anyone was looking for me!"*

Instead of going to a hotel in Yorkshire like Agatha Christie, she'll go to Paris and stay incognito in an elegant Airbnb while she prepares for her role. If she goes outside on occasion, she'll wear a big floppy hat and sunglasses. She's going to change her hair for the part anyway. Dye it black and cut it into a bob. She'll use a different passport to fly—get one in another name. Easily done if you have the right contacts. Which she does. And she'll go by private jet. When you fly private, it's so different to flying commercial... they pretty much leave you alone. Her own passport? She'll leave that at home with the shattered phone and her credit cards, along with the drops of blood and the smashed-up lamp. Itty-bitty clues that she can always shrug off later as being inconsequential. And if things get really complicated, she'll wiggle out of it by saying she's lost her memory.

If there's one thing she's learned during her lifetime: people forgive movie stars for almost anything.

# FIFTY-SEVEN

## CLAUDIA

*So this is what it's like to be murdered?*

Claudia is locked in the trunk of her car. In the dark. Ava is in the front seat, gloved hands, hair tucked up into a cap, sock-footed—so she doesn't contaminate the future "crime scene" with traces of herself. Claudia is kicking and screaming inside the closed, claustrophobic space. This wasn't supposed to happen. Seconds ago, the hatch was wide open. At no point was it meant to click shut. "Help! Get me the fuck out of here!" she yells at the top of her lungs.

The trunk is supposed to pop open easily. Since the beginning of the millennium, US law requires all cars to feature a glow-in-the-dark release latch inside the trunk compartment whereby you can open the trunk from inside in case of an emergency, since several children have perished that way in the past.

There is nothing glowing in the dark. Fumbling for a latch, Claudia cannot see or feel anything remotely resembling a latch!

She is trapped.

Her heart is hammering against her ribs so hard it hurts. She takes in sips of measured breaths to try and calm her panic. The smell of dried bleach is burning her throat. Someone has fixed it so she can't get out.

Claudia is going to die. Poetic justice has been served all right. But to Claudia herself!

The trunk hatch slammed closed, seemingly on its own. The latch clicked with a horrifying fatal clunk.

How did she not see this coming?

Has her stalker been let out of prison? No, he still has a couple of years left to serve, because he had other misdemeanors too. Or did a new stalker, following her car, abduct Ava and slam the trunk hatch shut? Will the car screech off any minute? What the hell is going on? Or—oh my God, is it possible?—that Ava tiptoed around the car and clicked it shut without being seen?

Because why the hell isn't she coming to her rescue?

*It must be Ava. It has to be.*

Is Claudia being double-crossed? Her mind is scrambling, and scraping at the barrel for an answer.

What had Claudia been thinking? Her convoluted plot she had masterminded—as simultaneous payback for Lucas and a way of checking herself out for a while—is turning out to be a suicide mission. She put all her trust in Ava, a woman she hardly knows, whose husband she was having an affair with! How and why in a million years did she cook up this insane plan, banking on her when she was probably the last person on earth she could rely on? Ava most likely hates her. Ava, who has spent enough time on movie sets to pick up a thing or two, and who trained as an actor for a while with a private coach, no less. Yes, Ava told Claudia how acting had been her dream and why she had come to LA in the first place. She is more than capable of playing a role.

She won Claudia over with her "sincerity," her "sweetness." She has played the role of a lifetime. Convinced Claudia she was a true friend. *A fangirl turned friend.* God. They are the most dangerous of all. Ava, not Minnie, is Eve Harrington in *All About Eve*. Why had Claudia not anticipated that? Why did she go through life trusting people, making the same mistake time and time again? The helpful, adoring fan who has an agenda... this is Ava. Part of their plan was for Ava to pretend to Lucas that everything was fine with their marriage, for her to act normal with him. And to make sure she got exactly what she wanted with the new marriage contract. Ava, over the last ten days, must have decided she's too in love with him to let go and wants Claudia out of the picture. And as for Crystal? Damn! Why did Claudia give Crystal another chance? Is she in on it, too? Crystal has betrayed her before, who knows what her agenda is?

And Minnie? What about her? Miffed because Claudia "ghosted" her?

Claudia's mind is racing, coming up with any and every possibility.

Her throat is parched with panic. "Let me out of here! Please, Ava! I'll give you anything you want!"

Her voice is hoarse, breathing in dust that must have found its way into the trunk of the car during the journey to this abandoned canyon rutted with holes, the paving destroyed by an earthquake and never mended by the state. Just ten minutes ago, they had parked the car, and Claudia had slipped into the trunk, latch and door wide open to the elements, the sky a searing blue. The plan was to roll around, kick her feet and leave footprints, maybe break a nail, leave her DNA, fibers and hairs as evidence for the police to discover. Ava was waiting patiently in the front seat (wearing surgical gloves and socks so as not to leave prints). Any moment, Crystal was to come and collect them in Lucas's car. Ava had gotten hold of a spare set of his car keys. If his Lexus left tire tracks in the grit, all the better.

But.

Claudia walks her fingers around the edges of the pitch-black compartment once more, feeling for this supposed safety latch. No phone. Her purse with all her cash and brand-new phone are in the glove box. That was another dumb mistake.

"Ava!" she yells. "Please."

But Ava doesn't respond.

# FIFTY-EIGHT

## MINNIE

The other day I got roped into more shit. Not Lucas this time but Claudia. And Ava and Crystal have gotten involved too. What is *with* these people? They're all such liars.

The other night when Claudia invited me over to her house she was all over Ava like they were best friends. Said they had a little plan to punish Lucas, but I didn't ask what it was. The less I knew, the better. I told her not to tell me, in fact.

"Don't tell me what you're doing," I said. "I don't want to know." She handed me cash up front. Like a brick of cash so big I didn't need to count it. All I had to do when the time came she said was to take a pair of Lucas's shoes that Ava would bring round to my apartment and then put them into Lucas's closet when she gave me the word. Let myself into their house with the set of keys Lucas had given me.

At the time I couldn't figure out what they were planning.

I knew it wasn't good. But I still did it anyway.

Looks like Claudia bet on the wrong horse with Ava though. Ava outsmarted her. Reneging on their plan. Because Ava is all lovey-dovey with Lucas and Claudia has truly vanished.

# FIFTY-NINE

## AVA

Sometimes you have to take control of things. Sometimes you have to be tougher than you want to be in life. Both Lucas and Claudia taught me that.

Poor Claudia. She must've been so terrified, locked up in the trunk of her car. And as for Lucas getting accused of her murder... well, what can I say?

Poor, poor Lucas.

As I sit with Ariadne and Sappho on my deck, looking out to sea, the sunset streaked like garnets and amethysts across the sky, I contemplate our marital situation and what has happened up until now, so thankful I had my wits about me and sorted out a new marriage contract before all this happened.

No more irritating prenup blocking my way. Claudia was instrumental in getting me to look at the small print of Lucas's upgraded contract. How fortunate she and I met before I signed.

You see, concerning that prenup—and the new contract that bumped it nicely out of the way—everything was planned by me, weighed up, strategized ahead of time. I was well aware how Lucas's mind was wired—the benefits of playing reverse psychology with him. I wanted the prenup gone with every fiber of my being. But it was crucial to never give him any inkling as to how I felt.

*The prenup? No big deal, honey*, I let him believe. *In fact, I love working for a living; it is my be-all and end-all. I intend to get up at four a.m. until I retire, drive in bumper-to-bumper traffic jams through LA and spend my precious time worrying about continuity problems. I just love waking up in a sweat in the middle of the night, panicking about the possibility that so-and-so-actor was wearing a red T-shirt in the last shot and turned up in the next in a blue T-shirt, with the director saying it didn't matter because the performance was good, and how I will be blamed later in the editing room.*

This is the kind of shit I was dealing with to earn a living. And when I saw Claudia swanning around in such splendor in her gorgeous home, I thought, *I want that too.*

Sure, I had fun on the movies I made and I was grateful to have a good job, but some people treated me like I was a loose dangling thread despite the fact that I, the script supervisor, was the very *fabric* of the projects we were working on! Making a movie is about being a team; we are all in it together, there should be no hierarchy. Tell that to certain sycophantic jerks in the business who pander only to the stars, who called me the "continuity girl" or "script girl" and asked me to bring them a coffee.

I wanted more with my lot in life. I *needed* more. I *deserved* more.

And now I don't have to work if I don't want to. I am financially independent—free! With or without Lucas. But *with* my baby. Always.

Don't get me wrong, on a good day, with a good production, I did love my job—that part was absolutely true—but I knew what getting rid of that prenup would mean for me. Choice. Freedom. Respect. I can even go back to acting if I choose to.

When Claudia and I came up with our plan to bring Lucas down, we discussed how I would carry on like normal. I played my part of the loyal wife standing by her husband's side beautifully. I knew exactly what I was doing... Taking on that job, telling Lucas I had planned to leave him, that I could take care of myself and my future child. Moving to Montana? My threats of cruising out the door like it was an easy choice? He fell for it, even resorting to threatening me in his desperation. I knew that would drive him crazy and he'd change tack. Even paying for that expensive dinner at Nobu sent my message loud and clear.

Procrastinating about signing the new marriage contract he was offering me that gave me fifty-fifty? Are you kidding me? I was *desperate* to sign, but I kept him hanging on, dangled the carrot just far enough away from him he thought the carrot was a golden nugget. Lucas thinks he's smart, and he is, but not as smart as I am. He was so easy to manipulate, so simple to fool. Tell a man like Lucas you don't need his money, you don't even *want* his money, and worse, you can take him or leave him, and he'll rethink his strategy.

Men like Lucas like being in control. I was derailing that control by working, by telling him I didn't need him. The only way to reel me in again was by offering a new, upgraded deal, a deal that would make him master and commander again.

But even that deal was stymied after Claudia disappeared, because he was terrified of winding up alone. And he needed his loyal wife by his side so he looked innocent. So, the deal got upgraded yet again:

*"Fifty-fifty, no conditions, no clauses. And if I get hit by a bus, you get it all."*

That, folks, is when I finally signed.

It all worked out perfectly. I got what I wanted. That old prenup done and dusted. Claudia out of the way. And Lucas arrested for her murder.

Perfect.

# SIXTY

Just as I am gloating over my good fortune, Jack calls. I hesitate, then pick up. I need to get this conversation over and done with.

"My God you're a sneaky goddamn bitch," he spews out.

I hold the phone away from my ear. "Language, Jack," I reply coolly. This small dig at my father-in-law's self-righteousness feels sooo good.

"Don't language me, you conniving, po-dunk piece of white trash. You set Lucas up, didn't you? He told me about the matchbook, how you had Claudia Spector's address. I'll get you for this."

"Don't threaten me, Jack."

*Po-dunk piece of white trash?* I think of my humble roots. The jobs I took to get myself through college, and even before that, as a teenager to support myself and my family. When your father splits and disappears when you're three years old and your mother ends up an addict, you don't have a choice. In contrast, the silver-spoon education Lucas enjoyed and the support he received from his parents, never doubting his place in the world, made him a different person altogether. His privileged birthright. His entitlement. And this makes me white trash in Jack's eyes? So we lived in a trailer park for a while when my mom was at her worst? But I built strength from that and became the person I am today. I am proud of the fact I do not come from money and I made something of my life.

And look at me now. A winner all the way. *Take that, Jack Fox!*

My calm silence has Jack worried. I can tell from the way he clears his throat, the tremor coming down the line. Perhaps he thinks I am recording this call? If I'd been thinking straight, I would have.

"I'm going to prove it was you, Ava, by God, if it's the last thing I do."

"Prove away, Jack. You have no proof of anything."

"That's why you never made it to the police station to give your statement. You set my son up, goddammit!"

"I was planning to go," I answer in a sickly-sweet voice, "but—"

"Liar! I knew he never should have—"

I wave my phone around so the breeze will cause static. I shout loudly, as if I can't hear him, "Sorry? Jack? You're cutting out. I can't hear you."

"I've just seen Lucas and I'm—"

"I'm losing reception. Jack? I can't hear you, Jack?" I press End with glee and a grin.

I hear him all right. His message is loud and clear.

Jack Fox would do anything to salvage his upstanding position in society. It's not Lucas himself he truly cares about, but what people are saying about "his" son.

I smile to myself. Jack, like Lucas, had it coming to him.

A little bit of karma goes a long way.

# EPILOGUE

## AVA

The funeral is quieter than I had expected, and I am more emotional than I imagined I ever would be. It is a small family affair. Nobody notified the press. Still, there is a helicopter hovering overhead. I am wearing black, with dark shades so people can't see the welts under my eyes from my inconsolable crying. Who would think, after all that has happened, that I would be affected quite this badly?

I was party to a murder, there is no way around it.

If I hadn't agreed to that stupid magazine article, none of this would have happened. Claudia would never have invited me to her home and we wouldn't have cooked up that crazy plot, because she would never have gotten wind of how much I admired her, and things would have worked out differently. Nobody would have died. I could have held my head high and walked away from it all.

Here I am, though, dressed head-to-toe in black, pregnant with Lucas's child, saying farewell to a person I never dreamed would meet their fate in such a horrible way.

Guilty.

I am guilty.

White lilies—Claudia's favorite, incidentally—adorn the little church on the hill, and the view looking out to the ocean is breathtaking. I don't look at the faces that surround me, how can I? Some children are playing tag, scurrying around, wildly unaware of the tangled pain in so many grownups' heads and hearts, trying to make sense of this tragedy. Jill is here, standing by my side. She has turned out to be a super-supportive friend, after all.

Claudia's face haunts me. It always will. That is the thing with famous people; they follow you forever, even after they're dead. Marilyn, Rita, Audrey, Cary Grant. They are still with us, aren't they? They are a part of your psyche, whether you invite them in or not.

Earlier, the pastor read out a bunch of meaningful prayers, and I stumbled through a stanza from an Amanda Gorman poem, "The Hill We Climb." Crystal had suggested it, and it felt quite apt. I feel a lump lodged in my throat, remembering that day at Claudia's house when I met her for the first time. Her charm. Her beauty. How I couldn't help myself feeling awed and impressed, and how all that changed when she fed me the truth about her affair and how Lucas still wanted her. Her relationship with Lucas was a living and breathing entity, so much more powerful than I had originally thought when I found that flip phone.

Forgiveness is a lot more complicated than people will admit.

I feel a shadow come up behind me. I turn.

"The service was beautiful," one of Lucas's lawyer friends tells me, his tall frame towering over me. He is dressed in an elegant black suit, with a red rose in his buttonhole. "Lucas is looking on from above, you can bet on it. He would've gotten a kick out of this view to the ocean. I didn't think the poem would suit, but you read it beautifully, Ava."

Jack and Barbara are standing as far away from me as possible, unthawable as ice in a freezer. Shame they'll never get to meet their grandchild, because they still haven't forgiven me for Lucas's arrest, which they believe inadvertently caused his death. They clearly don't want anything to do with me. Maybe, when things settle down and the truth is revealed, they'll change their minds and loosen up a little. Getting hit by a bus was something nobody could have possibly imagined, not in their wildest fantasies. Who gets hit by a bus in Los Angeles of all places? It was a freak accident, the press said. It happened outside the courthouse when Lucas was crossing the road to reach his parked car. Bail set at a million dollars. He was jaywalking, so the driver was exonerated. It happened so quickly, so swiftly. Instant death, they said.

It's a strange sensation, knowing that because we signed the new marriage contract—and got rid of the prenup—all Lucas's money, the house, everything, is now mine. My baby no longer at threat of being taken from me.

*"Fifty-fifty, no conditions, no clauses. And if I get hit by a bus, you get it all."*

Poor Lucas. I do feel devastated by what has happened. And sad for my baby-to-be that he or she won't have a dad.

With all the media surrounding his case, and Claudia still missing, I have been getting an unprecedented amount of attention. *The poor jilted, pregnant widow.* Isabella Mox wants me on her show. I have an agent now. Helena Ronstein, Claudia's agent. The offers are coming in, fast and furious. I need to think long and hard about how I want my acting career to go, moving forward. Do I want to be a celebrity or a serious actor? This is something she and I need to figure out.

Later in the evening, I take a plane to Paris. To avoid any hullabaloo, I fly private. Someone very special is waiting for me there.

When I arrive at the apartment where she's staying, a hidden gem tucked away in Le Marais, she greets me with open arms. I'm taken aback to see that, like me, she has a baby bump. She is pregnant. Very pregnant, in fact. I swallow, taking in the bare truth. It occurs to me she must have been this way for quite a while. She never did drink champagne the day I met her at her house, did she? She must have been bearing that child all along. Why did she keep it a secret?

Nothing can really surprise me anymore.

Wheeling my suitcase to her front door, I take off my shades, revealing the dark, weepy circles under my eyes.

I think of the day she was locked in the trunk of the car. It was all of three minutes before I realized what had happened and came to her rescue. The way she yammered on about it, it was like she'd been in there for hours. I never heard the end of it.

She notices how my eyes flit down to her stomach.

"Yep, it's Lucas's." She waits a beat, searching my face for a reaction, then adds, "Sorry I didn't tell you. It's for the best he's gone, for both of us, you'll see. The last thing we need—for the sake of our kids especially—is his womanizing getting in the way. You and I both know what it's like to have a deadbeat dad. Our kids will be better off without him, trust me, Ava."

My heartbeat slows. I never wanted Lucas to die. I loved him, whatever his faults. He deserved punishment, but certainly not death.

As I stand there, looking down at our matching bumps, it dawns on me.

Lucas's death was no accident.

Did Claudia take our plan one step further? Worse, maybe she had plotted it all along and hooked me in for the ride? Did she want him out of the way from the moment she found out about me?

I think for a moment before I speak, weighing up whether to be upset or not. Of course, now he's gone, it does make my life way less complicated. He can't get in the way of me and my baby. Plus, his death has made me extremely wealthy. As well as the money and house there is a fabulous bonus, too, which I had forgotten all about: Lucas's life insurance policy.

"The bus," I say. "That was taking things a little too far, wasn't it?"

Claudia looks at me wide-eyed, innocence personified. Her famous hair frames her face like a golden aura. "I swear I had nothing to do with that. Believe me, Ava, I would *never* do such a thing. It was poetic justice taking its course."

"Poetic justice? Are you sure?" I raise a brow.

She smiles her gazillion-dollar smile and looks me straight in the eye. "Poetic justice. Abso-freakin-lutely."

# A LETTER FROM ARIANNE

Dear Reader,

I feel honored that you have chosen *The Prenup* and have stuck with my story till the very end. If you are new to my books, I hope you had an entertaining ride and that I was able to offer a fun escape from the real world for a while. Ava is very close to my heart. I think we all have a little bit of Ava in us, don't we? And, as a once-upon-a-time professional actor, I can also really relate to Claudia. I hope you enjoyed her story, too. I have other books you may enjoy, so do check them out. And if you are a return reader, I am even more grateful! Thanks so much. I can't tell you how much I appreciate your trust in me as a writer to deliver an entertaining story.

I have more books in the making, so if you'd like to be the first to hear about my new releases, you can sign up using the link below:

*www.bookouture.com/arianne-richmonde*

I came up with the plot for *The Prenup* several years ago and was delighted when I found it on my laptop, lurking in the shadows! We are all liars, some of us to a much deeper degree than others. And just because someone lies, it doesn't make them (us) a bad person, yet some of the characters in *The Prenup* take lying to a new level! I wanted to do a deep dive into a dysfunctional marriage, where the players are all lovable but also despicable.

Thank you so much for joining me on this twisty adventure. I would be so grateful if you could spare a few minutes and leave a quick, spoiler-free review, even just a couple of lines; we authors are so grateful when people spread the word.

I love hearing from readers and am always available for an online chat and will reply to any emails, so don't be shy to reach out. Bookouture books go through a rigorous editing and proofreading process, but little typos can still sometimes escape. If you spot one, don't hesitate to get in touch.

Take care,

Arianne

facebook.com/authorariannerichmonde

twitter.com/a_richmonde

# ACKNOWLEDGMENTS

A huge thank you to my editor and publisher, Lucy Frederick, for helping me be a better writer and being so tough on me. This has not been an easy book to write and you have not let me get away with a thing. Your eagle eye has given me some sleepless nights, but I am grateful, I truly am.

Thank you, again, to ex-homicide detective and author Holly Roberts for vetting my detective chapters. Any mistakes are my own.

Thanks to everyone in the fabulous Bookouture team, including other authors in the Bookouture family who have been so supportive, especially my great friend Nelle Lamarr, whose beta read helped so much. Also, Freida McFadden, Sue Watson, Carla Kovach, Shalini Boland, Susie Lynes, Jessica Payne, and Ellery Kane. Our chats have meant the world to me, and you have spurred me on through a few dark nights. A big thank you, too, to Anne O'Brien and Becca Allen for your sharp, intelligent eyes, for catching any typos, inconsistencies, and embarrassing mistakes. To Noelle Holten, Kim Nash, and the marketing team for being fabulous. This book has been a real team effort. Oh, and to Lisa Horton for another fabulous cover.

I am so grateful to all the bloggers and Instagrammers who spread the word about my books. You are incredibly dedicated, squeezing in our novels between your busy lives and day jobs; what would we authors do without you? A special shout out to Stu, Sharon, Angie, and Lisa for going above and beyond.

Last but never least, huge thanks to my readers for making this wonderful job as an author possible. I know how lucky I am to have you.